DEATH OF A SECRET

SHARON ROWSE

THREE CEDARS PRESS

Death of a Secret
A Barbara O'Grady Mystery
By Sharon Rowse

Book cover designed by Sharon Rowse & Three Cedars Press
Published by Three Cedars Press
www.threecedarspress.com

ISBN-13: 978-1-988037-13-4

ALSO BY SHARON ROWSE

The Barbara O'Grady Series: (in order)

Death of a Secret

Death of a Threat

Death of a Promise

Death of a Shadow

Death of a Lie

Death of a Dream

Death of a Chance

The John Granville & Emily Turner Historical Mystery Series: (in order)

The Silk Train Murder

The Lost Mine Murders

The Missing Heir Murders

The Terminal City Murders

The Cannery Row Murders

The Hidden City Murders

The Dockside Murders

For my family

CHAPTER ONE

Have you ever had one of those conversations that feels wrong from the first sentence, but you're not quite sure why? That's how it felt at that first meeting with Cassie Stewart.

Which probably shouldn't have surprised me, since I don't usually meet prospective clients at art gallery openings. Quite the opposite, in fact.

I'm a private investigator these days, but I once had dreams of a career as a painter. I've never lost my love of that world. When I'm at a gallery, investigating anything other than the artist's vision and style was the last thing on my mind.

This particular show took place on a Saturday evening in early spring. I was standing in front of a sprawling canvas, enjoying the artist's contrast of pink cherry blossoms against a freeway interchange. Taking a sip of a surprisingly decent Cabernet, I was considering her use of light on very different surfaces.

I would have stepped back for a better perspective, but the press of people behind me wouldn't allow it. The din of rising and falling voices confirmed it—Yuriko Imry's opening was a success. That was the moment when my old world collided with my new one.

"Barbara?" The voice and accompanying touch on my shoulder startled me.

I swung around and smiled to see Ian Wong, the affable and well-connected co-owner of the Omega Gallery. But it was the woman standing beside him who grabbed my attention.

"Do you know Cassie Stewart?" he asked.

"We've never met," I said. I knew who she was, of course. Just like I knew about the works she'd bought and the artists she'd sponsored. Though I doubt she knew about the paintings that gathered dust in my spare room, where I'd once planned to set up a studio.

"You'll have heard that Cassie is the newest member of the Vancouver Art Gallery board?" Ian was saying.

I nodded. Of course I had. Because Cassie Stewart also collected works by new artists. And she'd been known to make or break careers. There was a time when I'd have given anything to meet her.

"And Cassie, this is Barbara O'Grady," he continued. "Formerly one of our promising young artists, she now runs her own investigative firm."

I couldn't decide which part of his description embarrassed me more. "It's a pleasure," I said automatically, not yet sure if I meant it, and shook the slim hand she held out to me.

I'd seen pictures of Cassie Stewart at various events and fundraisers, but grainy images in two dimensions don't say very much. In person, she was polished, discretely blond and very poised. Though she wasn't tall, probably five or six inches shorter than my five ten, she held herself as if she was a finalist in a supermodel reality show. She looked younger than the fifty-something I knew her to be, though her eyes were tired and there was tension in the line of her shoulders.

"I'm pleased to meet you, also," Cassie Stewart said. "Thank you, Ian."

With a nod, he departed, leaving Cassie and I considering each other. She must have asked him to introduce us. Before I had a chance to wonder why, she leaned towards me.

"I'd like to hire you," she said in an undertone.

Here? Now? I really hadn't expected that. And it set off all my internal alarms.

Why me? With her money, Cassie Stewart could easily engage one of the bigger, better-resourced firms. And she couldn't have known that I'd be here tonight, since attending had been a last-minute decision on my part. Surely she wouldn't hire a P. I. on an impulse?

Curious now, I lowered my voice to match hers. "How can I help you?"

"First, I will need to know I can rely on your discretion."

"In my job, that's a given." If I wanted to stay in business, that is. I was a bit offended that she'd even asked.

"I've heard good things about you," Cassie Stewart said. Her eyes met mine. Hers were a clear blue, and cool. "But I'm well known in Vancouver, and people love to gossip. I dislike gossip."

I'd just bet she did.

"You have my word that I'll keep anything you tell me strictly confidential," I said. Wondering what she'd heard about me. And from whom?

"As long as we understand each other," she said with a sharp glance. "But we can't talk here. I'll meet you tomorrow morning at the Moka Café. At ten?"

I'd normally have asked her to come to my office, but the Moka is an oasis of calm on traffic-heavy Broadway. Plus they make the world's best dark chocolate cherry scones, with decent coffee to boot. Meeting a potential client there was no hardship. I found her abruptness grating, though, so I asked for details on the case before I agreed.

"I need a background check done," she was all she'd tell me.

I should have said no right then and there. I knew it. And from her frozen look she probably knew it too. But curiosity has always been my undoing. And everything about Cassie Stewart intrigued me.

Even without her almost legendary ability to spot a good artist early in their career, she seemed just too elegant for the edgy modern art I knew she collected. And she had about as much human warmth as an iceberg in Glacier Bay.

But as I watched the subtle changes in her face, my fingers suddenly itched for a drawing pad and some charcoal. I wanted to catch the contradiction between that fragile blonde surface and whatever emotion was seething beneath it. It would have made a terrific portrait. Though probably not one she'd have cared for.

And it left me wanting to know more about the person behind that facade.

"Ten is fine," I said. My questions—and my curiosity—would have to wait.

"Good. I will see you then." And with a sharp nod, she moved on, leaving me to continue my viewing of Yuriko's work. And to wonder about Cassie Stewart and whatever job she really needed done.

CHAPTER TWO

Tuesday morning found me sitting in one of the booths at the Moka Café, a sixteen-ounce mug of dark-roasted Sumatran in hand. The opening door let in the usual cacophony of sound as taxis, buses and delivery vans raced by outside. I looked up to see my potential client walking towards me, haloed by the thin spring sunlight streaming through the windows. The deceptiveness of that image had me hiding a grin.

Cassie Stewart was one of those women who are elegant down to their fingertips. Pale blond hair was pulled smoothly up and back and pearl studs gleamed in her ears. She was wearing something beige and ivory, that draped fluidly and gave her a regal air. Of course, perfect posture didn't hurt, either.

When Cassie Stewart reached the booth where I sat, she paused, sizing me up. Then she slid gracefully onto the seat opposite me, waving away the server as she did so.

"Good morning, Barbara," she said. "I hope you're prepared to begin work on my case tomorrow."

Again that combination of impatience and arrogance. This was the woman that as art students we'd whispered about and schemed to meet—while our work was being rejected by one gallery after another. "If Cassie Stewart likes your stuff, you're on your way." It was gospel in our small world.

Now she was a potential client. And it was my decision as to whether to help her. I've always been a fan of irony, but this was pushing it, even for me.

"I'll need a few details first," I said. "What kind of background investigation did you want me to do?"

"I'd like you to investigate my husband," she said, her face carefully blank.

I stared at her, caught off-guard for a split second. "You want me to investigate your husband?" I repeated, just managing to keep the disbelief out of my voice.

No wonder she was hiring an obscure PI. She couldn't use any of the bigger firms without word getting back to him almost immediately. For a big city, Vancouver can be a pretty small town.

Cassie Stewart placed long-fingered hands with French manicured nails on the table and studied them, perfectly mascaraed lashes fanning against her pale cheeks. "I believe Brian is having an affair. I'd like you to follow him and find out with whom."

I noted her perfect diction and grammatical correctness. The right schooling did make a difference, it seemed. She didn't meet my eyes as she toyed absently with a spoon. Her face was pale, composed, and very still.

It was that stillness that worried me. She was holding herself too tightly. Put together with the brittleness I'd noted earlier— what I was seeing wasn't embarrassment, or shame, or even anger.

It was fear.

Fear tightly controlled and forced into submission, but fear all the same.

"You want me to find out the name of the person your husband is having an affair with?" I asked, watching her closely. I wasn't about to leap to conclusions about gender.

A flash of cold blue fire as she glared at me, then her eyes were focused on her hands again. "Yes."

She was lying to me.

I'd had too many clients talk about too many cheating spouses—and they didn't look or sound like this. She was doing her impressive best to hide whatever she was really feeling, but I was willing to bet money it wasn't a philandering husband.

"What did you have in mind?" I asked her.

"I would like a full report of his actions from tomorrow morning until Saturday night."

"You want to hire me for four days?"

I nearly told her that was a waste of my time and her money, but some residual sense of awe at who she was stopped me. Or maybe it was curiosity.

"You need to understand that a case like this can sometimes take a day," I said. "But it can also take a couple of weeks."

"If you find something in less than four days, I'd still like you to follow him through Saturday night," she said. "If you find nothing, we'll review your contract the following Monday. And if that is not satisfactory to you, I'll find someone for whom it is."

Her request made no sense, which intrigued me and concerned me in about equal measure. What was she really up to?

And why was I even discussing it with her?

Still, this was Cassie Stewart. Reactions left over from the years when I'd have given anything to attract her attention seemed to have taken over. "What can you tell me about his schedule?"

"Until Friday you'll need to follow Brian only until he returns home from work. On Saturday I'd like you to follow him all day as we're going to the theater that night. And I expect you to attend the theater and follow him there, also."

Okay, that was officially the weirdest surveillance schedule I'd ever heard of.

"As long as you understand that I may not have answers for you in that time frame," I warned her.

"Those are my terms."

Clearly she didn't like being questioned. Never a good sign in a prospective client. Well, it was her dollar, and there would be quite a few of them. But it was my time, and ultimately my career.

I'd already failed at one career—I didn't plan to do so a second time.

I drank coffee and let the silence stretch.

She didn't flinch.

Point to her. And I just couldn't let this one go.

Telling my intuition to shut up, I met her eyes and said, "When did you begin to suspect something was wrong?"

Her mouth tightened but she held my gaze. "The changes in his habits have been subtle, over a period of perhaps a month. It is nothing anyone else would have noticed. But we have been married nearly forty years. I know him rather well."

Or at least she thought she did. "Have his actions changed?" I asked.

"He—it is his attitude more than anything. He seems distracted, distant."

She'd been about to say something else, but had changed her mind at the last moment.

As I watched her guarded face, I wondered about the Stewart's sex life, and whether those "habits" she seemed so reluctant to discuss were sexual preferences. I nearly asked her, but I had the feeling a direct question about her sex life would end our association immediately.

Which might not be a bad thing, except that by now I was intensely curious. More about my contradictory would-be client than the case.

"So what makes you think he's having an affair?" I asked, suppressing a grin.

"What else could it be?"

Surely she wasn't serious? Brian Stewart was a high-powered lawyer in a prestigious downtown firm. I wondered if he shared details from that part of his life with her.

"Any number of things. Problems with work, legal issues, health concerns, money problems..."

"You do know who I am, don't you? And who my husband is?

Money problems are not something Brian or I will ever have to worry about. Not with my trust fund."

Must be nice. Was she really this arrogant, or was it the stress talking? "What about his work? Has his schedule changed in any way?"

She shook her head. The closed look on her face told me she'd finished talking. Too bad, because I hadn't nearly finished asking questions.

Now it was up to me. Was I going to take this case, knowing she'd lied to me about everything from why she wanted her husband followed to what she really wanted me to find out?

Apparently I was.

My intuition still wasn't happy, but I ignored it. This client was far too intriguing to pass up. Besides, most of my clients lie.

"What time do I start?" I asked.

Cassie looked pleased, and she didn't even blink when I told her what four days of surveillance was going to cost her. Even though I'd cheerfully upped my fee by thirty percent—I call it the pain-in-the-ass tax, and she definitely qualified. Not that she cared.

She just signed the contract, then wrote out a check.

Looking at the flourishes of her signature, I tried to imagine getting a check like this for one of my paintings. And felt a flash of pain at the realization that I never would—the price of choosing security over dreams.

Ignoring the feeling, I filled my new client in on how I'd handle reports and billing and she filled me in on the basics of her husband's routine. We shook hands, and she left. I watched her go.

When I was twelve, my mother sent me for ballet lessons. I'd just grown to my current height and I think she hoped it would get me over my gawkiness. I loved the class, but I could never get my arms and legs to do the right things at the right time. I was never sure whether the teacher gave up, my mother got frustrated or the money ran out, but after a year or two, there were no more lessons.

I've always been glad of those early lessons, though, because not only did they give me terrific posture—which showed up when I finally grew out of the gawkiness—ballet also trained my eye so that when I watch people, I see them as bodies moving in space. All those art classes only sharpened that perception.

Now I automatically notice how a person moves. Often I can read a client's state of mind in their movements before I even talk to them.

Cassie's departing back looked as elegant as when she'd arrived, but she was holding her head a little less stiffly. Maybe she was relieved she'd hired me to help take care of her problems. Whatever they were.

I just hoped I wouldn't come to regret it too much.

CHAPTER THREE

Half an hour later, I was back in my office, sitting in my vintage but gorgeous burgundy leather chair and thinking about the case I'd taken on. A sudden rainstorm pelted against the big windows on the far wall, and the chill rolled off the glass.

I reached for a sweater, then watched the patterns the rain made on the window. And wondered about Cassie and Brian Stewart and their life together.

I'd seen the articles and smiling photos of the two of them in the social columns. They were almost always photographed together. "Cassie and Brian Stewart, attending the opening of the new wing of the Art Gallery—Mrs. Stewart was the Chair of the committee that raised the funds". "Cassie and Brian Stewart at the Opera's fundraising Gala."

She was definitely a presence in her own right, not like those sad women whose only function seems to be as "and wife" at social events. So what was she hoping I'd find?

The Perfect Couple not being so perfect didn't surprise me— few things are as seamless as they appear on the surface, and certainly not society marriages. Call me cynical, but I've been involved in one too many cases where the only thing holding a marriage together is fear of splitting the assets.

If the guy is a lawyer like Brian Stewart, an ex-wife with a good divorce lawyer can end up with half the value of her husband's practice. But in this case, the money and the connections were Cassie's. From what I'd read about the Stewarts, I didn't think that any lawyer, no matter how successful, could afford their lifestyle on his earnings alone.

Brian Stewart stood to lose more than his assets in a divorce action—he could easily lose his social standing and a lifestyle he'd become accustomed to. Why would a man jeopardize all of that? Love? Middle-age crisis? Who knew?

Assuming that he actually was having an affair.

And based on what I'd seen from my client, that was a big assumption. One I was in no hurry to make. I flipped open my laptop and did a quick computer search. Then I reached for the phone.

"Trusted Temps, Andrea Fisher speaking."

"Hi, Andrea, it's me."

"Barbara?"

My best friend sounded slightly wary. Not that I blame her. She's known me for too many years not to recognize that tone in my voice.

I needed a favor. And she knew it. But we've always traded favors back and forth.

Though I have to admit since I got my P. I. license the favors I need have become slightly more complicated. Which Andrea would call the understatement of the year.

"Have you got a couple of minutes?" I said.

"I've got exactly ten minutes before my next interview. What's up?"

Andrea runs the best temporary help agency in town, and I swear she has a second sense when it comes to hiring exactly the right person, then matching them to exactly the right job. That unerring instinct for people was the reason I'd called her.

Well, that plus the fact that she always seems to know what's going on in this city weeks before the rest of the world.

"I'm working on a case, and it looks like a local couple may be peripherally involved," I said. "I'm wondering what you might know about them?"

She gave an exaggerated sigh. "Names?"

"Cassie and Brian Stewart."

"Not the 'if-only-I-could-swing-a-meeting-with-her-I-could-get-my-career-off-the-ground' Cassie Stewart?"

"That's the one."

"Wow."

"Yeah. So, what do you know about them as a couple?"

"Hold on a minute. How do you feel about finally meeting her? I assume you've met her?"

"Yes, I have. It's no big deal."

"Really?"

She didn't sound convinced.

Not surprising, given that I wasn't exactly convinced either. But I wasn't ready to talk about it yet. "So, what do you know about them as a couple?"

"Hmmm."

I could picture her pursing bow-shaped lips. Andrea looks a little like an old-fashioned kewpie doll, which belies an incisive intelligence and a killer business instinct. But it's look that works for her—especially with men—and she knows it.

Did I mention her killer business instinct?

"They're very well connected. Cassie's family, the Grantleys, are old money," Andrea said. I could hear her keyboard clicking in the background.

"Or at least what passes for old money in Vancouver. Which means a hundred years or so," I said.

Andrea ignored me. She's heard my "Vancouver is still a pioneer city" speech before, most recently at the last party we'd attended. I hate small talk, so I tend to trot out my favorite theories. And once in a while that leads to a great conversation.

Andrea tells me I'm not nearly as funny as I think I am. Which entirely misses the point. Not that I'll ever convince her of that.

There was a pause while I heard keys clicking in the background. I wondered what sources Andrea was using.

"Cassie went to all the right schools and then to the right university," she said.

The University of British Columbia, locally known as UBC. My computer search had already told me that. She'd studied art history and organizational behavior, which had struck me as an interesting combination to have chosen, especially given the influence she now wielded in the art world. "Go on."

"They met at university and married right afterwards. Then he graduated top of his law class and joined the city's most prestigious law firm, of which, not incidentally, Cassie's father was a partner. They have two, no three kids, two boys and a girl, I think."

"And money?" I had the general outline, but Andrea always seems to know the details.

"Cassie inherited millions from her maternal grandfather on her twenty-fifth birthday. Brian does quite nicely himself as a senior partner. They are definitely not hurting. They're seen everywhere. And very generous to a number of causes, Cassie in particular to the arts. Which you already know."

It sounded like the perfect life, but sometimes things that look good on the surface can hide some pretty ugly secrets. "Any rumors about them?"

"None that I've picked up."

"What about affairs? Or tension in the marriage?"

"They've always seemed a very happy couple and I've never heard any gossip to the contrary. Don't be so cynical, Barbara."

"What, me? Cynical?"

"Yes, you. You think there's no such thing as a good relationship, let alone a good marriage. It's why you're thirty-three and still single."

"That is not true." Well, not exactly, anyway. I just haven't seen very many of what I'd consider good marriages, but I wasn't making the mistake of telling Andrea that.

"Speaking of relationships, what happened to that guy?"

"What guy?"

"You know, the cute blond one who was giving you the eye the last time we went to Guido's."

"I don't remember any guy."

"See, that's your pattern. You not only don't believe in relationships, you deliberately ignore potential ones when they're under your nose."

"How can you deliberately ignore something? That's an oxymoron."

"Stop trying to change the subject. You know what your problem is?"

"No, but I'm sure you're going to tell me."

"You're still looking for that perfect partnership. And you're still running scared after that disaster you called a relationship with Jayson."

No way I was getting into another discussion about Jayson. "Jayson who?"

"Very funny. You know I'm right."

"That was more than four years ago."

"My point exactly. And how many dates have you had since then?" my incorrigible—and still single—friend wanted to know. "Whoops, look at the time, I've got to run. Bye." And she disconnected.

Which was a good thing, because I didn't want to think about her questions, much less answer them. I was much more interested in knowing what my new client was really worried about. Not a question either Andrea or my computer could answer.

I checked out Benton, Grantley, Baynes and Stewart's very spiffy website, typed in Brian Stewart. Back came the photo, biography and an impressive list of deals on which he had advised. His specialty was corporate law.

I studied the photo for a moment. They'd gone with black and white, giving everyone that formal corporate look, but Brian was handsome anyway, with silvered dark hair and chiseled features. I wondered what color his eyes were.

"So, what are you up to?" I asked out loud.

Since he didn't answer, I settled for designing a surveillance schedule. With only me to follow it, a schedule wasn't exactly necessary, but I hated to waste all those hours of poor Sid's patient mentoring.

So I had only myself to blame when the completed schedule said I had to be outside the Stewart residence the following morning at six-thirty a.m.

CHAPTER FOUR

At six twenty the following morning I sat shivering in my car, parked across the street and a discreet half block up from the Stewart place. Brian and Cassie live in one of those stately old homes on the street known as The Circle, the most exclusive location in already exclusive Shaughnessy.

It's an enclave of mansions, most dating from the turn of the century, surrounding a circular park. The entire area has the feel of wealth and privilege. Every house is set well back on huge grounds, with walls, fences or hedges designed to ensure maximum privacy.

The Stewart place was no exception—screened by old, well-tended trees and shrubbery on three sides and across most of the front. Which unfortunately meant that all I could see was the front entrance and the garage door. I fixed my eyes on the side view mirror, watching those glossy black doors.

It looked like it was going to be a nice day, but at that early hour there was a slight fog on the ground and it was damp and cold, with the kind of cold that seeps into my bones and sort of sits there. My hands were cupped around a *venti* cup of Starbuck's French Roast coffee, as I endeavored to get both caffeine and warmth in the same place.

The radio was playing something soothing, with no beat to it and I switched stations until I found some oldies rock. I forced myself to quit drumming my fingers in time. There's no room for inattention while doing surveillance.

That moment or two when your mind drifts off elsewhere is always the moment when the target chooses to slip out a side door.

I glared at those glossy black doors. "So, where is he?" I muttered.

Inaction and waiting are not really my strong points.

As if on cue, the front door opened, and a man I recognized as Brian Stewart stepped out. He looked very dapper for this hour, in a charcoal gray double breasted suit that fit him admirably. This was a man who had kept himself in shape.

His silvered hair was nicely styled, swept back from tanned chiseled features. I couldn't tell what color his eyes were for this distance, but I was betting they were blue.

Clearly, Brian Stewart would have no problems finding willing participants for an affair. The question was, had he done so?

Moments later a gray Mercedes sedan emerged from the double garage. He took the most direct route into town, with me following a carefully judged distance behind him.

My client had briefed me thoroughly the previous day, so I followed Brian Stewart's car into the parkade, and found a parking spot two floors below his reserved spot. Which probably meant that he'd have left the parkade before I was even parked.

I waited impatiently for the elevator, hoping he'd gone straight to his office and not out of the building before I could catch up with him. To my shock, the elevator doors opened on a pair of very bright blue eyes.

I knew this man had to have blue eyes.

"Good morning," he said as I stepped into the elevator.

"Morning," I mumbled, not meeting his eyes. Too dangerous, on several fronts. Even his cologne smelled good—the freshness of citrus offset by something warmly woodsy. Andrea was right, I needed to start dating again.

I glanced over and noted that Brian had pushed fifteen. "Sixteen, please."

He pushed the appropriate button.

I fixed my gaze on the little numbers winking on and off, announcing the floors. I find elevator etiquette vastly amusing—I've been known to strike up loud conversations with complete strangers on elevators, just to see them squirm—but it is handy on occasion.

And staring at flickering numbers instead of noticing an attractive man was perfectly in keeping with my current disguise—a navy jacket worn with a knee-length pencil skirt and round-necked blouse, both dark gray, low heels and a pair of too-large for my face oval glasses.

As a disguise it seemed to be one of my more effective efforts.

His eyes took in the tightly pulled back dark hair and bland attire, then moved on. I'd been judged, categorized and passed over. Just one of those nameless, faceless hordes of "temps" that keep the wheels of business oiled.

Not worth a second thought.

I was conscious of a slight feeling of pique at being so easily overlooked. Which annoyed me. The whole point was for this guy not to notice me—I'm supposed to be completely unmemorable when I'm on surveillance.

The elevator lights flashed twelve, then fourteen.

The law firm of Benton, Grantley, Baynes and Stewart occupied all of the fourteenth and half of the fifteenth floor. Brian got off on fifteen. I waited impatiently for the elevator to reach sixteen—jointly occupied by an engineering firm and a property management company—then raced through the fortunately deserted hallway and clattered down the stairs.

If Brian was meeting anyone this early, I wanted to know about it.

By the time I reached fifteen, there was no sign of him. At least there were no sleep-deprived interns or associates in the lobby, and the receptionist seemed to have vanished too, which was a relief. I'd rather not have to explain why I'd taken the stairs.

I took a deep breath and turned down the hall to my left.

In most offices, if you look like you belong, no-one questions you, so I'd left both purse and coat locked in my car. If someone did stop me, my story was that I was temping on a special assignment on fourteen, and I'd been sent up to fetch extra pens and legal pads for an early meeting.

I saw no-one as I walked purposefully down the hall. Brian's office was in the far corner. The corridor wall of his office was all glass, with huge windows on two sides giving a view of the harbor and the clouds still obscuring the North Shore mountains.

The interior curtains were drawn back. I could see him seated behind his enormous desk, talking on the phone. He looked angry.

I was curious, but I couldn't afford to linger.

Spotting a promotional pamphlet in the lobby, I grabbed a copy then took the elevator back down to the parkade. I moved my car up a floor so it was in view of Brian's, set up the spy-cam on my dash—disguised in a small plush penguin—and checked that I was getting a clear feed on my cell.

That car wasn't going anywhere without my knowing about it.

———

BACK AT STREET LEVEL, I walked briskly through the cavernous lobby towards the coffee shop—all dark wood and glass—where I indulged in a latte. Then I found a seat on a stool by the interior window.

From my perch I could see people leaving the elevators and making their way across the lobby to the outside doors. I could also both see and hear the coffee shop's patrons. What I couldn't see was anyone who chose to take the stairs.

It wasn't much of a vantage point, but it was all I had. Did I mention how much I hate surveillance?

Setting the iPhone for easy viewing, I opened the pamphlet I'd picked up upstairs, which turned out to include the names and photos of the firm's one hundred plus lawyers. I paid particular attention to the lawyers who worked in Brian's section.

Stowing the pamphlet in my grey slouch bag, which I'd retrieved from the car, I pulled out a small notebook and a soft lead pencil. As I watched the crowds flow across the lobby, I made quick sketches of the faces and the people—an expression here, a way of walking there.

Sketching makes a great cover when you have to sit idly for several hours at a time. And it keeps my eye for detail sharp. Since I started bringing a sketchpad along, it's as if I've become invisible.

Occasionally someone will stop and ask to see what I'm drawing, but mostly they just give me a nod and a smile and leave me alone.

I didn't know what—or who—I might be looking for, but I didn't spot anyone that set off my radar.

At exactly eight-thirty I phoned and told a very chirpy receptionist that I needed to speak with Brian's admin. Cassie hadn't been able to tell me much about Brian's schedule. I hoped a little subterfuge would yield something useful.

My call was transferred immediately, and this time the voice was mature, confident and firm.

"Brian Stewart's office, Janet Adams speaking."

"This is Mary Jenkins. I'm calling on behalf of the CEO of Interco West. He's asked me to set up an appointment with Mr. Stewart."

"I'm sorry," Janet said. "Mr. Stewart is not accepting new clients at the moment. However, I'm sure he can recommend one of our other partners to help you."

"No, it's Mr. Stewart we're interested in working with. And we are in a position to need, and pay for, his level of expertise." Would that make a difference?

It seemed so. There was a pause and I could hear keys clicking. "I can set something up for the end of the month," she said.

Nearly four weeks from now? His schedule must be booked solid. "I'm afraid the matter is urgent."

"I'm sorry, but that's the best I can do."

"If Mr. Stewart can't accommodate us, we'll need to find another firm who can."

More keys clicking. "That's the earliest appointment available."

"I see. Thank you for your time."

I disconnected, and stared at the phone for a moment, thinking.

Given his high profile, I'd have expected Brian to be busy, but I hadn't expected to hear that he had no openings for nearly four weeks, especially for a new, and potentially lucrative, client. That lack of flexibility made me uneasy.

I'd love to get a look at his appointment book, but that wasn't likely to happen anytime soon.

CHAPTER FIVE

By one-fifteen, when Brian Stewart finally strode through the lobby, an intent expression on his face, I'd begun to wonder if Cassie was wrong when she said he ate lunch out most days. Of course, I was also worrying that I'd somehow missed him and would have to admit failure on day one, and to Cassie Stewart of all people.

And I had a pounding headache from trying to look for his face in the river of people who had already flowed by me. No matter. He was here now.

Brian was alone today, and empty-handed.

Tucking my notebook and phone into my purse, I gulped down the last of my coffee, and followed him into the sunshine. I dug for my sunglasses, appreciating the subtle hint of spring flowers over-lying the heavier smells of traffic and construction. Following him was easy—Brian walked quickly to the Sterling Hotel, seemingly oblivious to everything around him.

I kept a careful half block behind him, just in case.

The dining room at the Sterling is beautiful, and it's one of those that aim for a European level of service and style, with prices to match, of course. Everything is understated and designed to soothe the senses—chandeliers, rich fabrics, crystal and silver.

What I like most is that it's possible to sit in the elegant bar and have a view of most of the dining room.

So as the maître d' showed Brian to his table, I chose a cushy chair in the bar, and an attentive waiter popped up with the menu. I ordered a San Pellegrino and the lemon chicken and basil panini, then sat back to watch the dining room.

It was nearly full. Brian was sitting at the near end—I could see him and his companion clearly. The other man was in his late seventies, nearly bald, but with strong features and a forceful presence.

He was also Senator Ed McMather, still one of our city's key players. McMather had started in provincial politics, then graduated to national roles. He'd been in the spotlight, one way or another, for more than fifty years.

There had been the occasional rumor of shady business dealings and gossip about his relationship with a number of somewhat questionable backers, but I'd never heard anything concrete.

From where I sat I could only partially see their expressions, but their body language spoke volumes. This didn't look like a social occasion. They were sitting facing each other across a small, square table and neither man looked relaxed.

McMather was leaning forward, emphasizing a point by tapping on the table with a blunt finger. Brian was leaning back in his chair and the perfect cut of his suit emphasized the lines of tension down his back. Under the table, his feet angled away from McMather.

The politician had his own feet planted squarely beneath him. He leaned forward most of the time, and the set of his jaw was belligerent.

Was this business, then? Benton, Grantley, Baynes and Stewart are a very conservative firm—Ed McMather is anything but. And there was an intensity about the conversation that didn't suggest a client relationship.

Could this lunch relate to whatever was behind Brian's changed behavior?

I watched the two men for over an hour, without once seeing either of them smile. Twice McMather's face turned an alarming shade of red. What would Cassie make of their meeting?

My waiter re-appeared at intervals, brought my lunch—which was delicious—cleared it, brought coffee. I scarcely noticed, absorbed in trying to unravel the drama I was watching. I just wished they'd turn towards me a little, so I could figure out what they were saying.

As a kid I learned to lip-read because I wanted to know what people were talking about when they didn't want me to hear. I got quite good at it, and would sit for hours watching the television with the sound off, practicing.

My mother used to rush in and insist that I either turn the sound on like a normal person or shut the set off. Funny, our inter-actions haven't changed that much. Mom still has a tendency to rush in, and she still wants me to change—little things like my career, my social life, my marital status…

I wrenched my mind back to the job. Had either Brian or McMather been facing me, I could have 'read' half the conversation.

As it was, I could only watch in growing frustration until they finished that last cup of coffee. There was the usual gentlemanly dickering over who'd pay the bill. McMather ended up with it, after what looked like a very sharp remark. If he was a client, or even a potential client, shouldn't Brian have picked up the tab?

A half hour later, I was back sitting in the lobby coffee shop, whose stark trendiness I was coming to detest. Partly because the very of-the-moment chairs were not designed for patrons to sit in for an entire day. I shifted position again, checked the web cam and my e-mail, then Googled Ed McMather.

He'd been a very public figure for years, so there was far too much data to easily deal with on a small phone screen. I flipped through screen after screen of links, most dealing with senatorial duties, appearances and speeches. I followed the Wikipedia link, which had clearly been written by his PR people, checked into a few blogs.

After fifteen minutes I gave up. I hadn't found anything linking McMather to Brian Stewart, nor learned anything new about either man.

I'd have to do a deeper search when I had a bigger screen.

Maximizing the cam, I glanced around the coffee shop.

It was filling up again, with people seeking their mid-afternoon caffeine hit. Listening to the variations on coffee orders that people placed amused me, I'd try to see if their orders matched what I saw in their faces. Mostly they didn't.

The non-fat Matcha Green Tea Latte had a petulant look, rather than the well-yoga'd serenity I'd have expected. The Double Espresso with her was a better fit, with sharply cut dark hair and a narrow, focused face.

Her I'd like to paint. I sketched in a couple of quick lines, then looked at her again.

I knew that face. But from where?

Scanning my memory banks, I stuffed the iPod in my purse and grabbed my empty mug. I had a feeling I didn't want to miss a word of this conversation.

As I moved into line behind them, Matcha Latte's voice took on a shrill note. "He's shirking."

"With all he's contributed to the firm, he's entitled to reduce his workload occasionally," said Double Espresso in measured tones that suggested quite a bit of courtroom experience.

I'd placed her face—I'd seen it in the Benton, Grantley, Baynes and Stewart pamphlet.

Not only was she a lawyer, she worked directly for Brian Stewart. Which made it likely Matcha Latte also worked for the firm, though her face was less memorable. Maybe that explained the petulant look.

Could it be Brian they were discussing?

"Reduce it?" Matcha Latte was saying. "And exactly what workload is he handling, anyway? He gave you the Gelbart case. And the Crossman case. And the Venier case."

"Are you jealous of the exposure it's giving me, Gail?"

Matcha Latte's mouth tightened and she glanced impatiently at the barista. "Of course not. I'm concerned about you."

My fingers itched to capture the truth beneath their expressions.

"It's a great opportunity for me, and he needs the break."

"I know he's your mentor and you think the man walks on water, but look at you. You're exhausted."

For a moment Double Espresso looked as skeptical as I felt. "I'm fine," she said.

"You know I'm telling you this as a friend, Marcia. I'm just worried about the workload you're carrying." The first voice again, softer now.

As I paid for my order and moved a little closer to them, I wondered just how much of a friend Matcha Latte really was.

"It's a great opportunity," Double Espresso said, grabbing her to-go coffee.

As they walked towards the door, Matcha Latte said something else. Their body language was intense, but even straining my ears I couldn't hear a word.

I was losing them.

I mentally urged the barista to greater speed on my Americano, but to no avail. As they exited, neither looked pleased with the other, leaving me to speculate.

Whipping out the Benton, Grantley, Baynes and Stewart pamphlet, I flipped through the photos.

Double Espresso was Marcia Jaffer.

Matcha Latte was harder to place—her photo was overly flattering. Photoshopped?—but she was Gail Thomas.

Both worked for Brian. Which meant he'd reduced his workload enough that others had noticed. Yet his secretary said he wasn't accepting new appointments.

So what was he doing instead of the work he'd dumped on Double Espresso?

Was this what Cassie wasn't telling me? Or did she even know?

I made a few notes, then stared at the bright world beyond the windows while I tried to make sense of the facts I'd gathered so far.

What was Brian Stewart up to, and how was I going to find out?

When breaking into his office at midnight started to sound increasingly attractive, I sighed and got up to get a bottled water. Not good for the planet, but anymore coffee and I'd still be staring at the ceiling at dawn.

Trying to figure out this annoying case.

———

IT WAS past seven-thirty by the time Brian returned to his car.

The coffee shop had closed hours earlier and I'd been reduced to prowling the lobby while keeping a close eye on the camera feed from the parkade.

Since the elevators were empty, I made it down to my car in time to follow him out, then followed tamely as he drove straight home. A lack-luster ending to a thoroughly frustrating day.

I was no closer to knowing why Cassie had hired me than when I'd started.

Maybe I'd call Andrea, see if she was up for a movie. I could use the distraction. No such luck. The minute I walked in the door the phone rang. "Hello?"

"There you are, Barbara," said my mother. "I wanted to tell you I'm planning a family dinner for this Sunday. Susanna and her family are coming. Why don't you bring Jerry Hawald? It's been far too long since we've seen him."

Oh, great. Mom was matchmaking again, and with Jerry of all people.

Jerry and I grew up next door to each other, and we know too much about each other to ever be more than friends. Plus he's now a detective with the Vancouver Police, and even less thrilled about my current career choice than my mother is.

"You know it isn't like that with Jerry and me, Mom. And I'm in the middle of a case. I doubt I'll be able to get away."

"It's only a few hours. And it wouldn't hurt you to eat something healthy for a change."

I could just see it. There we'd sit, digging into vegetable stew and homemade bread, while she dropped little comments contrasting my sister Susanna's life, with her perfect husband and her two equally perfect children, and my single state. Having Jerry along would only make it worse.

No thanks. "I'm sorry, I really can't make it."

"Then maybe you and Jerry can come the following weekend. Or are you seeing someone else?"

I had to laugh.

Sometimes she's about a subtle as a sledgehammer. The irony is that while my mother would be thrilled to see me married—as long as the man in question had a decent job and a good insurance policy—she'd be equally happy to see me stay single as long as I had a high-pressure corporate job with career prospects and a solid pension plan.

Her dreams, my nightmares.

Mom's not thrilled with what she perceives as the insecurity of my current career. She didn't like the previous one much, either, but as a reformed flower child, she had slightly less trouble with the idea of me as a struggling artist than she does with my struggling investigative agency. Go figure.

"No, I'm not seeing anyone. I'll let you know about next week, but I have to run now."

There was a short silence. "Barbara, have you talked to Susanna lately?"

What was this? "Not in the last week or so. Why?"

"I think you should call her."

"And I should ask her...?"

"Ask her about Godfrey. See if she'll talk to you." And she disconnected.

Another Perfect Couple with problems?

While I love my sister, and I think her kids are great—if more than a tad spoiled—the less I say about my brother-in-law Godfrey, the better. Still, Susanna and Godfrey had always presented a seamless surface to the world, and that includes me.

Which, to be fair, might be part of my dislike of the man. From the day she married him, my little sister stopped confiding in me. If they were having problems now, it was no surprise she hadn't told me.

It hurt, though.

Except that it didn't sound like she was talking to Mom either, and that was out of character.

I frowned over that thought, then dialed Susanna's number, and got the answering machine. No way I was leaving this kind of message.

Hanging up the phone, I recognized the familiar knot in my stomach, the one that should be labeled "family."

And after a day of remarkably unproductive surveillance of Brian Stewart, I was due for a relaxing evening.

Except I couldn't stop thinking about Susanna. I wouldn't have her life if you paid me, but she'd seemed happy with it, and I wanted that for her.

I considered taking a glass of red wine out on my small balcony, but I knew I'd just sit and worry about my case and about my sister.

So I changed into running gear and went for a long, hard run.

And spent most of it trying to figure out how a suspected affair and Ed McMather were connected.

And just what Brian Stewart was doing instead of working.

CHAPTER SIX

It was a sweltering day, and I was chasing a zebra through thick brush. I'd nearly caught him—until the alarm went off.

I tried to hit doze, but I misjudged my swipe, as usual, and the clock ended up on the floor. Which is why my downstairs neighbors hate me.

By the time I rescued the clock and shut it up, I was awake. Sort of.

I peered at the clock. It was ten after five. I'd overslept.

Bleary eyed, I stumbled towards the kitchen, and stubbed my toe on a furry lump. Furry?

I let out a squawk and lunged for the lights.

A pair of amber eyes blinked at me from the middle of my mud brown wall-to-wall, which I intend to change for bamboo flooring one of these days. The cat—if it was a cat—was the largest I'd ever seen, a mound of orange and white.

He hadn't even twitched when I'd walked into him, and was now regarding me as if wondering what I was doing in his living room.

"What are you doing here? And how did you get in?"

He blinked at me.

I live on the fourth floor. My balcony door was open a few inches, but this cat was at least eight inches wide. Plus the balcony doesn't connect to any of my neighbors' balconies.

I checked the hall door. Locked.

I glared at the cat. "Don't look so pleased with yourself. I don't know how you got in, but you're not staying."

He stared at me.

Oh, great. I was already running late and I had a cat in my living room. I like cats well enough—from a distance—but I have no close personal experience with them. And this one wasn't staying in my living room.

"Come on, cat. Shoo. Shoo." I said, waving my arms at him. Her. Whatever.

The cat closed his eyes.

I marched over and reached for him—and one eye opened. I hesitated. If I picked him up, would he bite? Scratch?

The eye closed.

That did it. Scratches or not, he was out of here.

Reaching down, I snagged both hands around his furry midsection, trying to keep teeth and claws as far from my body as possible, and lifted.

I nearly dropped him. The furry monster must've weighed sixteen pounds, most of it muscle from the feel of him. He didn't struggle, just draped limply from my outstretched hands, getting heavier with every passing second.

I was nearly to the balcony door when I realized the fool cat was purring. Shaking my head, I set him gently down on the balcony. The purring grew louder.

"Okay, stupid. You got up here, you can get out," I told him, quickly running my hand down his silky back.

The cat blinked at me as I closed the door, shutting him outside.

I went for my run. When I got back, the cat had vanished. Well, at least he knew a way down.

———

BY SIX-THIRTY I was parked just up the block from the Stewarts' place, a travel mug of Guatemalan coffee in my hands. I planned to keep digging into the McMather connection, but I needed more before I confronted the Senator.

For the time being, my best source of information seemed to be Brian himself. I settled in to wait for him to appear.

It was pretty much of a repeat of the previous morning, but eventually the glossy black garage door eased up, and Brian's steel gray Mercedes edged its way onto the street. I stuck close behind him as he took the now familiar route to his office.

———

ONCE I'D CHECKED Brian was safely ensconced in his office, I retreated to the lobby coffee shop. Just like the previous day. Neither e-mail nor Google searches occupied me for long, and by eleven, my patience was stretched thin.

There had been no sign of Brian, and neither Matcha Latte nor Double Espresso had shown up, so I didn't even get more office gossip. I called Andrea to see if she'd heard any whispers, but she wasn't available.

So I put another call in to Susanna, figuring I was on a roll. When she actually answered, I was momentarily at a loss for words.

"Hello?" she repeated.

"Susanna, it's Barbara. How are you?"

"Fine. Why?" She sounded defensive, which was unlike her.

"No reason." No way was I telling her Mom had told me to call. "We haven't talked in a bit, that's all."

"Oh. Well, we're all fine."

It came out too quickly, and I knew her too well. "Susanna? What's wrong?"

"Why do you always assume…" she began, then broke off abruptly. "Oh, what's the use? I might as well tell you."

"Tell me what?"

"It's Godfrey."

"Go on."

A broken sob. "I don't know what I'm going to do, Barb. I think he's having an affair."

Shades of Cassie Stewart. "Calm down. Tell me what's happened."

"Nothing's happened. Except he doesn't love me anymore," she wailed.

"Has he actually said that?"

"He doesn't have to say it. It's in his actions."

"So what's he done?"

"It's little things—you wouldn't understand."

No, probably not.

And I'd really rather not have to think about what went on between my sister and her obnoxious husband. But I couldn't just ignore her pain. "Have you tried talking to him? Told him how you feel?"

"That'll only make things worse."

I was out of my depth, but I took a shot. "How can you know what he's feeling if you don't ask him?"

Dead silence.

"Susanna?"

"You're not married. You don't know what it's like."

Ouch.

"True. But Susanna, you can't go on like this."

"I can't talk about it now." And she disconnected. Leaving me staring into my empty mug, trying to figure out where we'd gone wrong.

Susanna and I had fought constantly growing up, but we'd also relied on each other. After Dad died and with Mom working all hours, we'd had no choice. It hurt, knowing that now when something went wrong, I was the last person she'd call.

With an effort, I shifted my attention away from Susanna and back to my case. It was half past eleven, I noted with a grimace. I still had at least an hour before Brian would emerge for lunch.

What had I expected this little exercise to prove, anyway? Brian's new inamorata—if she, or he, even existed—could walk right by me and I wouldn't have a clue.

————

TEN MINUTES LATER, I nearly missed Brian's emergence from a crowded elevator. He was pushing through the lobby doors and out into the sunshine before I noticed him. And he was carrying a briefcase.

As I exited and joined the colorful, hurrying throng, I could just make out Brian ahead of me. He turned right and continued at a brisk pace through the usual lunchtime crowds. Was I finally getting a break?

I tailed him down the block, trying to anticipate where he was going. All the restaurants on this street were cafes and delis, which didn't seem his style.

Two blocks further and he turned left on Howe Street.

Where was he headed?

When he crossed Hastings, I started to guess that his destination was Sinclair Centre, one of the toniest of the downtown shopping malls. I was right. He turned into the Centre and I had to hustle to keep up.

Stepping through the carved double doors, I scanned the lunchtime crowd milling about in the central plaza. Just as I was getting panicky, I spotted Brian Stewart on the stairs at the far side.

I followed cautiously. If he noticed me here, it could be the coincidence that started him wondering.

By the time I reached the top of the stairs, I'd lost him. Luckily there were only three options: a bookstore, a store for travelers, and the passport office. It turned out to be fairly easy to find him.

He was seated on one of the hard plastic chairs in the waiting area for Customs and Immigration, a bored expression on his face. Judging by the number of people who were also waiting, he was going to be there for quite awhile.

Which meant so was I.

With a sigh I grabbed a number and a seat as far away from Brian Stewart as I could manage and settled in to wait. I watched him out of the corner of my eye as he worked on his Blackberry, and wondered why he hadn't just mailed in his passport renewal.

Unless he needed a new passport quickly? But why?

It was a long wait, and my stomach was snarling at me.

I nearly decided to use the time to retrieve my own messages, but luckily was still watching Brian when he pulled several pieces of paper from his pocket just as his number was called. He pulled a stack of papers from his briefcase, stuffing the papers he'd been holding inside.

Only he missed one.

If I hadn't been watching so carefully, I'd never have noticed the crumpled scrap of paper coming to a rest just behind his chair leg.

Brian, busy with various forms, didn't notice, just strode to the designated window and began answering questions. I kept a wary eye on him as I stood, stretched, and sauntered over to the window behind his vacated chair.

Dropping the pen I was holding, I bent to retrieve it, capturing Brian's scrap of paper at the same time.

A quick glance showed me a scribbled phone number. The 604 area code said it was local.

Pay dirt.

Things seemed to be in order with Brian's papers, because he was pulling out his credit card. I casually moved to peruse a rack of pamphlets just beside the exit.

Several minutes later Brian was heading back downstairs. I followed, keeping a careful distance between us on the expansive marble stairwell.

As we reached street level, I considered the puzzle Brian Stewart had just presented me with.

Why was he renewing his passport?

Was he the kind of person who had to have a current passport, no matter what?

I am, but that's to maintain the illusion that I could travel on a moment's notice. Actually I could, as long as I didn't mind declaring bankruptcy when I got back.

I doubted that was Brian Stewart's motivation, though. He'd never have to worry about bankruptcy.

Could he be planning on an international trip soon? And if so, did Cassie know?

Or maybe he was planning a trip with someone other than Cassie? If he was having an affair, and so far I'd seen nothing to suggest that he was.

So why had Cassie really hired me?

———

I TRAILED Brian back to his office tower, and watched him get on the elevator. I hated that I had no way to be sure he'd actually returned to his office.

Resuming my seat in the coffee shop, I pulled out the scrap of paper he'd dropped. Keying in the phone number, I held my breath as I counted the rings. One, two, three. A female voice answered.

"Vancouver Public Library," she said. "How may we help you?"

Completely frustrated now, I started searching online for any connection—no matter how remote—between Senator McMather and my client.

Ignoring the din around me as stressed-out staff popped by for their afternoon dose of caffeine and sugar, I tried every combination of searches I could think of. Twenty-seven google screens in, I found a small newspaper item that made the back of my neck prickle.

I nearly missed it—just another grainy photo of two men shaking hands while two frock-clad women with bouffant hairdos stood demurely by. But even in the poorly scanned image, the man on the left was clearly a very young not-yet-Senator Ed McMather. I didn't recognize the figure on the right, but the caption identified him as Robert Grantley, McMather's brother-in-law. And Cassie's father.

Even then I wasn't sure, but another quick search confirmed it.

Ed McMather was Cassie Stewart's uncle, or to be precise, her uncle-in-law.

I'm not fond of coincidences at the best of times, and this one was a stretch.

Maybe Uncle Ed knew something about whatever Cassie wasn't telling me? Or maybe Brian just thought he did.

In either case, it was time to talk to Cassie again. Her reaction to hearing about their lunch date should tell me quite a bit.

Maybe I could turn that lunch into informational gold.

CHAPTER SEVEN

I tracked Cassie down at the Zanthus Gallery, where she was studying a new installation by one of Vancouver's edgier artists.

The Zanthus is a highly respected gallery with an international reputation. They've stayed cutting edge for years, and have maintained a reputation for finding up-and-coming young artists and helping them build their careers.

It was Cassie's kind of place.

The piece that had caught her attention seemed to be constellation of flashing lights mixed in with broken pieces of metal, all forming some kind of twisted pyramid. The significance of it escaped me—but then I was pretty focused on the problem of her husband's actions.

Cassie looked up just then and saw me. She didn't look particularly pleased. "Were you looking for me?"

"Yes. We need to talk, but not here. Have you time for a coffee?"

Her lips tightened, and she glanced at her watch, then shook her head. "I'm sorry, I have an appointment in less than fifteen minutes. What is it?"

I glanced around. The gallery was almost empty. No-one was near enough to hear us. "Ed McMather."

She looked at me blankly, though I saw her eyebrow flicker. "Uncle Ed?"

Okay, this wasn't quite the reaction I'd expected. "Yes. What kind of relationship does your husband have with him?"

"Almost none. My father and my uncle were—estranged. Uncle Ed didn't even come to my wedding. Brian and I have run into him at the occasional function, but nothing more. Why?"

Now there was tension in the line of her shoulders and she'd shifted her weight forward a little, as if preparing for an attack. I'd hit a nerve. But why?

"Your husband and your uncle Ed had lunch together yesterday," I said, watching her closely. "The conversation grew quite heated a couple of times. Any idea what that might be about?"

"No, none at all." She managed to look puzzled without even the slightest wrinkle appearing on her too smooth forehead.

I wasn't buying it. "You don't know of any reason for them to be meeting?"

"No."

"When was the last time you saw your uncle?"

She paused. Over her shoulder one of the installations pulsed pale blue, then neon green. I focused on Cassie's face.

"It must be six or seven months ago," Cassie said.

"And your husband?"

"The same, as far as I know." She glanced at her watch. "I'm sorry, but I really must go. Unless there was something else?"

"Yes. Actually there is something else. I think it's time you told me what you're really worried about."

She looked—stunned is the best word I could come up with. "I don't know what you mean."

"You're holding something back, and I can't do a decent job unless I know what that is."

"I really don't know what you're talking about."

I kept my gaze level, and said nothing.

The silence stretched, then she gave a small sigh and said, "Brian ordered a DNA testing kit."

Not what I'd been expecting to hear.

Still, it did explain the time frame she'd set for the investigation. I knew from a previous case that DNA test results could take as little as three days. My gut said she was still holding something back, though.

"Is it possible he ordered it for a current client?" I asked. It seemed a logical place to start.

"And hid it in his golf bag?"

Okay, maybe not.

I nearly asked why she'd been looking in his golf bag, but given that she'd just hired a P. I., the question was probably redundant.

"Could he be trying to locate ancestral origins through DNA?"

"Then why keep it from me?"

I didn't have an answer for that one, either. "Which company was the test kit from?"

"One called Gene-test."

Now her words rang true. I asked her to spell it, and she did so. Then she paused slightly. My radar quivered.

"If my husband is going to tell me he has fathered a child with someone else, I want to be prepared," she said.

Again, not what I'd expected to hear. My mind raced, considering and discarding possibilities.

What did she mean by prepared? And why had she leapt to that conclusion?

Her face was so tight and tired that I actually began to feel sorry for her.

Me, feeling sorry for Cassie Stewart. Not something I'd ever imagined possible.

"And if he doesn't say anything?" I asked her.

"Then I'll have to confront him. And I'll need the facts to do so. That's why I hired you."

Good to know. I even mostly believed her.

I still didn't think she'd told me everything, but I couldn't figure out what she was hiding. At least I had something new to go on.

"If that is everything, I will see you on Saturday evening," she said, not giving me a chance to respond.

She was an enigma.

She gave a little nod and walked towards the rear of the gallery.

I watched her go, wondering what it was that I was missing. And more than a little curious about whether she planned on buying a piece from this exhibit. I glanced around me once more and grimaced.

Maybe my paintings were exactly where they should be. Gathering dust. They definitely weren't in the same category as these pieces.

I just wished I was sure that was a good thing.

———

WITH CASSIE'S newly generous sharing of information about what her husband was really up to, I headed back to my station at the coffee shop. Hoping Brian hadn't gone somewhere in my absence. Which wasn't all that likely. Not based on his activity—or lack of it —to date.

Cappuccino in hand, I settled in on my stool and googled Genetest. Their website laid out all the different DNA tests available, and told me how to order them. Which was nice of them, but not much help. It seemed anyone could order a simple paternity test online, if they had four hundred dollars and could wait three to five days for results.

With a couple of clicks, I ordered a basic kit. Might as well see exactly how simple the process was. And it counted as a billable expense. I doubted Cassie would check the "miscellaneous" items too carefully. I went back to reading the website.

Apparently if you needed a paternity test to stand up in court, the complexity of the process and the cost increased. Likely Brian-the-lawyer would be familiar with court processes regarding DNA evidence.

Or would he? His specialty was corporate law—which meant he wasn't likely to have much experience with the legal ins and outs of DNA testing.

So I did a search on genetic testing. Which gave me screens full of information on various diseases.

I knew that advances in gene technology have given people a lot more information, including some pretty scary choices, especially around genetically linked diseases like Huntington's chorea and some forms of breast cancer, but I hadn't really thought about it. Not in any personal sense.

Now I did.

What would I do if I learned I carried a gene for something particularly nasty? Something that could kill any child I might have? That could kill me?

It would stop me in my tracks—and it certainly put the frustration of sitting in a coffee shop trying to decipher Brian Stewart's motives in perspective.

Could that be why Brian had ordered the DNA kit? Was he looking for information about some form of genetic disease he was afraid he might carry?

I googled DNA testing, and was rewarded with reams of information about paternity testing, ancestry testing and the legal implications of paternity testing. I settled in to read. Not an easy thing to do while keeping one eye out for Brian. I was soon a little awed and a lot overwhelmed by how much information was available. And how accessible much of that information had become.

If I was going to understand enough to figure out what might be going on in this case, though, I needed an expert. I checked my watch. Four o'clock. Still more than two hours before I'd expect Brian to leave for the day.

I scanned my contacts list, made a couple of calls, pulled a few strings, and managed to secure a meeting for the next day with Dr. Arthurs at UBC Faculty of Medicine. Who just happened to be one of their top researchers, and an expert in DNA and genetic testing.

CHAPTER EIGHT

I was twenty minutes into the meeting with Dr. Arthurs when I knew I was in trouble. I glanced around the small office, taking in shelves crowded with books with unpronounceable titles and a whiteboard with scribbles that meant nothing to me before settling with relief on the green courtyard beyond the windows.

It wasn't so much that my eyes glazed over. More that he'd lost me on the fourth sentence. And I hadn't caught up again. I'd thought I had at least a basic understanding of DNA—after multiple seasons of CSI, who doesn't? Turned out I was wrong.

That's the problem with interviewing a research scientist—they're often so deeply immersed in their area of interest that concepts can only be expressed in technical terms.

What I needed was a translator.

Lucky for me Dr. Arthurs was a perceptive man, as well as an obviously brilliant one. He was cute, too, in a preoccupied, there-are-more-important-things-than-style way. He paused, looked at me for a moment, and smiled.

"I'm sorry, I tend to get a little carried away," he said. "Why don't we move on to another question."

For a moment I considered flirting with him. I hated to admit it, but Andrea might be right. I hadn't been dating enough. I did return his smile, though.

"Why would someone order a DNA testing kit?" Since a general question had got me too much highly technical information, I went for the specific.

For a moment he looked baffled. Then he was off again, explaining testing for specific genetic weaknesses, paternity testing, sibling testing, ancestor testing, and the intricacies and challenges of each. Still way more information than I could use—I needed the broader picture first.

Until I knew what I was looking for, this kind of detail was just so much noise. Fascinating, but noise. I tried again. "How accurate are the DNA testing kits an individual can order online?"

"It isn't the kit that's the issue, though a sample could easily be contaminated if the person collecting it is careless. If it's a buccal swab, for instance," he glanced at me and added, "that's a swab taken from the inside of the cheek, then it should be fine. The real issue, though, is how the lab at the other end handles the specimens. Still, most of them will be accurate enough."

"So they could tell if there was a genetic predisposition to a particular disease?"

"Yes, very often."

If there was some serious illness in Brian's family history, that could be worrying him while he waited for test results. But not enough to cause this sudden, overwhelming change in behavior, surely? Unless he'd been showing symptoms.

What else?

"And they could tell also tell if someone had fathered a particular child. Or not fathered it."

"In most cases, yes, and very accurately."

So if he'd been having an affair—or had one previously— someone could be threatening to sue him for child support. Probably not something he'd want made public. But was it enough to stop him working?

And what was the meeting with Cassie's uncle about, anyway?

"What if he were looking at the paternity of three children who share a mother? Would the answer be clear if all were fathered by the same person?" It was too early to eliminate the possibility that it wasn't his own indiscretions Brian was concerned about.

"I'd say it would be very clear."

And that was how Brian could walk away with a good chunk of her money if he wanted to divorce Cassie. Supposing one of their children wasn't his biological child. If he threatened to tell that child the truth, I suspected Cassie would pay a substantial amount to keep him from doing so. And as a lawyer, he'd know exactly the angles to play.

I wasn't sure that explained his current behavior either. But I had one more question.

"Would DNA results stand up in court?"

"For that, you'd have to ask a lawyer, I'm afraid."

I knew just the lawyer to ask. And I had a few more questions for Cassie, too.

I thanked Dr. Arthurs, and he generously agreed to answer further questions if I had them.

The way this case was unfolding, I was pretty sure I would.

I walked across the leafy campus, weaving my way through the swarms of fresh-faced and impossibly young students, most of whom were connected to an electronic device of some kind. When did they lower the age of university admission, anyway?

Had it really been that long since I'd been a student here?

With a rueful grin, I punched in Claire Chan's office number and was put straight through. Amazing. As a litigator and barrister with her own practice handling both general and family law, she's one of the busiest people I know, yet she always takes my calls, and I've never seen her look flustered.

"Barbara? What can I do for you?"

"I have a case that involves DNA testing, and I need some advice on the legal implications."

There was a beat of silence. "Would you care to join me for tea?" she asked.

Claire's mid-morning tea ritual is sacred to her, and usually solo. An invitation to join her is an experience not to be missed. "I can be there in half an hour or so."

"I look forward to seeing you then."

———

CLAIRE CHAN WAS AS SLEEK AS EVER, wearing a cream silk suit that was perfect with her dainty frame and shiny cap of dark hair. She greeted me at the door of her office with a spontaneous hug and a skeptical smile. "What's this about DNA testing?" she asked as she closed the door and waved me to a chair.

I breathed in the peace of her office.

Bone white walls, painted with leaf patterns from the cherry trees outside, set off sleek black furniture. Pale gray accents contrasted the pot of flourishing bamboo in the far corner. I don't know how she'd done it, but just blocks from the rawness of the Downtown East side and the clamor of Chinatown, Claire had created an oasis of calm.

Smiling, I filled her in on the general scenario, or at least as much as I could say without breaking my client's confidence.

"You always have the most interesting cases."

I shrugged. Not from my perspective.

Most of it's pretty dull—cheating husbands and insurance fraud. It's just that the ones I talk to Claire about are the unusual ones. And there have been a few of those. "Have you had any cases involving DNA testing?"

"A few. One is now public record, as it went to trial. It may be of some relevance for you."

"Because...?"

"It was an issue of inheritance, where an unknown half-sibling came forward to claim a share of the estate after the father's death," she said.

"It must have been an ugly case."

"It was."

"And you represented?"

"The family. That is, the legitimate offspring. We lost."

"Ouch. Based on DNA testing."

A small smile. "Yes. The claimant, a woman, was definitely his child. It wasn't a pleasant situation, for anyone."

"Was there a will?"

"Yes. Leaving the estate split evenly between his children. His wife had predeceased him," Claire said.

"Ah. Let me guess. He didn't name the children, or state how many there were."

"Exactly."

What were the implications for my case? Since all three Stewart children were Cassie's, or at least they were as far as I knew, all three would stand to inherit her millions. Any child Brian had fathered outside the marriage would have a claim only against his estate, wouldn't it?

I made a note to look into what kind of money he had.

"Hypothetically, if the money were the wife's and the husband had an illegitimate child, would that child have any claim against the wife's money?"

"It would depend on who predeceased whom. Hypothetically speaking, how long a marriage?"

"Nearly forty years."

"Then it might make an interesting case. It could depend on the wife's money—inherited or earned?"

"Inherited."

"It could depend on the terms of that inheritance. And how good the illegitimate child's lawyer is."

I made another note. "What if one of the couple's own children was not fathered by the husband?"

"And the money is the wife's?"

"Yes."

"Then the child would still inherit, obviously. But the husband would have an interesting claim to make in divorce court."

That's what I'd suspected. "How much could he walk away with?"

"Depends on how good his lawyer is."

In his position, Brian would undoubtedly know exactly who to retain. "And if he had a barracuda representing him?"

"Let's just say he could walk away a wealthy man. Very wealthy."

It fit with my second scenario, where Cassie was the one who had cheated.

Claire cocked her head to one side, smiled. "You look like you're ready for our tea."

I nodded, and watched as she brought out the matcha powder, the whisk, the bowls. Watching the ritual, the change in her face as she poured and swirled, I realized it wasn't just the décor that made her office so calming.

It was Claire's own insistence on taking this pause in her day, the complete focus she brought to it.

I tried to imagine bringing the same kind of attention to my coffee ritual, and gave a wry smile.

Better I just enjoy what Claire had created here.

CHAPTER NINE

Saturday morning I was slouched back in my battered Civic outside Cassie and Brian's house. Again. I'd come prepared for a long wait, armed with the paper, a tall Italian Roast coffee and a chocolate almond croissant. The wonderful smell of coffee permeated the car, the early morning sun was bright through the windshield, and I was in weekend mode.

I needed to look nothing like temp Brian had met in the elevator, or the one he might spot around the office. So I was wearing my oldest jeans, a well-worn navy T-shirt, a Canucks cap with my hair pulled through the back in a curling pony tail and large sunglasses.

By the time Brian showed up, I'd scanned the headlines in the first two sections and read the sports page, the comics and the arts section. I'd finished my croissant and most of my coffee, so I was feeling human.

I'd even just about forgiven him for that phone number. Which had messed up my sleep all night and which I was still trying to figure out.

I wasn't so inclined to be forgiving when he turned up in running shorts, though.

Oh, don't get me wrong, it wasn't an unpleasant sight. Quite the opposite. I'd been right, the man had kept himself in very good shape.

That wasn't the problem.

If he was planning on running, though, I'd have to follow him, and that was a problem. I hate running after I've eaten.

And naturally I wasn't even wearing my good running shoes, just my old battered Nikes. But I didn't have much choice. With a resigned shrug, I ditched the paper and sunglasses, tucked my phone and credit card into a pocket and set off after him. At least it wasn't raining.

Several miles later, I was still following him. I'm in pretty good shape, a fact for which I was thanking my lucky stars, because Brian Stewart was fit. He didn't even look winded, nor did he look like he was going to stop anytime soon.

I wondered how he managed it on his schedule. Then pictured his house. He probably had a complete gym in the basement. It was big enough.

We wound our way through the quiet, tree-lined residential streets. Just as he seemed ready to turn back, he headed towards Oak Street, one of the major arteries into the city. Now what?

Brian picked up his pace. If he kept this up for very long, he was going to lose me. Hoping that his burst of speed didn't mean he knew I was following him, I dropped back even further. Half a block further on, he turned onto a narrow path and disappeared.

I sped up, my breathing harsh.

Reaching the path, I stopped and listened for a moment.

All I heard was the pounding of my heart and over it, a distant rush of traffic and closer, the wind in the leaves and somewhere a bird singing. The lilting sound ceased abruptly, as though someone or something had disturbed it.

Bending forward to avoid a low hanging branch, I moved forward as quickly and quietly as I could, listening hard for any sound. The last thing I needed was to run right into him.

I'd begun to wonder if I'd lost him, when just ahead of me I heard something.

Voices, talking softly.

I moved in.

Just beyond me, the path widened into a small clearing. Brian was talking to someone. She was wearing Lululemon yoga gear, which in this part of town has become mandatory weekend wear, regardless of sport.

The black, figure-hugging suit left no doubt that she was both female and very attractive, despite the fact that she also sported one of those ugly indestructible hats with the floppy brim that hides most of your face if you wear it right.

Was Cassie right about Brian's other woman? And was this her?

I skirted the edge of the clearing, staying behind a screen of trees, and watching how I placed each foot in the leaves that mounded beneath the thick trunks.

I strained to catch what they were saying, but they were talking too softly. I could barely see her lips move.

Every now and then I could guess what she was saying, but the disjointed words didn't make much sense. I lip-read "wife" and "time" and then "too long".

All I could see of her face was her lips and chin, but the lips were firmly set and the chin was determined. Whatever this lady wanted, she was prepared to get it.

They seemed to be arguing, and Brian made a furious gesture. She didn't even flinch.

I made out "money," then "problem" and "soon". Could she be threatening him? But about what?

My gut told me that whatever this meeting was about, it wasn't an affair.

They were standing too far apart, with none of the subtle leaning towards each other that signals sexual attraction. Brian wasn't touching her and her stance and movements were impatient, not amorous.

Definitely not an affair. So what was it?

The conversation ended. I ducked behind a large bush as Brian turned back towards the path we'd come in on.

Decision time. Who did I follow?

Brian, who might be expected to go home and take a shower before going anywhere else? Or the unknown woman, the first breakthrough I'd had on this case?

It was a no-brainer.

I'd take my chances on catching Brian later.

Once he was out of sight, I took off after the woman. She headed across the clearing at a brisk pace, then cut through the park. I was close enough to see her get into a late model gray Prius. I even caught the license place.

Maybe my luck really was changing.

I ran back towards Oak Street and the hospital, then called a cab, which came almost immediately. The cabbie dropped me off a couple of blocks from the Stewarts'.

I'd just settled back in my car with sunglasses firmly in place when I spotted Brian returning from his run, looking tired and hot at last.

Wishing mightily that I was also headed for a nice long shower, I sat back to await his reappearance.

———

SEVERAL HOURS LATER, I was still waiting. As the day got warmer, I was really wishing I had access to a shower. Even with the windows cranked open, my Civic was beginning to resemble a sweatbox.

I was also wishing it wasn't Saturday. I have a friend at ICBC, Rod Zabel, a fellow I went to high school with. He's always willing to check out the odd license plate number for me on the QT, and I could find out more about the lady in Lululemon. Unfortunately, Rod doesn't work on weekends.

Finally the door opened, and Cassie Stewart left the house, with Brian right behind her. They were dressed casually, Brian in chinos and a golf shirt, his wife in a full-skirted sundress and light cardigan.

Moments later the Mercedes with Brian at the wheel headed towards town. I followed.

Brian dropped Cassie off on Fourth Avenue, outside What Else?, one of the city's more interesting women's clothing boutiques. I browse there occasionally, just to see what's in fashion, but their prices are way out of my range.

Keeping up with the latest styles is not one of my priorities—every item I buy does at least double duty, and will be worn until it literally wears out. What Else? has wonderful end of season sales though, and there are a couple of infinitely versatile items in my wardrobe that have resulted from those sales.

I was guessing Cassie would be there for most of the morning. Much as I wanted to ask her a few pointed questions, I had other priorities.

Brian continued down Burrard, and across the bridge, finally turning onto Georgia. Where was he going? I was four cars behind him, trying not to lose him in the snarl of cars.

Ahead of us Georgia opened out, and I could see the distinctive curve that resembles the Roman Coliseum. Not the library again!

What was it with him and the public library?

Sure enough, Brian drove into the library's underground parking lot, and I followed. Then someone backed out in front of me, very slowly, and I lost sight of him.

"Figures," I muttered, and started my search. I just hoped he'd gone into the library itself, and not out onto Robson Street. I'd never find him then.

CHAPTER TEN

I finally found Brian Stewart on the fifth floor of the library. He was seated at one of the cubicles in the newspaper stacks, looking through microfilms. And judging by the number of rolls piled on the table beside him, he was serious about it.

So what was he checking out so intently?

He was so focused on the screen in front of him that I took the chance of walking behind him, as though I were checking the reference volumes there. From that vantage, I could see that he was working his way through what looked like twenty years of back issues of the *Vancouver Sun,* mostly from the sixties and seventies.

He was going to be there for quite awhile.

He didn't look up as I took down a volume, opened it as though checking a reference, then keyed the information on his search into my phone. He seemed totally engrossed, scrolling quickly through the pages, sometimes pausing to scan a page.

I took down another volume, watching him over the top of it. It made me dizzy just watching the pages roll by. I couldn't see any pattern to his searching, either.

What was he after?

And how did it relate to that DNA kit he'd bought?

———

TWO HOURS LATER, Brian was still sitting in the same spot, staring at the same screen. He'd barely moved, except to shift the stack of microfilm from one side to the other.

Finally, with a huge sigh, he sat back, stretched out his shoulders and looked around the room. He checked his watch, ran a hand through his hair and rolled his head back and forth.

I could just imagine how stiff his back and neck muscles must feel. I've spent my share of time poring over microfilms. It isn't fun.

He picked up the last two rolls, checked the dates. Then he put them down, stood up, stretched again, and left the room.

He'd taken me by surprise, and I had to hustle not to lose him.

As I followed the familiar silver Mercedes onto the madness of Georgia Street, I wondered what he was up to now.

Was this finally going to be the information I'd been watching for?

Of course not.

Brian Stewart was merely going to get his hair cut.

It would have helped if Cassie had told me about the appointment. It was probably a weekly habit. A style like his doesn't stay neatly trimmed all by itself, and somehow I couldn't see Cassie with a pair of barber's shears.

So there sat Brian, ensconced in the one of the high-tech chairs at Axel's, while I scrambled to find an inconspicuous vantage point.

He emerged forty minutes later looking very sharp, collected Cassie and went home.

I sat outside their house until nearly six-thirty, but there was no further sign of them.

As I put the car in gear, I had that panicky feeling that I was going to miss something important, but I still had to get ready for the play, and by now I badly needed a shower.

———

JUST OVER AN HOUR and a half later I was mingling with the crowd of theatergoers jamming the semi-circular lobby of the Playhouse. *Blithe Spirit* had been getting good reviews, and Noel Coward's brand of witty sophistication always goes over well in this city.

I was wearing my classic 'little black number,' one of those What Else? sale items that had more than justified its cost. I always felt good wearing it with sexy shoes—about the only time I do wear them—though I draw the line at heels higher than three inches.

I'm already tall enough, thanks, and I value my ankles. Especially if I have to chase after someone I'm supposed to be tailing.

I don't get to plays often enough, but I thoroughly enjoy the experience when I do. I confess I find people watching often more entertaining than the play itself. Playgoers arrive dressed in everything from sequins to Gortex—this is the Wet Coast, after all. Some are clearly enjoying themselves, while others are quite blasé about the whole thing.

Brian and Cassie fell into the latter category.

They had dressed to kill, he in dark Armani, she in a knee-length sheath of eggshell silk and shimmery bronze stilettos with four-inch heels. Her posture was too perfect, though, and I didn't think it was the heels—she was practically brittle with tension, like a too thin spun-sugar glazing that will crack if you look at it wrong.

Cassie hadn't looked like this the last time I'd seen her—was she expecting something to happen tonight?

Was that why I was here?

I hovered close enough to their group of eight to catch a few stray remarks. All of them had seen the play many times—it was going to take spectacular acting or directing to catch their attention. For them this was primarily a social occasion, a chance to see and be seen.

As the bell rang to announce the first act, I followed the Stewart party into the theater.

I'd managed to get a single seat ten rows higher than the seats that Brian and Cassie held for the season. For the first few minutes, their heads were tilted towards each other and they seemed to be continuing an earlier conversation. Even from behind, I could see the lines of tension along her neck and in the angle of her head.

Once the curtain rose, Cassie focused on the play.

Brian began to gaze around the theater. He'd check the action on the stage for a moment or two, then scan the rows. He seemed oblivious to Cassie's tension, but I couldn't tell if he was too unsettled to concentrate, bored with the play or looking for someone.

Lululemon Lady, perhaps?

At intermission, Brian and Cassie rejoined the group they'd been with earlier. Both of them chatted easily with the others, though I could still see the tension in the way Cassie was standing. Then Brian touched her on the arm, said something and headed for the bar.

I followed him. Discreetly, of course.

He exchanged nods with a number of people on his way, but didn't stop. He joined the line-up of theatergoers patiently waiting for their glasses of Scotch and warm chardonnay, but his eyes moved constantly, scanning the crowds. Even standing motionless in the bar line-up, he gave the impression of being in motion.

There was a lot of pent-up energy there. What was going on with these two?

Reaching the bar at last, Brian ordered two gin and tonics. He took a long swallow of one, then headed for the lobby, where he rejoined his friends. There was no sign of Cassie.

Brian didn't seem worried, just held her drink while slowly emptying his.

I could easily guess where Cassie was. And if the line-up was as long as the last time I was here, she'd be there for a while. Why are there never enough stalls in the women's washrooms at these places? Don't they know what will happen at intermission?

As I watched Brian and kept an eye out for Cassie, I wondered what Cassie hoped I'd accomplish by being here tonight. Brian made no effort to leave the group he'd rejoined. When the first bell rang they all drifted off, leaving him standing there holding the untouched gin and tonic.

Where was Cassie?

If it weren't for that G&T, I'd have suspected she'd gone home with a headache or some such. But Brian was clearly expecting her back.

I'd just started to think she'd abandoned him when she appeared on his left, looking flustered. She accepted her drink, downing more than half of it with an air of relief. Then set it aside.

The two of them hurried into their seats just as the curtain rose.

The remainder of the evening passed without incident. As far as I could tell, Brian didn't meet up with whomever he was looking for. And Cassie's tension didn't lessen.

If anything, it had increased.

They watched the rest of the play, then went down to the parkade for their car. Following them, I expected they'd join their group for a drink or a late supper, but no. They went straight home.

Parking outside the house, I watched for about half an hour to see if Brian would go out again, with or without Cassie. About twenty minutes later, the lights in the house went out, one by one.

I waited another half hour, then gave up.

It had to be one of the shortest Saturday nights on record.

———

BACK IN MY CONDO, I considered my options. My assignment was over and I was already dressed to impress. Plus I didn't want to sit home and think about whether I'd missed some key event this evening.

The last was enough to decide me. Grabbing the invitation I'd stuck to the fridge, I headed out.

My compact apartment is located just off South Granville Street, which gives it two advantages—it's decidedly cheaper than trendy Yaletown, and it's around the corner from Vancouver's gallery row.

Most of the city's important art galleries are represented along this ten block stretch, interspersed with coffee shops, restaurants, antique stores, bookstores, delis and a heritage theatre. That particular evening, the exclusive Courtland Gallery was having an opening for a one-man show of Jayson Ho's work. I'd received an invitation, complete with puffed up quotes about "this exciting young artist".

This in itself was not surprising—Jayson sends me invitations to all his openings. I can never decide if this is for old time's sake, or just his need to rub it in now that he's "someone who matters" in the local and even the national art world.

Usually I ignore the invitations, but sometimes I put in an appearance, just to prove that Jayson and his world no longer affect me. Then I end up wishing I hadn't gone.

I hadn't intended to go this time, but I wasn't ready for the evening to end. I was feeling restless—partly glad the Stewart case was over, partly frustrated by my failure to decode it. Since it wasn't like Cassie to miss a major opening, the persistent part of my nature wanted to see if she and Brian showed up after all.

And Jayson and I were over a long time ago. I was just going to see what kind of stuff he was doing now.

Who was I kidding?

I was curious about how the Courtland Gallery would handle Jayson's work, but basically I couldn't resist an opportunity to immerse myself in that world.

I don't get time to paint much anymore, and mostly I'm okay with that. It was my choice, after all, and I already feel more successful as an investigator than I ever did as an artist. But sometimes I just need a hit of the scene.

It's part love of art, part nostalgia and part some indefinable shiver I get when I walk in the door.

Nearing the gallery, a cloud of cigarette smoke and the rising and falling din of a great many people talking at once rushed out to greet me. I paused just inside the door to get my bearings.

Success at a gallery opening is measured by the number of people packed into every available inch of space, and it looked like this one was a success. From where I stood, the press of people was so great, all I could see of the art was the tops of some of the canvases, stretching towards the ceiling in great swaths of black and orange and gray. Jayson must be feeling very proud of himself.

As if the thought had conjured him up, the artist himself appeared in front of me. "Barbara. You came," he said, dark eyes agleam, smiling the smile that every woman he's ever met has found mysterious and intriguing. It irks me to realize I still found it so.

As he leaned closer to kiss me on each cheek, I caught a waft of his cologne, spicy with just a hint of musk. At least Jayson's scent no longer had any effect on me. I blame the fact that our relation-ship lasted as long as it did on my unaccountable reaction to his cologne.

"Jayson," I said.

He waved a slim hand towards the crowded room. "Isn't this unbelievable? Jennifer-my-agent tells me they haven't had an opening like this in years."

"Mmmm," I said, scanning the crowd, hoping I'd see someone to save me. No such luck.

"I find it hard to believe they're all here just to see my work," he went on. "All those years of struggle, and now this."

Too bad there wasn't a reporter handy.

I wondered uncharitably whose autobiography Jayson had been reading—modesty isn't his usual style. Giving him a half-smile, I murmured something about finding the bar, but I wasn't going to get away that easily.

"I need another drink myself," Jayson assured me, taking my elbow and moving towards the back of the room. "I've done nothing but answer questions about my work all evening, and my throat is getting dry."

As we moved through the crowd, people were congratulating him on every side.

He nodded acknowledgment to everyone who spoke to him, but continued towards the bar without slowing, keeping a firm hold on my arm. I noted with some amusement that even in this kind of crowd, when Jayson decides on a destination, no one stops him. None of the people he didn't stop to talk to would feel slighted, either, such was the nature of his charm.

I've never quite figured out how he does it.

He produced a glass of red wine for me and single malt for himself and steered me towards one wall. I went along—it wasn't worth the struggle it would take to oppose him.

As we went, I noted that the Courtland Gallery had done him proud. His works were beautifully displayed and subtly lit. He's an incredible artist, with an intelligence and an energy that leap off the canvas.

Though I seldom like his work, I am in awe of his talent.

"So, Barbara," he said when we'd reached a relatively quiet corner. "What is new with you lately? When will I see a Barbara O'Grady showing?"

"I'm no longer painting, Jayson. You know that."

"But it is such a waste. Painting is in your blood, as it is in mine. Can you stop breathing?"

"I wasn't getting anywhere as a serious artist," I broke in, knowing he was quite prepared to go on forever in this melodramatic fashion.

"Barbara, you sell yourself short. Your art is so much a part of who you are. And it is very—pleasing."

I winced, but managed to smile pleasantly at him and shrug, a gesture I know infuriates him.

I'd heard his views, as well as the subtle put-downs, often enough before.

I still found it sad that what had originally drawn me to Jayson was his understanding of how important painting was to me.

Jayson's eyes narrowed.

Before either of us could say something we'd regret, his agent came looking for him. Something about a prospective buyer for several canvasses. Jayson's expression changed instantly, and the two of them disappeared into the crowd, leaving me to sip my wine and survey the scene.

There was no sign of Cassie or Brian Stewart. Not that I'd really expected them to be there.

I wandered through the crowd, looking at the enormous canvasses with their frantic sweep of colors and listening to snatches of conversation. Most of it was complimentary. There was no doubt Jayson had a hit, though one or two people seemed to share the acute unease that all of Jayson's work had begun to engender in me.

When I'd finished my wine, I put the empty glass down on a side table already littered with empty glasses, and quietly departed.

I walked slowly south on Granville, testing the chill of the night air and clearing my lungs of smoke and my mind of the contact with Jayson and his works.

I was too wound up to go home, so I continued on past my street to Guido's, which is one of my favorite places, a bistro that serves an odd mix of Italian and Creole food, all of it good. On a Friday and Saturday night they have pints of local micro beers on special and the place is always hopping.

I needed a little of that good-hearted energy.

Guido himself met me at the door, and enveloped me in a hug. "Barbara. It is good to see you again. Tonight we have the Granville Island Pale Ale on special. For you a pint?"

I nodded, returning the hug. Guido's one of my favorite people, and a more genuine person doesn't exist. There couldn't be a more complete contrast to Jayson's pseudo warmth.

I sat at the bar with my beer, chatting to Guido when he wasn't bustling about the small room. One or two of the regulars were there and we exchanged a nod and a smile.

A crowd of twenty-somethings at one end of the room were having themselves quite a party, and the noise level was as loud as it had been at the gallery. To my ears it was a friendlier sound, underlaid by the old-style blues that always plays through the sound system, and I could feel myself relaxing. It was after one by the time I finally left.

CHAPTER ELEVEN

Sunday I slept in, then staggered into the kitchen and made a pot of Viennese coffee, slathered toast with ginger-pear jam. Blearily I carried my cup and plate into the living room. Rain was pattering against the French doors and the light was thin and gray.

I looked warily about. No cat. Good.

I was tired and I was looking forward to a leisurely read of the paper—cat wrangling was simply not on the agenda. But no sooner had I sat down on the sofa and opened my paper than a large warm lump landed on my lap. And began to purr.

"And just what do you think you're doing?" I asked him as I tentatively scratched him behind one ear. "You can't stay there. You weigh a ton, Cat."

The purring stopped. One eye opened. He just looked at me.

"Oh, all right. Just until I finish the paper, though."

The purring resumed. I grinned.

Bested by a cat.

It figured.

I opened my paper again. The front page headline instantly wiped out my smile.

"Local Senator Murdered," it screamed in seventy-two point type.

We have more than one local Senator, but I had a nasty feeling this was related to my current case even before I read the first paragraph.

Ed McMather had been found dead late Saturday night.

I sat and stared at that name for at least thirty seconds.

Maybe this had nothing to do with the meeting between Uncle Ed and Brian Stewart on Tuesday, or with Cassie's long disappearance during intermission. Maybe, but my intuition wasn't convinced, not even for ten of those thirty seconds.

Taking a deep breath, I scanned the article. It described the murder scene in graphic detail.

Another reporter with a secret desire to write murder mysteries. It would have amused me under other circumstances.

McMather had been shot to death in his kitchen. The body was discovered at midnight. By whom? I scanned further.

Jerry Hawald was named as the investigating officer.

I turned to the obit, which was extensive, detailing the late Senator's accomplishments and affiliations. I read somewhere that newspapers keep biographies of well-known people on file, so that when they die, most of the story is pre-written. I wondered who the poor reporter was that had to dig out pertinent facts at one a.m.

McMather had lived a colorful and very public life.

He'd been affiliated with a wide variety of business interests and had represented two political parties, one local and one national. Back in the late-forties and early fifties he'd been involved with a number of B.C.'s big resource companies, particularly in mining and exploration, as well as a venture capital firm.

There was no mention of McMather's family or of his wife. Cassie's late father was described as a business partner of McMather's in the mid-fifties, but there was no mention that they were brothers-in-law.

I read the story again, slowly, then swallowed hard.

Was I going to have to tell the police about my latest case?

If either of the Stewarts had anything to do with the murder, I was obligated to share what I knew. Which wasn't very much, admittedly, and it would mean breaking my client's confidence.

I could still hear Cassie's voice in my head. "I dislike gossip."

I could just imagine how she'd feel about my telling the police she'd had her husband followed. And with her connections, that would not bode well for my current career.

The only thing worse was if one of them was actually connected to the murder. Cassie had disappeared for half an hour or so during the intermission. I had a horrible moment picturing a trial with me as witness for the prosecution.

I didn't even want to think about how testifying against my own client would play on the local rumor mill.

I considered the tension I'd seen in my client all evening. Surely she hadn't been gone long enough to commit murder? And her cream gown was unstained.

What motive could Cassie Stewart possibly have for killing an uncle she barely knew?

McMather had been a man who made enemies—likely the police already had a suspect. I was letting my unease around whatever my client was keeping from me get out of control.

I dumped Cat off my lap and stood up. Offended, he stalked off down the hall, tail very straight and twitching slightly. I ignored him.

I needed the straight facts on McMather's demise, and I wasn't going to find them in the paper. And the detective in charge was none other than my old buddy Jerry, the guy my mother thinks I should be dating.

Yeah, right. Jerry's the closest thing I have to a brother. The idea of dating him is just too weird.

But he can be a very helpful friend.

———

THE MAIN VANCOUVER police station is a low, red brick and glass building next to an on-ramp for the Cambie Bridge and across from a Canada Line SkyTrain station. It isn't a memorable building, but it is secure. Unless Jerry signed me in, I didn't have a hope of getting much past the main doors.

With McMather's murder on his plate, Jerry wasn't going to do that anytime soon.

That's where being old friends comes in very handy. Jerry's a creature of habit, and if he wasn't actually at the murder scene, I had a pretty good idea where to find him.

With the advent of the Canada Line, this part of Cambie is gentrifying fast, but there are still holdouts from a more hard-scrabble neighborhood, including several small, increasingly rundown strip malls.

Tucked away behind a nondescript storefront in one of the least prosperous malls is probably the world's best bakery. I can never resist their chocolate almond croissants, and Jerry is a sucker for their gooey, pecan-spiked cinnamon buns.

He swears he finds the connections in his cases when fueled by those cinnamon buns. And who am I to argue with him—his solve rate is one of the best on the force.

Shaking off the rain, I pushed open the glass door and stepped into the steamy warmth. The yeasty smell of baking bread mingled with the rich scents of cinnamon, caramelized sugar and coffee. I drew in a deep breath, savoring it as my eyes searched the small, nearly empty room.

Jerry had chosen an isolated table in the far corner. I grabbed a coffee and a croissant for me and a refill plus a second cinnamon bun for him and headed over.

He was deep in thought, and didn't notice me until I'd actually put the fresh coffee and roll in front of him. Then he looked up and frowned.

Jerry's no fan of my new career, and he's always wary when I track him down here.

When he's not scowling, Jerry's a nice looking man—tall and

dark with craggy features. He looks like someone you can depend on, and he is.

When he is scowling, though, Jerry looks like an offended orangutan. Something I wasn't planning on telling him this morning.

"Thanks, O'Grady. But what are you doing here at this hour?" Before I could answer, his eyes narrowed. "Not my murder case?"

I nodded.

"Damn. What are you involved in now?"

"Sorry, Jerry. Client confidentiality."

"Don't mess with this one, O'Grady. Whoever shot him was serious about it. That kitchen was a mess, and the poor guy was lying there with a look of surprise on his face. You do not want get anywhere near…"

"He looked surprised?"

Interrupted mid-rant, Jerry glared at me. "Yeah. The man looked almost stunned, as if he couldn't believe what was happening to him."

Which makes sense, in a warped kind of way. Most corpses probably don't start the day expecting to be dead. But still, most of them don't end up looking surprised about it. "Have you ever seen a body look surprised before?"

He ignored me. "Murder is police business. You're way out of your league, O'Grady, so stay out."

My mind was putting the pieces together. We've been hit with a wave of violent inter-gang shootings lately, most of them drug related. Could McMather have been involved somehow? "Do you suspect drugs?"

"Tell me you didn't just ask another question."

"Calm down, Jerry. I'm not planning on getting involved in your investigation. I just wanted to be sure I didn't have info that you needed."

"Like what?"

"Someone I'm doing some work with crossed paths with your victim."

"Who?" he barked.

"Brian Stewart." I figured I could say that much without compromising my professional ethics or my client.

"You kidding me, O'Grady? Stewart's a top-notch lawyer. He doesn't need to murder anyone—he can sue them till there's nothing left."

I shook my head. Jerry's had a few run-ins with defense lawyers, and it's left him bitter. "Very funny."

"I thought so. Wait a minute. You don't have anything concrete —like a motive—do you?"

"Nothing like that. It's probably nothing, but I just wanted to check a few things. Can you tell me the time of the murder?"

"Yeah, I guess so. It'll be public today anyway. He died sometime between eight-thirty and ten-thirty Saturday night."

My stomach went cold. Cassie Stewart had disappeared from the QE lobby within that time frame. No way she had time to kill McMather, though.

And I still couldn't see any connection between McMather and Brian's DNA kit. "And McMather lived in Shaughnessy, right?"

"Shaughnessy? You're slipping, O'Grady. He moved to Yaletown last year, had the penthouse in that new place on Robson."

I knew the one he was talking about, a towering pillar of glass with imported hardwood floors and stainless steel everything. One of its selling features was being walking distance to a number of destinations, including the Queen Elizabeth Playhouse.

I felt sick. Could Cassie have killed McMather?

No. I was over-reacting. No matter what the man might have known, she wouldn't risk a life sentence to silence him. Not Cassie Stewart.

And not when she'd hired me to watch her husband, and by extension, her.

That sent my thoughts off on a new tangent. Maybe she'd hired me because she was afraid Brian needed an alibi?

No, that would imply she knew both that McMather was going

to be killed, and when. And surely no-one but the murderer would know that.

Which brought me right back to my original concern. Could Cassie…? No.

Unless she'd hired someone.

Just like she'd hired me to protect her husband?

While I was busy torturing myself with doubts about my client and this case, Jerry had gone back to his original question. "At least Stewart's no danger to you. Not like some of the cases you've taken on. And I think you can rest easy about him being connected to this one."

Of all the times for him not to take me seriously. Unless…" Does that mean you have someone in custody?"

"Not yet."

"But you've got a suspect?"

"You know I can't tell you that. Let's just say I'd be very surprised if we wanted to know where Stewart was last night. Your conscience is clear," he finished with a wicked grin.

But was it?

My mind froze for a second, then went back into overdrive. Cassie had been insistent I keep a close eye on her husband on that particular Saturday night, which meant I was now in a position to vouch for his actions during the entire time frame in which McMather was likely killed. Those were facts.

"What do you mean, my conscience is clear?" I said.

"You've advised me of a possible connection. We'll take it from here. Now, if you don't mind, I have a murderer to apprehend." And he drained his coffee and polished off the last of his second cinnamon bun.

If they really did have a suspect, then maybe I was creating theories from thin air and worrying about nothing.

I absently wrapped a paper napkin around my croissant, which I hadn't yet touched, and drained my own coffee. "Yeah, yeah, I'm going. Oh, by the way. You did know that McMather was Brian Stewart's uncle-by-marriage, didn't you?"

"Oh, that's right, he married Grantley's daughter, didn't he?"

"Yes, Cassie Stewart." Who couldn't possibly be guilty of murder. Not wearing four-inch heels. Could she? "What was the murder weapon?"

".38," he answered absently. "Still, I doubt the relationship is relevant."

I hoped he was right.

I pictured Cassie as I'd seen her at the theater last night. She'd been carrying a heavily sequined baguette bag in the same shimmery bronze as her heels. Could she have fit a .38 in that bag?

I pictured the bag, the gun. It was possible.

It wasn't likely, though—this was Cassie Stewart, after all. She didn't strike me as someone who would choose to settle things with a gun. "Who found the body?"

"Ted Hewitt. McMather's PA."

"And Mrs. McMather?"

"Divorced. She lives in Venice," he replied, obviously still pondering the McMather-Grantley connection.

"Only the one ex?"

"Yes—wait a minute. Why are you asking me all these questions?"—then as he replayed his answers in his head—"and whatever you do, don't talk about the murder weapon, we haven't released that yet."

"Of course not."

"And exactly why did you want to know about the ex-Mrs. McMather?"

"I'm not sure." And I wasn't.

But I still had a bad feeling about this death. It wouldn't hurt to learn what I could about McMather and his connections. "Is she still using his name?"

"As far as I know. Our information doesn't show her remarried."

"How long had they been divorced?"

"No idea."

I made a mental note to check what had happened in that divorce. It was too bad she was so far away, and that my finances wouldn't stretch to a trip to Venice. I'd have loved an excuse to revisit that city.

"The ex isn't a suspect, if that's what you wanted to know," Jerry stated, startling me out of my reverie. "She's been out of the country for years. We're looking at events a little more recent than that one. It's no secret that McMather had some rather unsavory connections."

"Thanks, Jer." He wasn't about to tell me anything else and I had what I needed to know my client was in the clear.

We walked out together, into a driving rain that had me lowering my head and dashing to my car.

CHAPTER TWELVE

It was nearly ten on Sunday morning by the time I parked in the now too-familiar spot across from the Stewart mansion. After thoroughly drenching me the rain had let up and the clouds were clearing, but there was no sign of movement from the house.

Had Brian and Cassie already left? Were they still asleep? Half an hour crawled by. I was beginning to wonder if they were dead too. They'd turned in before midnight the previous night.

Before my imaginings got too macabre, the front door opened, and Brian appeared, wrapped in a heavy cotton robe with his feet bare. He retrieved the paper and went back inside.

I'd been hoping he'd at least glance at the headlines on the porch where I could see him, but no such luck.

Twenty minutes later I was basking in the unexpected sunshine when Brian dashed out, looking like he'd just run a mile in a high wind. Anything more unlike his usual immaculate self would be hard to imagine. His hair was still wet and standing on end, his shirt was untucked and he wasn't wearing socks.

If I were a wagering woman, I'd bet he'd just seen the front page of the paper. I'd hoped for a reaction, but I hadn't expected this.

As I followed the now-familiar Mercedes through the downtown core, I wondered if he was heading for the police station, but no. He made a left turn onto Georgia Street and we proceeded through Stanley Park at its greenest and across the Lion's Gate Bridge.

Even in the present circumstances the panorama of mountains and ocean with the span of the bridge arching through it caught my attention. Sunlight reflected off the water, and a flotilla of sailboats filled the bay. We Vancouverites are an odd lot—it rains so much here that the minute the clouds part, everyone in the city is outside —sailing, biking, walking the Seawall.

Not Brian, though.

He followed the long curve off and beneath the bridge, turning up Taylor Way and then onto the Upper Levels highway. I was following three cars back, half expecting him to turn down the hill into West Vancouver.

He didn't.

Ten minutes later I was still following him along the highway, wondering where he was heading. And why?

At no point in this last week had I been able to figure out Brian's motivation, and now I was more in the dark than ever. I knew he hadn't killed McMather, but that was the only thing I did know.

I had no idea why news of McMather's death had triggered this journey. Was it possible he also suspected Cassie?

After we'd passed all the other turnoffs, including the one to Whistler, I realized Brian had to be heading for the ferry terminals at Horseshoe Bay. Great. All I needed was for him to take a ferry to the Island, and I'd be stuck there overnight.

If it weren't for the frequency with which my car gets broken into, I'd leave a packed overnight bag in my car.

To my relief, it soon became clear that Brian was headed for the Bowen Island ferry. Only problem was, though Bowen Island is only about twenty minutes away, the ferry that services it is small, eighty cars or so.

The odds of Brian spotting me tailing him onto the island were high.

After a quick internal debate, I decided that it didn't much matter. I wasn't on the meter anymore.

If I chose to take a day trip to Bowen, so what? And given the state Brian was in I doubted he'd recognize the Prime Minister himself.

Still, once I'd been directed to my parking spot on the open deck of the ferry, I stayed in my car and buried my face in my newspaper to lessen the chance that he'd spot me.

When we reached Bowen, the procession of cars wound off the ferry and up the single street. Brian was a dozen cars ahead of me, but now the size of Bowen was working in my favor. There are only two ways to drive from the ferry terminal—either you go straight, or you turn right at the first corner along the road that curves around the island.

Brian turned right.

I followed him, gradually dropping back as the cars between us turned off one by one. We'd gone right around the far curve of the island before he slowed.

When I saw his taillights flicker, I eased off the gas and allowed the battered Civic I've been driving for years to drop even further back. The car is unmemorable, to put it kindly, and with so many Civics around, people tend not to notice them. For a P. I., that's an asset.

My car also has the distinct advantage of a paint job that's faded over the years to mottled brown, a color Andrea refers to as theft-proof beige, usually when she's trying to convince me I need a new car. With my bank account? Not likely.

Brian turned into a driveway that was all but obscured by over-hanging cedar trees. I continued on for several hundred yards before stopping and turning the car.

Retracing my route, I slowed down well before those cedar trees. I caught a glimpse of silver at the bottom of the driveway that told me where Brian had parked the Mercedes, but nothing to tell me who lived here.

Some of the houses along the way had those cutesy wooden signs announcing 'Betty and Marvin Jones' or 'The Funk Family,' but this place didn't even seem to have street numbers. I parked my car around the next bend and walked back.

Finally, I found what I was looking for—a faded cedar board with the numbers fourteen-eleven etched into it, all but invisible against the graying bark of a huge pine. The house itself wasn't visible.

I double-checked to make sure that silver gleam was indeed Brian's Mercedes. It was.

In the back of my head, I could hear Sid Fluxgold's nasal voice repeating impatiently, "Always make sure of your facts. Check, double check and check again. Don't ever assume you know what you're seeing," as he tried to instruct his newest recruit in the tough world of private investigation.

Thanks again, Sid. You taught me well.

Back in my car, I headed for the ferry terminal and the few shops and services that served as Bowen's social center. Bowen is basically a suburb of Vancouver, but because it's an island, it has the features of a small town and an island mentality.

Everyone knows everyone else, and a fair bit about everyone else's business. Sitting in the cheery coffee shop, with a surprisingly good cup of coffee, I'd get an update on the island social life just by listening in.

I also had a clear view of the hand drawn map of the island that covered one wall, showing the various properties and the names of the owners. Number fourteen-eleven was listed as belonging to one Gregory Rutledge.

I knew the name, of course.

Rutledge sat on the Provincial Court bench for a number of years before his retirement, which must have been fifteen years or more ago. I wondered how Brian knew him, and why he'd run to the Judge now?

Whatever the reason, I was pretty sure I wouldn't find it on the island. Not that it mattered.

It really wasn't my case anymore.

CHAPTER THIRTEEN

Monday morning found me sitting behind my desk, with sunlight streaming through the office window and a rich blend of Italian and French coffee gently steaming in my cup. I was staring at the to-do list I'd made on the ferry the previous day. Topping the list was writing my final report for Cassie Stewart.

I hesitated, then added 'call Susanna' on the bottom of the list, right after 'set up meeting with Cassie.'

I wasn't looking forward to either conversation.

Occasionally I sit in my not too messy office, with the sign on the door that says 'Barbara O'Grady Investigations,' and feel a sense of pride. It makes all the days of hard, tedious slogging—and even leaving my painting behind—seem worthwhile. Then one of my cases takes a wrong turn, and I'm left wondering exactly how I ended up here.

Today looked like being one of those days.

After fortifying mouthful of coffee, I focused on writing the report for Cassie. Nearly an hour later I realized I still had no information on the woman Brian had met with.

I could hardly submit a report without that detail. I grabbed a refill, checked my watch, then Rob's number at ICBC, my least favorite insurance company.

"Zabel speaking."

"Hey, Rob. It's Barbara."

"Barbara. Good to hear from you. And what can I do for you this morning?"

"As if you need to ask."

"You never know. You might actually be wanting to date me, one of these years."

"Yeah, right." We both know his preferences go in other directions.

He laughed. "Okay, B., let 'er rip."

"The number's triple L, 937."

"LLL 937," he repeated. "Half a mo." I could hear the clicking of keys. "Plate belongs to a Lisa Stern. 200 East Fifteenth Street. That's Vancouver."

The name rang a faint bell. I prodded at my memory, tried to connect it with the little I'd seen of her face. Nothing.

I noted the address. It was a decent part of town, nothing fancy. "Can you spell that?"

"F,I,F,T…"

I could almost hear his broad grin. "Funny, Rob."

"Okay, here we go. Lisa as it sounds, S, T, E, R, N."

"Thanks, Rob. I owe you one."

"You sure do. And somewhere there's a steak with my name all over it."

"When this one's done, you can collect. I'll call you."

"You do that, B. Later."

I disconnected, unearthed the phone book from under a stack of papers, and looked up Lisa Stern. There was no Lisa or L. Stern listed, but there was a D. Stern and the address was right. I dialed.

The phone was answered on the third ring.

"Stern residence," said a heavily accented voice.

"Lisa Stern, please."

"Mrs. Stern is not home. May I take message?"

"Can you tell me when you're expecting her back?"

"No, I'm sorry. Is there a message?"

"No, I'll call back, thanks." I disconnected, and thought about what the call might have told me.

The hour and the presence of what I was guessing was a live-in nanny suggested the woman worked full time, somewhere. I Googled her, but couldn't find anything relevant.

Now what? At least I had a name for my report, but for anything more I'd have to follow her. If, and it might be a big if, Cassie was prepared to pay for it.

Who knew—perhaps she already knew the woman.

Downing the rest of my coffee, I turned back to the report, typed in the relevant information and pressed print.

With a sigh I checked my list. I'd written in Ted Hewitt's name with a question mark.

He'd been McMather's assistant, he'd found the body. He obviously hadn't been home when McMather was killed, or someone would already be in custody, but he might know something about the relationship between McMather and the Stewarts.

Technically I didn't need to talk to him unless Cassie renewed my contract, but I hate loose ends. And I still had some niggling questions about her motives, particularly around McMather's death.

Of course, Jerry would have my head if he found out that I'd talked to Hewitt, but what he didn't know wouldn't hurt him, as my father used to say. Which turned out to be ironic, given the manner of his death.

I checked directory assistance, found the only T. Hewitt in Yaletown, dialed.

After three rings, he picked up. "Hewitt here."

Perhaps my luck had turned. "Mr. Hewitt, my name is Barbara O'Grady and I'm an investigator. I understand from Detective Hawald that you found Senator McMather's body. I'd like to ask you a few questions, if that's convenient for you."

"More questions?" He sounded bone weary. "Yes, alright. How's ten-thirty?"

"Perfect. I'll see you then."

"Sure." He sounded distracted. "What was the name again?"

"Barbara O'Grady."

"Fine, see you at ten-thirty, Ms. O'Grady. Just buzz 2780."

"Thank you, I will."

———

HEWITT'S APARTMENT was a tiny but immaculate studio with a slice of an ocean view between two neighboring towers. Located just around the corner from the glass tower where McMather had lived, it must have been convenient to be so close to his work.

Knowing the kind of light, space and spectacular views you can expect from a downtown penthouse like McMather's, though, I had to wonder how Hewitt felt about the comparison between his own cramped space and McMather's expansive one.

When he answered the door, Hewitt looked drained. A shock of rusty hair topped pale, expressionless features. Shock. I saw it in his face, skin pulled too tightly against bone. "Thank you for seeing me, Mr. Hewitt."

"Come through here," he said, leading the way to a bistro table bathed in morning light. "I'm sorry I can't offer you anything. I haven't had the heart in me to shop."

"I can understand that. I gather you were the one who found him."

"Yes," he said, turning even paler. I hadn't thought that would be possible.

"Was he alone that night?"

"As far as I know he wasn't expecting anyone. Though I found two brandy glasses and a small plate of cheese in the living room."

"That would be Saturday night?"

"Yes. He'd asked me to come back at nine to go over his schedule for the next week."

"Was this usual?"

He shrugged. "It depended. He had several appearances on Sunday, so it suited him to do the weekly preview on Saturday."

It sounded odd to me. And as if Hewitt hadn't had much of a life. "Did you work for him long?"

"Nearly five years."

Okay. So maybe he was used to the schedule. Or maybe he'd got very tired of the Senator's expectations. "The brandy glasses you found. Were there lipstick smudges on either of them?"

"Lipstick? No, nothing like that."

Of course there are some pretty good smudge-free lipsticks on the market, and Cassie could afford the best. "You have no idea who his visitor might have been?"

"No, no more than I did all the other times you people've asked that question."

Was he lying?

He obviously thought I was with the police and I wasn't about to correct that assumption. But I'd be careful not to say anything deliberately misleading. "Bear with me. Did he have enemies?"

"McMather? Oh, yeah."

That was a great help. Not. "Had he seen or talked with any of them recently?"

"No, actually he'd been pretty anti-social, for him, anyway. Usually there were people coming and going—the man liked a good party."

"And that changed?"

"Yeah. He seemed to have something on his mind. He'd cancelled a bunch of appointments the previous week. Well, except he had tea with his niece the other day."

Oh no. "His niece?"

"Sure. Cassie Stewart."

Cassie had been one of the last people McMather had met with before his death? "Which day was that?"

"Saturday afternoon."

The day he'd been murdered.

I remembered the tension I'd seen in her that night. My skin chilled. "When was the tea arranged?"

"He told me to add it to the schedule late on Friday."

After I'd told Cassie about Brian's lunch with McMather. "Did McMather set it up, or did she?"

He shrugged. "Don't know. McMather liked to invite the ladies in to tea, though."

Somehow I didn't think this had been a typical invite-the-ladies-for-tea occasion. "What time was it arranged for?"

"Two-thirty."

While I was watching Brian read microfilm, Cassie was taking tea with a man who'd be dead in less than eight hours. "Any idea what they talked about?"

He started to say something, but then held it back and shook his head. "I'm afraid not."

"You're sure?"

"Uh huh."

"How was the relationship between the senator and his niece?"

He shrugged. "Can't say."

Can't or won't? "Did they meet often?"

"Don't know."

Something was off there. What?

I asked Ted Hewitt a few more questions, but his answers were now guarded, mostly mono-syllabic and distinctly unhelpful. I'd clearly got everything I was going to out of him, at least for now.

And I had a few new things on my urgent list.

Item one was presenting my report to Cassie, which would end my relationship with her. Couldn't happen soon enough for my taste—if she hadn't set me up.

If she had, she'd regret the day she hired me.

I'd make sure of it.

CHAPTER FOURTEEN

The next morning found me in my office, watching Cassie Stewart read the report I'd prepared for her. I hadn't expected her to be willing to come to my office, but she'd insisted on it. As she sat in the armchair across from my desk, she was immaculately turned out, but the face exposed by her smooth French braid was stretched tight, the bones too prominent.

It was raining again, and in the slanting gray light I could see the ghost of the woman she'd become at the end of her life.

After a long silence, broken only by the sounds of rain and pages turning, Cassie Stewart looked up from the report, her face pale. "Brian actually met with another woman."

I nodded. "You don't know her?"

"No," she said, and bent back to the report.

Finally she flipped the last page. It was several long moments before she raised her head, and gave me one of the bleakest looks I've ever seen. "He isn't working?"

"Not as far as I could tell."

"I can't understand it." She swallowed hard, and her voice steadied. "I knew something was wrong, but nothing like this."

"What do you mean?"

"Brian lives for his job. I would have said nothing was more important to him."

I had to ask. "Not even you?"

She glanced at me, then away. "He grew up poor."

It wasn't quite an answer, but I couldn't bring myself push her on that point. Not when every scrap of her poise and confidence seemed to have drained away. It was a hard thing to see.

"What do you think is wrong?"

"I wish I knew."

"Do you still think he's having an affair?"

"No."

"Despite the blond?"

She shook her head.

"Why not?"

She gave me a look I couldn't read. "The sex is too good."

I had a sudden glimpse of her as a young woman coming of age in a post-Pill and pre-AIDS world that had reveled in its own sexuality. It was an intriguing contrast to the image she now presented.

Yet that very history should have told her that good sex was no guarantee her husband wasn't also having an affair.

I was beginning to feel protective of her as well as sorry for her. Which worried me. It's always a bad sign when I start feeling that way about my clients.

Especially ones who might be murderers. "So what does his not working tell you?"

"That something is more wrong than I feared."

"And you have no idea what that might be?"

"None. I just wish I did."

I didn't know what to say as she struggled to regain her composure. I was beginning to realize that if I'd painted her portrait back when we first met, I might have been the one most surprised by what it revealed. This wasn't the stainless steel society princess I'd thought I was dealing with.

Under that layer of permafrost was a load of hurt.

"I'm sorry," she said eventually.

"Don't worry about it. But I do have one question."

"Yes?"

"Why were you so insistent I follow your husband Saturday night?"

"I thought Brian's actions at the theatre might be telling."

I wasn't convinced.

Time for a little plain speaking. "He didn't do anything worth watching, but I find I've conveniently become his alibi for McMather's murder. After all, I was following him at intermission. You know, when you vanished. Right around the time your uncle was murdered."

She stared at me for a second, then began to laugh. It sounded genuine, but there was an edge of hysteria underneath. "You can't think…"

She put a hand over her mouth, as though physically stopping the sound. Drawing in an audible breath, she met my eyes.

Her gaze was direct, her eyes compelling. "You really think I could have killed my Uncle Ed?"

"Did you?"

"No, of course not."

She said it calmly enough, with a little smile.

I'd have believed her immediately. Except for all the research I'd done on sociopaths, after I'd run into a very plausible one on an earlier case who came very close to costing me my license. If you have no moral judgment, it's easy to lie, easier still to persuade someone of the truth of that lie.

It's not that I thought Cassie Stewart was a sociopath—I just didn't know her well enough yet to be sure that she wasn't. The fact that I respected her, was half-way to liking her, meant I had to be even more cautious. Sociopaths can be charming, even charismatic. "Your husband didn't seem too fond of McMather. What about you?"

"I didn't know him all that well. But I certainly didn't hate him enough to kill him."

"People kill for all kinds of reasons."

"I wouldn't know. And I did not kill my Uncle Ed. Clear enough for you?"

It was the edge of hurt behind the outrage in her voice that made the difference.

Well, that plus the fact that I'd never been able to figure out what she stood to gain by killing her uncle, especially with me right there to notice she'd gone missing.

She still could have been manipulating me, but I was inclined to believe her, on this at least. She was still lying about something, though. "Why didn't your husband like McMather?"

"They had nothing in common. I don't even understand why they had lunch together."

I didn't either. "I was hoping you'd be able to tell me."

Cassie shook her head. Looking down at her hands, neatly folded in her lap, she let the silence stretch.

Finally she looked up, met my gaze. "Barbara, I'd like to hire you to continue this investigation. With no end-date this time."

I hadn't expected that. "For what purpose?"

"To find out what is bothering my husband."

"You're serious?"

Reaching into her purse, she pulled out a leather-bound check-book. A few quick scrawls and she handed me a check.

My eyes widened. It came to three weeks work at the outrageous fee I was charging her.

She was serious.

"Let me know if you need more money," she said.

I couldn't even imagine it. "Just so we're clear, I'll be doing it my way this time."

Her lips tightened a little, but she didn't even argue. "Fine."

———

WHY WAS I even considering this? But I couldn't just leave this case half-done.

"Then we have a deal," I said, and tucked the check away. "So.

My following Brian around isn't telling us enough. I'm going to have to start digging into his background, probably into McMather's murder. Are you okay with that?"

Cassie's body tensed, but she nodded.

"What was your husband's relationship with McMather?"

"They had little to do with each other."

"Even though McMather was your uncle?"

"By marriage. I hadn't seen much of him since I was ten or so."

"Then why did you meet with him on Saturday afternoon?"

"I was told you were good." She smiled, though the tension in her body hadn't eased any. "Because he asked me to tea."

"What did he want to talk about?"

"I still don't know. It was mostly platitudes. How are you, how is your husband, your children. I sensed there was something he wanted to ask me, but he couldn't quite work up to it."

"And you have no idea what that something might have been?"

"No. I wish now I had just asked him."

It felt like another lie. "It's important, Cassie."

She gave a little sigh and relaxed back into the cushioned chair. I don't think she even realized she'd done so. "He might have wanted to know about my aunt."

"His ex-wife?"

"Yes. He asked how my mother and my aunt are doing, if I ever see them." She sipped at her coffee. "I don't think he and my aunt have seen each other since she divorced him."

"Your aunt divorced your uncle? Not the other way around?"

"No, she left him. I'm not sure why. It's another one of those things that no-one in my family would talk about." She gave a rueful half-smile. "It seems there were a lot of secrets I never questioned."

"You might have to start questioning some of those secrets now."

"You mean with the murder."

"And the timing of the murder. It seems highly coincidental that McMather should be murdered just when you've hired me to investigate your husband's changed behavior, and after Brian met with McMather last week."

"When you put it like that, it does. I wish I did have an explanation, but all I have is the sense something has gone very wrong for my husband. And I need to know what."

"Can you think of any link between your husband and McMather? Anything Brian might have stumbled into?"

Cassie shook her head.

"You talked about changes in your husband's behavior. Is there anything more specific you can tell me?" Now that she'd decided to be honest with me.

She hesitated, gave me a sideways glance and a little grin.

For the first time I could see the girl Brian had married, a girl I could have been friends with. "When we make love lately, he's so intense. I'm not complaining, mind you, but there's an edge there that feels almost desperate."

"Desperate?"

"It's the only word that seems to fit."

Desperate. What was going on in Brian Stewart's life that his wife would describe his lovemaking as desperate? "And you have no idea why?"

Cassie shook her head and wouldn't meet my eyes.

"Are you sure?" Pushing her.

She looked up. "I'm sure, Barbara. I really don't know what is wrong with him. For him. That, more than anything, is why I came to you."

Oh boy. If I was any judge of character, and I like to think I am, she was telling the truth. She really didn't know what was going on. She was counting on me to find out.

But she was still holding something back.

I took a hasty swallow of coffee, and let a silence fall between us.

Cassie sat and sipped her coffee, like she was at a garden party or something. No trace of her recent emotions showed on her smooth face. She'd make a great diplomat.

But I had no intention of letting her cement that façade back in place. "Do you know any reason someone would want Ed McMather dead?"

It shook her up, I could see it. But she just shook her head.

We were at an impasse. Again.

I watched Cassie's pale face, her smooth expression. Her level eyes. "Is there anything else you can tell me that would help explain your husband's behavior? Anything at all?"

"I wish there was something. I can't think of anything that connects Brian and Uncle Ed, nor any real reason anyone would want my uncle dead. Except for Aunt Vivianne, of course," she ended with an attempt at lightness.

"What about the passport renewal?"

"Brian's passport expired six months ago. I had been nagging him to do something about it, but it wasn't important to him. I have no idea why he'd be renewing it now."

"Is there a trip he's planning on taking, or needs to take?"

"Nothing that I know of."

"Do you have any idea why he'd be researching the old copies of newspapers from decades ago?"

"I have no idea."

"What about his health? Has anything changed? Is he showing any kind of symptoms?"

"I don't think so. And I pay attention, because he won't. But what kind of symptoms?"

Something serious enough to send Brian Stewart off to get his DNA tested. "Symptoms of any of the nastier hereditary illnesses. Does anything run in his family?"

"Nothing that I know of. But he's an only child. And his parents died years ago."

At my questioning look, she added, "Accidental."

So another dead end. "What about his history from before you met him? Is there anything that he might be worried about?"

"Well." Cassie looked thoughtful. "I know he grew up in the interior, in Kamloops. His parents were not well off—I believe his father was in the construction industry. I never met them. They died the year I met Brian."

Wait a minute. "Both of them?"

"Yes, there was a car accident in the Fraser Canyon. Brian was devastated. We'd only been dating a couple of months then, but we married the following year. So the accident must have been almost forty years ago..." Her voice trailed off. "Barbara, do you think there might be a connection?"

One glance at my face told her that I did think there was a connection. Or at least something worth exploring.

"I'll check into it," I said, making another note. "Do you know anything else about them?"

She turned faintly pink. "I'm ashamed to admit I don't. Brian won't talk about them, and I've always assumed it's too painful, so I never pushed him."

"Anything else?"

"I don't know much about his childhood, either," she said. "I should probably have asked, later, but somehow the timing never seemed right and I didn't want to hurt him even more."

How could she have been married to him for so long and know so little about his formative years?

If it had been me, I'd have asked, dragged it out of him if I had to. No wonder she couldn't figure out what was going on with Brian now, when she knew so little of where he'd come from. It seemed an odd way to conduct a marriage.

"Who might your husband know that lives overseas?"

"My mother lives overseas. And there are some cousins on my father's side, but Brian only met them once."

"Did your mother know Brian's parents?"

"No. Brian and I met a couple of months before they died."

This wasn't helping. Back to McMather. "What was Brian's reaction to McMather's death?"

Cassie fingers whitened on the cup she still held. "He went paler than I've ever seen him. He threw on his clothes and dashed out without a word to me. I had to read the paper he'd dropped to even guess what was wrong."

"He didn't say anything to you?"

She shook her head. "Not a word. Barbara, what do you think it means?"

And now fear was stark on her face.

She'd surprised me again. When Cassie came out from behind the wall of her composure, she had a vulnerable side that was very appealing. "I don't know what it means. But that's why you've hired me."

"I wish I knew where he'd gone."

There was no help for it. I'd have to admit I'd tailed him. "He took the ferry to Bowen Island and visited Judge Rutledge."

She gave me a considering look. "You had better consider yourself re-hired as of yesterday, then."

Worked for me.

"Brian went to see Gregory Rutledge?" she asked then.

"Yes. How does Brian know him?"

"He, more than anyone, is Brian's mentor. Gregory was Brian's favorite professor in law school and they've stayed close. I know Brian still respects his judgment, even relies on him at times."

My thoughts made a leap. "Did Judge Rutledge know Brian's parents?"

"I don't think so. The accident was long before Brian started law school. Gregory probably knew Uncle Ed, though."

Close enough. "Do you have any problem with me talking to him?"

"No. Except I don't want any of this to get back to Brian"

"That might prove difficult."

She smiled. "Not if I tell the Judge I've hired you to write a family history as a surprise for Brian. Do you know anything about history?"

I managed not to grin. "I majored in art but minored in history."

She gave me a thoughtful look. "I keep forgetting you're an artist."

"Former artist."

She gave me another look, almost as if she could see the prepped canvas with the roughed in outlines of ocean and forest that had taken over my spare room when I wasn't looking.

Something about this case, probably working so closely with Cassie, had brought all the old dreams back, and I didn't know what to do with them.

"Does any artist ever really give up?" she said.

Fortunately for my peace of mind it seemed to be a rhetorical question. But that flare of interest in her eyes made me as uneasy now as it would have made me ecstatic once.

"Judge Rutledge is a passionate amateur genealogist," she said, refocusing on the current problem. "He traced his own antecedents back as far as fourteenth century England, and helped my daughter Jenny when she was working on a family tree as a school project some years ago. I'll set up an appointment for you."

"Do you still have that family tree?"

"I think so. I'll find it for you. It may be useful in the conversation with Gregory."

Even if it was only a prop, having it couldn't hurt, right?

CHAPTER FIFTEEN

Several hours later I was back on the fifth floor of the Vancouver Library's main branch. This time I was sitting in a cubicle and practically cross-eyed from staring at microfilm as it whizzed by. Since I was officially back on this case, I wanted to know why Brian had run straight to Judge Rutledge as soon as he read about McMather's murder. Cassie hadn't yet arranged my meeting with the Judge, so the only lead I had was the microfilm Brian had been searching on Saturday.

McMather's obituary mentioned that he and Grantley had been partners in the early sixties, so I started with the *Vancouver Sun* from those years. I was looking for any mention of Robert Grantley, Ed McMather or Gregory Rutledge.

Several months in I found a society page photo of the McMathers and the Grantleys at a gala dinner. The caption listed Grantley as a 'prominent lawyer' and McMather as a 'financier,' whatever that meant.

I looked at the accompanying picture. It showed the two men on either end, with the two women in the middle.

The men couldn't have been more different. Grantley looked suave, polished, while McMather looked bluff and uncomfortable.

The two women were smiling into the camera, all lacquered hairdos and elegant frocks. I stared at the photo for a moment.

Genevieve Grantley was brunette and Vivianne McMather blond, but otherwise they were nearly identical.

I flipped through the rest of the year, finding more social mentions of the two couples, but nothing on the two men. If they had been business partners, I might need a business name to find anything. I kept scrolling forward.

In the business section the following year, I found a long article about a new mining venture, Triple Diamond Investments, headed by Robert Grantley and Ed McMather. Shares were to be made available to the public through the Vancouver Stock Exchange. There was a photo of the two men shaking hands, and a long interview with Grantley, who was to be instrumental in taking the stock public.

I rolled my eyes.

Small mining ventures listed on the VSE had a terrible record and a worse reputation for most of the twentieth century. Even today, savvy investors are wary of penny stocks on the TSX-V, which replaced the VSE. I had a bad feeling I knew what was coming.

I wasn't disappointed.

There were two follow-up articles later that year, each just a couple of inches of type. The creation of the company and the plans to sell stock were proceeding, but slowly. I wondered about the dynamics of that partnership, and whether Grantley or McMather held the real power.

Late that same year, the first issue of public stocks was announced. One million shares would be available at ten cents per share. Triple Diamond Investments was in business. There were no further articles for several months, but the stock appeared to be trading steadily, with prices between twelve and fifteen cents per share.

In May of the following year, a half page article in the business section announced a spectacular find at the mine just north of Castlegar. They'd been working a site that had been abandoned years before, mining for copper mainly, and they'd found gold.

There were quotes from assayers, quotes from an old-timer that remembered the original mine, and, of course, quotes from Robert Grantley. Triple Diamond Investments stock shot up to a high of four dollars a share almost overnight.

Then news of another discovery pushed it up again.

By the end of the summer, the stock was trading between eight and nine dollars a share.

During the winter the stock prices leveled off to around six dollars—no mining was being done, so no new finds were reported. I learned most of this from checking the weekly stock market summaries, because very little showed up as news.

The following year started well. The stock held steady just under ten dollars and the McMathers and the Grantleys started the year at the Grantleys' annual New Year's Ball, followed by several galas and fundraisers through January, February and March. In April, there was a small article about labor problems at one of the mines.

Then nothing until May. When the bombshell fell.

Amid allegations of fraud, accusations were made that one mine was all but played out and the other unworkable. The future of Triple Diamond Investments was suddenly and dramatically in question, and the bottom fell out of the stock. Prices crashed to five and then two dollars a share.

As more evidence emerged, it became clear that there was no recoverable gold in the mines. By mid-June, the stock could be had for pennies a share.

In July, trading was halted.

There was an investigation, of course. Despite allegations of fraud and cover-up, nothing was proved. Both of the principals in Triple Diamond Investments protested ignorance and pleaded good faith.

Somehow they were believed.

The chief mining engineer was fired, and eventually the scandal died away.

I pieced the timing together with the facts from the investigation. Ed McMather had sold much of his stock the previous summer. He'd sold all of it before the end of March, while prices were still strong.

Robert Grantley sold out in mid-May, just as the first rumors began, but before stock prices had fallen very far. He'd probably lost hundreds of thousands of dollars in potential gains compared to McMather. And he'd lost his good name—it was Grantley who'd been so prominently associated with the stock.

Intrigued, I scanned forward several more months.

There were no more photos of the Grantleys and McMathers together. Genevieve Grantley continued to show up organizing the occasional fundraising event, but Vivianne McMather seemed to have dropped out of sight.

Several months later I found a small piece on Ed McMather, who had been chosen as the Social Credit Party's candidate for the next provincial elections. His backers included several Vancouver stock promoters and the union who had represented the Triple Diamond Investments miners.

It reeked of fraud to me.

Had McMather set up his partner?

If Robert Grantley had still been alive, he'd top my list of possible suspects for the murder of Ed McMather. But was his daughter harboring a long standing grudge on her father's behalf? I doubted it.

Robert Grantley had still come out quite a bit richer than he'd started. And he'd still been a partner in the law firm he co-founded.

So where did all this shady history leave me? Nowhere, that's where.

And I'd not found even a single mention of Gregory Rutledge.

I pictured Brian sitting here surrounded by a mountain of microfilm boxes. What had he been looking for?

It could have been the Triple Diamond fiasco. The time frame was right. What else had been happening for the Stewarts during those years?

Cassie had said Brian's parents died nearly forty years ago, and that she and Brian had married the following year. The timing fit. It was another place to start.

I went searching, and found the article on Brian and Cassie's wedding. It would have been hard to miss—it was a page and a half long. Their wedding had evidently been the social event of the season. I was amused to note that Brian's hair had been on the long side, while Cassie's was twisted up on her head in a complicated style. She wore a long, full-skirted white dress and lace veil.

I scrolled backwards. Countless blurry pages later, I found a small article dated from the previous year. Joe and Maria Stewart had been killed when their car plunged into the Fraser Canyon.

They'd been traveling along Highway One from Vancouver to Kamloops when they apparently failed to navigate a sharp corner. The police investigation had shown no sign of foul play, and the deaths were declared accidental.

I pictured the winding Canyon Highway, with steep, heavily forested mountains on one side and a sharp drop to the Fraser River far below on the other, and shuddered. One bit of black ice in the wrong place, and you were history.

Had the roads still been icy that April?

I flipped a few pages. No, the weather had been sunny and unseasonably warm, the roads clear. Highway One was listed as "good driving condition".

An adjacent article caught my eye, detailing extensive improvements to the Canyon highway the previous month, "particularly on some of the more dangerous corners." So why had their car gone over?

I didn't find an answer to that question.

I did find an obituary dated two days later. It simply said that Joe and Maria Stewart were survived by their son Brian, and that the service, to be held that Friday, would be a private one. Very little information on what must have been a shattering event in so many people's lives, Brian Stewart's life most of all.

He would have been at university that year. I wondered if they'd been in Vancouver to visit him.

Was this what Brian had been searching for?

But if so, how did it tie into the DNA kit? And I couldn't see how any of it was relevant to McMather's death. Or Cassie's fears, whatever they were.

My stomach growled, and I realized I was starving. Checking my watch, I was amazed to see it was nearly six. My mind was churning with the facts I'd uncovered and I didn't feel like talking to anyone. Might as well pick up a sandwich, head back to my office and keep working.

I wasn't going to be able to think about anything else tonight, anyway.

———

MUCH LATER, I sat in my shadowy office holding a half empty coffee mug, eyeing the remains of a ham on rye with Dijon mustard and the notes on my computer with almost equal disfavor. Taking another mouthful of coffee, I reviewed the things I knew.

The people Brian had met. The places he'd gone. The events and non-events in his life. Cassie's behavior. Her father's relationship with McMather.

Still no inspiration came to me. All I could see was a collection of facts, with nothing tying them together.

"Come on, Barbara, think," I said aloud, my words echoing slightly in the silence of the empty building.

It was no good. With a shrug, I dialed Andrea's number. Her bubbly optimism would be a welcome relief.

I ended up talking to her voice mail and left a brief message, then pushed the notes aside. Time to call it a night.

The phone rang. I pounced on it, glad of the distraction. Only to hear my mother's voice. "Barbara? Is that you?"

Uh oh. "Yes, it's me."

"You spend too much time working—it isn't healthy. You need to get out more, meet people."

Ah yes, lecture number one hundred and three. I knew this one well. For people, read eligible men. "Why did you call, Mom?"

"Did you call your sister?"

"Yes, I did."

"So what are you doing about the situation with Susanna and Godfrey?"

What did she expect me to do? "I suggested she and Godfrey talk."

"That's it?"

"It's what she needs to do."

"No, Barbara. What she needs is help from her big sister. You need to call her again. She won't listen to me." And she disconnected.

What was going on? I knew getting involved in a marital dispute was a mistake, but there was a note in my mother's voice that worried me. Had I missed something?

What was really going on with my sister and her husband?

I checked my watch. After ten. Too late to call now. I'd ring her in the morning. With an uneasy feeling, I went back to my notes and began to list the things I needed to do next.

When the letters began to blur in front of my eyes, I realized I was done for the night. I needed a good night's sleep for a change.

CHAPTER SIXTEEN

By three the next day, I was ensconced in Gregory Rutledge's cozy, slightly too warm front parlor on Bowen Island, sipping a cup of tea. He'd greeted me warmly at the door, invited me in with old-fashioned courtesy.

Despite his age, for he must be well into his eighties, he remained a charismatic and charming man, elegantly slim with an upright carriage and a shock of beautiful white hair. And he seemed more than happy to discuss the Stewart family genealogy with me.

It wasn't my thing. I was glad it appealed to him, though.

Sipping my tea, I listened with focused attention as he explained what he'd found to be the finer details of compiling a family tree and what he'd told Cassie and Brian's daughter Jenny—where to start, whom to contact. He seemed pleased to have an audience, and brought out sections of his own family tree, explaining some of the remoter connections in great detail.

When he seemed to be running down, I drew out Jenny's chart. Removing the protective plastic, I unrolled it on the coffee table in front of us.

Jenny had gone back four generations on Cassie's side, but

seemed to have run out of steam when it came to Brian's antecedents. His parents' names were there, with dates of birth, death and marriage, but that was all.

I tapped my finger on the missing section. "I'll need to start here. I gather Brian's parents died before he started law school?"

"I'm afraid so."

"It might help to talk to someone who knew them."

He gave me a look I couldn't read. "It is certainly unfortunate that Ed McMather is dead, then. I gather he and Joe Stewart knew each other well when they were young."

McMather and Brian's father? Did Brian know this? "Cassie didn't mention that. How did they know each other?"

His broad forehead puckered slightly, the movement almost lost amongst the furrows. "I believe they worked together, though it was so long ago I may be wrong."

"Can you think of anyone else who might have known them?"

His eyes searched mine.

I'd noticed his clear gray eyes, so alive in that heavily lined face, when he opened the door to my knock earlier, but I hadn't recognized how piercing they could be. I had the sudden conviction that I wouldn't have wanted to be on trial before this man if I had something to hide.

"I knew Maria Stewart slightly," he said.

"You did?"

"Yes. I knew her when she first came to Vancouver, long before she met Joe Stewart. Maria Delorme she was then, the most beautiful and one of the most brilliant law students I'd ever taught. I taught at the law school for many years, you see, before I was appointed to the bench."

"Brian's mother was a lawyer?" How had I missed that?

He shook his head. "No, no. She dropped out after completing her first year. Quite a waste of potential."

She must have been bright, to have him remember her in those terms after all these years. Fleetingly I wondered why she'd dropped out.

But I was more interested in Joe Stewart, and his relationship with McMather. Unfortunately McMather was not part of Brian's family tree. "Did you know Maria's family? Or if she had siblings?"

"I'm sorry. As I said, I knew her only slightly."

"And Brian's father? Joe Stewart?"

"Joe was not a law student," he said, as if that answered everything.

"Is there anyone else you can suggest I talk to?"

"I think you're best to go straight to the genealogical records. There are a number of very good ones."

I had a better idea, but I listened as he explained the sources that he thought I'd find most useful, then thanked him profusely as he showed me to the door.

———

BACK AT THE FERRY DOCK, I took a minute to smell the salt breeze and enjoy the sun on my face. Just past the pier, the ocean was a brisk blue, only slightly choppy, and the pale green of poplars leafing out stood bright against the dark cedars across the bay.

I had half an hour before the Bowen Island ferry arrived, though the three mile crossing back to Vancouver would take only twenty minutes. Rolling the windows down for a cross breeze, I dialed my sister's number, expecting to leave a message. When she answered, I was momentarily at a loss for words.

"Hello?" she repeated.

"Susanna, it's Barbara."

"Barbara. What's up?"

"I wondered how you were doing."

"Mom called you, didn't she?"

"Yes. But I would have called anyway." Just not today. "Did you talk to Godfrey?"

"Yes."

"And?"

"He's left me."

"Why?"

"My sister the detective," she said. "Thanks for the sympathy."

"You know you've got my sympathy, Susanna. But sympathy isn't going to solve anything. Why did he leave?"

"He says he's being stifled. That I'm stifling him," she said in a voice that broke on the last words.

"Susanna, I'm so sorry."

"Thanks, Barbara," she said. There was a small silence, which neither of us was in any hurry to break.

Finally I had to ask. "Do you believe him? That he left because you're stifling him, I mean."

I heard Susanna draw in a sharp breath. "What are you saying, Barbara? What else could it be?"

Shades of Cassie Stewart. "Any number of things could be going on. It sounds like an excuse to me, and a pretty feeble one. Has his behavior changed?"

"Well, he's never walked out on me before."

Just when I think Susanna's completely lost her sense of humor, she surprises me. "True. Anything else?"

There was a small silence. Then a decided sniff. "I think there's someone else."

Ah, Susanna. I felt helpless. "Is there anything I can do?"

"No. The last thing I need is you poking your nose in." Then, as if realizing how that had sounded, she said softly, "But thanks, Barbara. If there is something, I'll call you."

"You promise?"

That drew a reluctant chuckle, as it was meant to. When we were kids, we'd never break a promise to each other, but we'd do anything to get out of making one.

"Yes, I promise," she said in watery tones. "Thanks, Barbara. And I do mean that." And my little sister disconnected.

I didn't feel quite as bleak as the last time we'd talked, but I still felt useless. It's not a feeling I'm comfortable with.

I reached over and flicked on the radio, just in time to hear the announcer say ...with this breakthrough in the McMather case.

Police have refused to release any further information. In other news…"

I skipped through the stations, hoping I could find a station that hadn't finished talking about the case. Three stations later, I did. Apparently Ted Hewitt had been arrested and charged with second degree murder. No details were given.

Ted Hewitt? The pale, shocked man I'd interviewed? He'd shot McMather? I wondered why.

Then I wondered what Jerry hadn't told me. I resolved to pump Jerry about Hewitt's arrest. Tomorrow.

Tonight I'd earned a long soak in the tub, to ease some of the kinks a frustrating day had put in my shoulders, and an early night.

But first I had to talk to Cassie.

———

CASSIE and I met at the Moka again, since it's fairly near her home and her schedule was too tight to allow for a meeting at my office. The café was half empty, so I chose a seat on the far side of the room, where we wouldn't be overheard. She slid into the booth opposite me, waved away my offer to get coffee.

"I don't have much time. What did you want?"

I summarized it for her. "I suspect whatever is going on with your husband has something to do with the death of his parents."

"But that was so long ago. Why now?"

I shrugged. "I don't know yet. But can you think of any other reason he'd be searching through the papers from that era?"

"No." She narrowed her eyes, assessed me. "But that isn't why you wanted to meet so urgently, is it?"

"No. I just met with Judge Rutledge."

"And?"

"He tells me Ed McMather knew Joe Stewart. If that's so, then I need to talk to someone who knew them both. And that would be your aunt, McMather's ex," I said.

"Why the focus on Brian's father?" Cassie asked, then held up a hand. "Never mind. It's good enough that you think you need to know. But I don't know whether Aunt Vivianne would have known Brian's father."

"I need to speak with her anyway."

"She's in Venice, with Mother. I can give you the number, if that would help."

"Your mother and your aunt are both in Venice?"

"Yes. Aunt Vivianne moved to Italy right after the divorce. I think there was an Italian Count involved at the time," she added with a half smile, "but after that ended she just stayed. Mother joined her after Father died."

"When did your aunt and uncle divorce?"

"More than thirty years ago.

"So your aunt left McMather for an Italian count?"

"I've always thought the count was an excuse. I had the impression that Vivianne and Ed were not happy together. She seemed to hold him responsible for something, and she was in no hurry to forgive him."

Cassie paused. "Of course, my children—Grant, Jenny and Julie —were all very small then. I didn't have the time or the energy to notice very much what was happening with an aunt that I saw a few times a year. Most of what I know I heard from my mother."

"Your mother and aunt kept in touch?"

"Yes. After the business collapsed, my father forbade her to see either Aunt Vivianne or Uncle Ed. He wouldn't talk about it," Cassie said. "Mother tried to reason with him, but he refused to listen, forbade her to speak of her sister. She tried tears, cajoling, but nothing worked."

"They stayed close, though. The only people in the entire town who didn't know that they kept in touch must have been my father and my uncle. My mother and Aunt Vivianne went to the same hairdresser at the same time each week, then they'd go for coffee or go shopping for the rest of the afternoon." Again the thoughtful look.

"I'd never realized how hard it must have been on Mother when

Aunt Vivianne moved to Venice," Cassie said. "No wonder Mother moved there after Father died."

"Any idea what Vivianne blamed her husband for?" I asked.

"Other than alienating her brother-in-law to the extent that he forbade his family to associate with her, no," was Cassie's answer. "But I think perhaps you need to talk to her in person."

"In Venice?" I asked, startled.

"Well, Uncle Ed's death seems to be figuring rather largely in whatever is going on. At one time, Aunt Vivianne knew Ed McMather better than anyone. As you reminded me earlier, Barbara, I am paying you to find the answers."

Correctly interpreting my expression, she added dryly, "Don't worry, I can afford the expense. And if it helps you sort out what is going on with Brian, it will be well worth the cost."

And as quickly as that, I was going to Venice, to meet with Vivianne McMather and Genevieve Grantley.

Cassie gave me the address, and said she'd phone her mother that night, let her know I'd be coming. Cassie also planned to tell her mother that she had authorized me to ask any questions I felt were necessary.

Of course, that didn't guarantee that the two women would want to answer those questions.

I dismissed that as a minor detail. Somehow the events of forty years ago were key to whatever was bothering Brian Stewart now. And I was going to get to the bottom of it.

———

THAT NIGHT I packed my bags, which primarily consisted of putting a spare pair of jeans and a couple of T-shirts in a soft-sided carry-on. This was complicated by the reappearance of Cat, who arrived out of nowhere to deposit his considerable bulk in the middle my favorite black tee.

"Cat. I don't have time for this. Get lost."

He purred, loudly, making that odd in and out motion with his claws that cats seem prone to. It couldn't be good for the fabric.

"Cat, I am not fooling. Get off my T-shirt and go home.

A blink, and more purring.

"Look, Cat. I really don't need this. You get one more warning. Get off."

He put his head down and wrapped an orange tipped tail around his nose. That did it.

"Look, if I wanted a bad mannered male cluttering up the place, I could have found one. And he wouldn't be furry," I informed him as I gingerly picked him up around the middle.

He did the boneless trick again, but this time I was ready for him. I carried him to the balcony, put him outside, and slammed the door before he could scamper back in.

Not that I could picture him scampering.

Shaking my head and muttering about other people's pets, I returned to the bedroom. I brushed the cat hair off my favorite T-shirt, packed it, then contemplated the contents of my suitcase.

After a moment's consideration, I added a short, straight black skirt, a couple of silky tops, a narrow black belt, hose, and a pair of low black heels. Then I threw in my black rayon jacket, the dressy one that looks like silk. I was going to Venice after all, and despite the urgency I was starting to feel, I couldn't spend my entire time questioning Cassie's aunt.

And I've never been one to pass up an opportunity.

Finishing, I stretched and considered going to Guido's on the corner for a glass of wine and something to eat, checking out who was there. A yawn caught me unawares. That decided me—after all those early mornings, I deserved the luxury of a quiet night.

I changed into my most comfortable pair of jeans and a sweater, and picked up the phone. I was overdue for a long chat with Andrea.

"Hello?"

"Hey, you're home. I was beginning to think you didn't live there anymore."

She laughed. "I'm glad you called. I was just packing."

Talk about coincidences. "You were? Where are you going?"

"Barbara? It's May."

"Oh. It's your week to visit your Gran." Andrea had made this pilgrimage every year since I'd known her. I really was working too hard. "How old is she now?"

"Just turned eighty-seven, as spry as ever. And she's still living on her own."

"She has spunk, your Gran."

"She had to have. Nelson back then was no picnic."

She had that right. A small town in the interior of British Columbia, Nelson had been mostly a resource and farming town. It took hard work, determination and no small measure of staying power to carve out a living from what had then been mostly wilderness.

"Especially coming from London. Say hi to her for me, will you? Though come to think of it, maybe I should just come with you."

"Your case really must be going badly."

"It is. Plus I really love your Gran. I used to wish she was my Gran too."

"She'd love to see you, Barbara. You know she always asks about you, wants to hear how you're doing. That painting you did for her still hangs in pride of place in her living room."

I groaned. "That thing? D'you know how long ago I painted that?"

"So? Paint her something new."

"Yeah, right." I wasn't getting sucked into that argument. Andrea thinks I should paint more. Sometimes I think she might be right, but it's not something I'm about to admit.

"Why don't you come, Barbara? Just for a weekend. Gran would be thrilled, we'd have a blast and it would be good for you just to get away."

I grinned. "Well, actually, I'm just packing for my flight to Venice tomorrow morning. It's for this case"

"How can you say the case isn't going well if it takes you to Venice?"

She had me there. "I don't know how long I can stay, or if I'll get the chance to see anything."

"I know you, Barbara. You'll make the time."

She was right. I would. "Still, the way this case is going, I think I might be better off going to Nelson."

"You're kidding me."

No, actually I wasn't. "If you've finished packing, d'you feel like meeting me at Guido's for a bite? We can toast our respective journeys."

"I'd love to, but I thought I'd hit the road tonight so I don't have to contend with all that traffic through the Fraser Valley in the morning. Raincheck when I get back?"

"Sure. Have a good journey. My love to your Gran."

"Thanks. You have fun. And don't forget to look for a gorgeous Italian."

"Cute, Andrea. I'll be working, remember?"

"You can always look. It's time you met someone new."

Uh huh. "Bye, Andrea. We'll talk when you get back."

"Sure. I want all the details."

Still laughing, I disconnected and I headed for the kitchen. A furry weight twined around my ankles, purring madly.

"Now how did you get back in?" I reached down to stroke him. The purring intensified. I rubbed a hand down his neck. Louder still.

"I guess I should have closed the window, too."

With Cat right behind me, I reached the kitchen and poured a glass of Cabernet. Then I poured him a saucer of milk. He seemed pleased.

"Should I be feeding you, too?" I asked him, watching his pink tongue flick in and out. Judging by his bulk, someone was already feeding him plenty. But I'd had a tough day, even if he hadn't. With my T-shirts safely packed, I could use the company.

I got out the crackers, opened a can of tuna, and shared it with him.

I took mine out on the balcony and sat in the old teak chair I keep out there, leaning my head back against the window glass with a sigh and staring out at the thin clouds hanging over the ocean as the sunset painted the sky in pale pinks and oranges.

Cat followed me, flopping at my feet and leaning his furry bulk against my ankles. I could feel his purring reverberating against my skin. It was oddly comforting.

"You know, Andrea would laugh her head off if I told her about you," I told him.

Cat purred harder. Hey, at least he was company.

We sat and watched the sky darken while I sipped my wine and ate my tuna and crackers. Cat ate almost as many as I did, lying at my feet until I finally yawned, stretched and got up. Then he vanished.

One of these days I was going to figure out how he got in and out.

CHAPTER SEVENTEEN

To my eye, Venice is one of the most beautiful cities in the world. Visiting Venice on an expense account, rather than backpacking as I'd done on my last visit, was an unimaginable treat. I found a hotel by the Arsenal that was clean and spacious rather than fancy, but it overlooked the lagoon.

Even on someone else's ticket I'm not comfortable with luxury. I like small splurges—red tulips in winter, a glass of good Sauvignon, a Kolinsky sable paintbrush, a cup of real coffee.

My room wouldn't be ready for hours.

I dumped my stuff with the concierge and headed out. Sauntering along the canal, I feasted my eyes on the rich color and texture of the old buildings, with their faded, peeling plaster and tiny wrought iron balconies made festive by pots of geranium and begonia in full flower. A gondola lazed by, followed by a *vaporetto*, creating small waves which lapped darkly against the buildings.

The scent of decay carried by the waves reminded me anew of the fate that threatens all this beauty. Venice is sinking, and the more visitors she has, the more quickly she fades.

But they say to be in Venice is to celebrate life. I can see why.

I chose a tiny café, went in and ordered that coffee I'd been promising myself, a genuine Italian cappuccino, with strong rich espresso and properly steamed milk. No matter how good the cappuccino is elsewhere, and I make a point of trying a cup in every city I visit, it's never as good as in Italy.

I don't know if it's the way the beans are roasted, or if the milk is different. Maybe it's the air that's different. I do know that first sip was exquisite.

It was early, so the cafe was empty. I sat back, closed my eyes and savored the quiet.

Only to open them again seconds later as the other two chairs were pulled out at my table.

Two women with lined faces and beautiful posture seated themselves at my table. Both were stylishly dressed and coiffed. At my stunned expression, the blonder of the two smiled gently at me.

"Barbara O'Grady?" she asked.

I could only nod. Jet lag often hits me that way—my social reflexes weren't functioning yet. Not that they're ever what you'd call stellar.

"I'm Genevieve Grantley. Cassie's mother," she introduced herself. "And this is my sister, Vivianne McMather."

I nodded at the two of them, still speechless.

"Cassie told us you were coming in, so we talked to Luigi at the airport, customs you know, and he told us you'd been cleared. Our chauffeur's cousin was your taxi-driver, and he told us what hotel you were staying at. Marcus, the concierge, told us you'd gone this way and what you were wearing—so we came looking for you," she said. "I hope you don't mind."

Finding my tongue, I asked the first thing I'd thought, "Why go to all this trouble? I'd have found you later today in any case."

Genevieve and Vivianne exchanged glances. Neither spoke for a moment as the waiter put cups of cappuccino in front of them.

"Yes, you would have found us. Eventually. However, this situation is more complex than either you or Cassie realize. There may be no time to waste." It was Vivianne who spoke.

"Ed, my ex-husband, was a dangerous man," she continued, "but he protected his own, after his fashion. With him gone…" She broke off, and seemed uncertain how to go on.

Genevieve patted Vivianne's hand gently, then said, "We're concerned that Brian is now in danger. If he has any inkling of this situation, he must be frantic with worry. He'll be trying to find some way to protect himself and Cassie."

I looked from one sister to the other, feeling as if I'd just stumbled into a bad suspense movie. They were looking at me with equally concerned expressions. I had no idea what they were talking about.

I took a hasty sip of my cappuccino, hoping to fight back the jet lag, and burned the roof of my mouth. "Why don't you start at the beginning. I'm a little unclear on all of this."

Genevieve looked startled, then flashed a guilty smile. "Oh, of course. Vivianne and I are so used to each other, I forget other people can't always follow our conversations."

She paused, as if collecting her thoughts. "I guess I should begin at the beginning. It's a long story…" she said, then looked at me inquiringly. When I nodded, she continued.

"Really, it began more than sixty years ago, the year Vivianne met Ed McMather."

The sister exchanged glances.

"I find it so hard to believe it's been that long. In any case, I was already married to Robert, and pregnant with Cassie. I wasn't around much for Viv." Another exchange of glances. "She was eighteen, had graduated from high school the year before. She was working part-time at Holt Renfrew,"

"Selling girdles, if you can imagine," Vivianne said with a conspiratorial smile.

"Viv was thinking about going to university in the fall. It was sheerest coincidence that she and Ed met at all—he was working as a longshoreman, and she was enjoying being Vancouver's favorite debutante. They met at the public library, of all places. Got stuck in that rickety elevator together for three hours. That was all it took."

"Did he already know Joe Stewart, Brian's father, when you met him?" I asked Vivianne. I wasn't at all sure this ancient history was relevant.

Vivianne nodded, with a glance at her sister that I couldn't read. "Yes. They'd worked together on the docks. They were both long-shoremen."

Brian's father had been a longshoreman?

"Ed was a handsome man in those days," Genevieve said. "And vital, with thick wavy black hair, dark eyes blazing with energy and that indefinable bad boy air about him. Viv was—well, Viv was beautiful. I mean, look at her now, and imagine her sixty years ago. Eighteen, with all her life ahead of her. They married three months after they met. I convinced Robert, my husband, to name them as godparents in an effort to make peace in the family,"

Cassie hadn't mentioned that McMather was her godfather as well as her uncle-in-law. Why not?

"My parents were horrified that Viv had chosen a longshore-man, and for a time refused to have anything to do with the marriage, or with the happy couple," Genevieve continued. "And they were a happy couple. For at least the first six months. "

"The sex was good," Vivianne said.

Genevieve actually grinned at her sister. "Even preoccupied with a brand new baby, not getting enough sleep and worried that I wasn't cut out to be a mother, I noticed things weren't going well with between them."

"Any new marriage takes adjusting to. Didn't Mother give you that advice too?"

"And look how well that worked for me," Genevieve told her. Then to me, "We didn't see much of them for a time. I had my hands full with Cassie, and Ed and Robert had nothing in common. Viv seemed happy again, though, so I just assumed that whatever problem there was had been resolved. I saw what I expected to see, what I wanted to see."

She shook her head, her face sad. "Ed stopped working as a longshoreman, took a job with a firm downtown that made some kind of investments."

"He used my money as leverage," Vivianne said. "Since I had 'no head for figures.'"

"Were McMather and Joe Stewart still friendly, once McMather was no longer working on the docks?" I asked.

"Once Ed changed careers, so to speak, I don't think he saw much of him. He continued to speak well of him, but didn't mention him often," Vivianne said. "I only met him once."

"When the Stewarts died in a car accident, did you ever suspect your husband might have been involved?"

A flicker of glances between the sisters. "No. Never," Vivianne said.

I was pretty sure she was hiding something. What was it with this family and their secrets?

Genevieve had been watching me closely, but she made no comment. "Viv and I were close," she said, "but she had her life and I had mine. Then Ed approached Robert with a business proposition. He wanted them to be partners in a deal he was brokering.

I'm not sure when the two of them first began talking. Robert didn't tell me about it for a number of months. He was firmly convinced that the less I had to worry about business matters, the better. I did know that he usually invested only with people or companies he knew and trusted. I've never understood how Ed convinced him to partner with him."

Genevieve Grantley shook her head slightly, then looked at her sister. "From here, it's Vivianne's story to tell, Barbara," she said. "If anyone understood Ed McMather and the role he played in all of our lives, it's Vivianne."

"ED WAS CHARISMATIC, especially when he believed in something, and most especially when that something involved making money," Vivianne began. "Making money was Ed's favorite thing. His next favorite thing was becoming 'somebody'.

He grew up in a small fishing village up the coast, the third son of a shrimp fisherman. There were seven children in his family and never enough of anything. He was determined to succeed and to him that meant money and social recognition.

It was probably obvious to everyone else, but I was eighteen, and headstrong. I wasn't listening. By the time we'd been married for ten months, I'd finally understood that Ed had married me for my money, my name and my social connections.

Oh, he was smitten with me, there was no question of that. But if I hadn't been a Delbert, he would never have married me. He'd most likely have persuaded me into an affair.

Ed could be very persuasive when he wanted to be, and I was in love, desperately in love, as only a rather naïve eighteen year-old can be.

I was blissfully happy at first. We had a tiny place, and I had to do all the cooking and cleaning, but I didn't care. As far as I was concerned, we had everything that mattered. Especially sex. Ed was a terrific lover, energetic and innovative.

In my circle, sex wasn't much talked about, and I thought I'd stumbled onto the secret of the ages. I was a virgin when I married, as most of us were then."

"Officially, anyway," Genevieve added.

Vivianne grinned at her, then continued. "Ed carefully introduced me to a subject he'd obviously made an extended study of. I was enthralled.

It didn't occur to me to wonder about the degree of experience he had. After all, I had nothing to compare it to. I just thought he was marvelous in every way.

Until we'd been married for six months or so, when I began to find little clues that Ed was seeing other women. Seeing them." Vivianne laughed shortly. "Even now I use the euphemisms.

Ed was having affairs, and not just one at a time. I denied it for as long as I could, telling myself it was my imagination, that a whiff of someone else's perfume does not always indicate an affair.

I finally admitted that there was someone else after my husband arrived home late every night for two weeks, smelling of alcohol and cheap perfume.

I cried myself to sleep for weeks. I tried to talk to him about it, but he'd either slam out of the house or make love to me until I forgot entirely what I was saying. But I always remembered again later, and hated myself for my weakness.

I finally hired a private investigator and had him followed.

To my horror, the investigator found that Ed was seeing two other women on a regular basis. I was miserable. I couldn't talk to my parents, and when Gen asked me what was wrong, I couldn't bring myself to tell her.

Finally I moved into the spare room and locked Ed out. He ranted and raved for awhile, but in the end I don't think it really mattered to him, as long as we seemed like the perfect couple to others.

Ed's attention span was never very long. Most of his women didn't last more than a month or two.

I distracted myself by volunteering. Ed had been investing the allowance from my trust fund in a variety of schemes, and he'd actually begun making money. We moved to a better location and bought a house. We became part of the social scene.

For the next few years, I was on every committee and involved in every fund-raiser I could find. It gave me something to focus on, but I wasn't happy. Somewhere in those years our parents retired and moved to Florida—and I had no choice but to be the adult I had sworn I was when I married Ed.

Then Ed convinced Robert to go into business with him.

That worried me. It's hard to imagine two more different people than Ed and Robert. By then I had discovered how ruthless Ed could be when he wanted something. I doubted Robert was capable of being equally ruthless.

In fact, I doubted Robert had any idea at all what he was getting into. Ed could be extremely persuasive when he wanted to be, and he had a level of enthusiasm that was contagious.

I tried to warn Gen, but she had about as much influence with

Robert when it came to money matters as I did with Ed. Oh, they managed our money, they just didn't discuss it with us. It's amazing either of us ended up with any money at all."

Here Vivianne broke off and she and Genevieve shared a smug look. I liked these two. They had an energy and a humor that I see all too seldom.

I was increasingly dubious about what I was really doing here, but I wouldn't have missed this for the world.

"Once Ed and Robert had formed their company," Vivianne resumed, "Things seemed to go along just fine for a time. Ed was full of himself, name-dropping and predicting how much money he was going to make, the way he always did at the start of a deal. We moved again, to a still grander house, and began to entertain more.

We were suddenly seeing a great deal of Gen and Robert socially, and Robert and Ed seemed to be the best of friends. Still, I was uneasy. I didn't trust Ed, but there seemed to be nothing I could do, except smile and pretend.

By then I was an expert at pretending.

For the first year, everything still seemed fine. The company was prospering, the stock was rising. Ed and Robert compared notes on how much their personal stock was worth every time they met. I began to wonder if I'd misjudged Ed, if this time, maybe, things could be different. I wanted so badly to believe it, I convinced myself it was true."

Vivianne smiled gently, and sipped her cappuccino. "Of course, like all lies, this one was going to rebound on me," she added.

Then she folded her hands in her lap, and resumed her story.

"After one particularly successful evening with Gen and Robert, I began sleeping with Ed again. I convinced myself then that he'd really changed, that we could start over. Later I told myself that it was the champagne."

"Now I can admit that I'd missed the sex." She gave me a sideways look, exchanged a smile with her sister.

"There we were, two happy couples, part of one big happy

family. Gen had her three beautiful children and I had just found out that I was pregnant for the first time.

Ed was attentive and concerned, in private as well as in public. If he was still seeing other women, he was doing a good job of concealing it from me. Life was good.

Then the first rumors began to circulate about the mines. It was some time before Gen or I heard them—women just weren't included in those kinds of discussions. Eventually, though, as the rumors grew closer to the truth, the gossip mill took over.

Finally I had to face my own fears, had to admit to myself that I thought Ed had set up an elaborate fraud.

I talked to Gen first, then we tried to talk to our husbands. First Ed and then Robert refused to discuss "business" at all. They didn't quite say we shouldn't worry "our pretty little heads" but they came damn close.

There was nothing we could do.

I felt helpless at first, then I began to be angry. It wasn't till years later that I recognized that anger as a first line of emotional defense. As long as I was angry with Ed, I could avoid recognizing the sense of betrayal I was feeling, and the deeper fear that all my hopes had just been proven wrong.

I was seven or eight months pregnant with Ed's child. I couldn't afford to know that he hadn't changed."

"I was angry with Robert, too," Genevieve said. "He'd ignored me as an adult, thinking human being for too long."

Viv reached over and patted her sister's veined hand. "We were tired of being excluded and treated as second class. We studied the financial community and the stock market, asked questions and listened when we socialized with Vancouver's business leaders. Then we began to shortchange our housekeeping funds.

Both Ed and Robert were generous. And why not? It was our money, after all.

They didn't notice the effects of "inflation". But every penny we could save or scrounge we invested—in penny stocks at first, much later in blue chip and in real estate. We did quite well, too.

I've never heard of financial ability being a genetic trait, but the two of us seemed to have our grandfather's legendary ability to pick an investment that would do well. The only stock we avoided buying or even researching was Triple Diamond. Looking back, I think neither of us wanted to face the truth.

Our investment plan was just beginning and the investigation into Diamond Mines had not yet begun when my son Michael was born. It was a difficult birth and I didn't get out much for a few months afterwards. He was such a beautiful baby, alert and alive. I lay for hours watching him, waiting for his elusive smile.

Gen came to visit when she could, and we'd discuss our investments while Michael napped. We'd begun to see results when the problems with Triple Diamond became too public for us to ignore.

Suddenly our husbands stopped speaking to each other, and all joint outings ceased.

Robert told Gen not to visit me anymore.

I felt so torn—I couldn't imagine not seeing Gen, but Ed, Michael and I were a family and I didn't want to risk losing that either.

Until the night I heard Ed on the phone, and from his conversation it became clear that the early finds had been "salted", to make the mines seem profitable. There was money to be made in running up the stock, not in profits from the bogus mines.

From Ed's tone it was clear that this was one of many such conversations he'd had over the months.

I listened in shock.

The family I had been so content with had no reality. Ed was as he'd always been, he hadn't changed. If anything, he was even dirtier than I'd once feared.

There was no-one I could turn to, not even Gen.

After a sleepless night and a day spent worrying, I confronted Ed. He admitted everything, the stock manipulation, the deals with the various promoters and financiers. He was even proud of it.

By the end of the conversation I was shrieking like a fool, and he lost control of his temper. He hit me across the face, and then hit me again.

The next day I packed my things and Michael's. I was leaving. I didn't think about or care how I'd survive, though I knew Ed would never willingly release my inheritance.

Our suitcases were out front, and I was just fetching Michael when Ed came home.

We met at the head of the long marble staircase leading to the foyer. Ed knew I was leaving and he was furious. He didn't even give me a chance to speak, he just cracked me across the face, hard.

I collapsed.

And dropped Michael.

Who fell all the way down that staircase.

The next few months I seldom left the hospital. I had forgotten completely about leaving Ed, all I cared about was Michael's survival.

When the doctors finally told me he would live, I was so thankful. I didn't really hear their cautious words about brain function and permanent damage.

It was months before I really realized that Michael would never again be a normal child. He was my child, and I cared for him as I'd never cared for anyone before.

When I was finally allowed to bring Michael home, Ed did everything for us. Nothing was too good or too much.

I scarcely noticed. My focus was Michael. All thought of leaving Ed was gone.

I had no interest in my husband, my home or my social connections. I still visited with Gen, but during that first year she handled the investing alone. I just didn't care.

Eventually I began to take an interest in my life again, but the question of leaving Ed never came up again. Michael needed the stability that my money and Ed's protection could provide. And Ed was protective—this was his son, his blood. Nothing and no-one would be allowed to touch him, cause him further harm.

I knew Ed's business methods and associates were questionable, but as long as it didn't touch Michael or me I didn't care about that either.

I chose to ignore what I learned about Ed and about his life. Once he entered the political arena, the things I knew became another layer of protection for me, for my son. Ed couldn't afford to have what I knew made public.

And even back then, you couldn't have news stories about politicians hitting their wives.

For a number of years, my life centered around my son, who never developed mentally beyond the age of two, and who was prone to every illness. He needed a great deal of care, but he was so sweet and so loving. Caring for him was my life.

The only time I spent away from him was for unavoidable things like doctor's appointments, and when I met with Gen. Choosing investments with Gen provided the mental stimulation I needed. Her company was my only social outlet.

Over time that changed too, and gradually I began to rebuild my life. Michael was admitted to a special school, which gave me more free time. When he was eighteen, my son suffered a stroke.

He battled back, and for a time seemed to improve, but it was too much, and he died.

"I'm sorry," I said.

She nodded, her expression momentarily closed and sad. "Thank you, Barbara. In a way, I was prepared. I'd always known his death could come at any time. But it was very hard.

I left my husband and moved to Italy. The investments Gen and I had been making all those years gave me the money to choose my freedom.

Ironically, when my divorce became final, I didn't need the money we had earned. Ed had made a lot of money over the years, and in many cases he'd used my inheritance as seed money. Between the divorce settlement and the return of my inheritance and some of its earnings, I was suddenly a very rich woman."

Vivianne took a sip of the coffee her sister had ordered for her. Then she looked directly at me.

"I know a great deal about the man my husband became and the connections he made along the way, Barbara. Some of them, if he'd been a threat to them in any way, would not have hesitated to have him killed.

And Brian Stewart may be next on their list."

———

I SAT BACK in my wrought iron chair in that Venetian cafe and stared at Vivianne McMather in disbelief. "You're saying you think Ed's murder was a contract killing?"

"Yes."

"And that Brian Stewart may be next?"

She nodded.

I felt a shiver run down my spine at the conviction in her tone.

It seemed unbelievable, sitting in a sunny cafe in Venice, with these elegant women, discussing contract killings.

In four years of investigating, I've come across some of the darker aspects of the human spirit, of the harm one human being can inflict on another, but it had always seemed more personal than this. Domestic violence, adultery, fraud, blackmail—each of them rises from emotion.

Paying to have someone killed is a business decision.

"But why?" I asked.

"Because Brian is Ed's son by a woman he had a liaison with several years before I met him. Brian never knew, he thought Joe Stewart was his father." She took a sip of her coffee.

I just stared at her.

I was still trying to decide if I believed her, but her words made an awful kind of sense, tying McMather to the Stewarts with unbreakable cords. "How did you find out?"

"When I confronted Ed with his liaisons, he admitted he had an illegitimate child. Of course, he said the children we'd have together were the only ones that mattered to him. I was incensed.

But I never knew who the child was until Cassie's wedding,

when I saw them together. Brian has Ed's ears, and there's some-thing around the eyes, too.

I confronted Ed with my discovery and he admitted Brian was his son. He also told me he'd kept in touch with Maria Stewart, though neither her husband nor her son knew about the rela-tionship."

"Did you believe him?"

"We'd been divorced for many years by then. He had no reason to lie to me."

"If Brian is McMather's son, do you think your ex-husband had anything to do with the deaths of Brian's mother and Joe Stewart?"

"In his own warped way, I believe Ed cared about both Joe and Maria. I don't believe he'd have hurt them," Vivianne said.

"So if Brian doesn't know McMather is his father, why is Brian in danger?"

"Because ironically Ed believed in protecting those of his blood, and he never left anything to chance. He made a lot of enemies in his day.

When Brian became a lawyer, Ed was determined to name him executor of his will. And you can be sure that in addition to the money he'll have left him, somewhere in all that paperwork is incriminating evidence against someone very powerful."

"What?"

Vivianne and Genevieve both nodded.

"But Brian wasn't named as McMather's executor..." I began, then realized Jerry might not have had information about McMather's will the last time I'd talked to him.

If Brian was the executor, Jerry must be finding my earlier questions extremely interesting now. My mind connected the two thoughts. "Might Brian's mother also have had information that was dangerous to McMather's enemies?"

"It's certainly possible."

A motive for the deaths of Brian's parents?

So it was possible Brian himself could really be in danger, though not until the details of the will were made public and his status as executor became known. Had that happened yet? "Do you know where McMather kept his will?"

"With his lawyers," she said. "He wanted to make very sure it was protected against all eventualities. He knew the type of people he was dealing with."

So the will could be made public any day now. "What exactly was Ed involved with?"

"I never knew exactly. On the surface he was a legitimate businessman, or at least as legitimate as most of the stock promoters in the city. I wasn't positive something was wrong until Ed managed to involve Robert in the Triple Diamond Investments scheme. Oh, both men made money, but if that had been Ed's primary purpose, there was no need to manipulate Robert to the point where he refused to speak to Ed again. Ever.

And it was right afterwards that Ed got involved in politics.

Ed was never in the news as an owner of the mine, you see. Once the company was set up, Robert became the spokesperson, he was the one the public associated with the mines. Robert was the one who suffered bad publicity and the wrath of the investors over the whole thing."

"The whole mess affected Robert's career for at least ten years." Genevieve added. "Fraud was never proven, yet years later many of the venture capitalists and stock promoters in the province would have nothing to do with his firm. And that had been quite a lucrative part of their business, before the Triple Diamond Investments incident."

"Another irony," said Vivianne. "Ed was the catalyst, yet he ran for office, was elected and eventually appointed to a cabinet post. It was the beginning of a very successful political career, and the beginning of his power base.

A dispassionate third party might have assumed that Ed had set Robert up, used him to make dangerous amounts of money without risking his own reputation. But if you knew him, you'd know Ed would never have done that.

That's really the double irony in all of this. You see, Ed

campaigned as the people's choice, someone just like them, from a background just like theirs. It was the last thing in the world Ed would have chosen to do. In his mind, that was just his background —one he wanted to leave behind.

Ed saw himself joining the ranks of the idle rich, or at the very least the well-to-do and socially prominent. Any scheme that involved alienating his well-connected brother-in-law and running as a populist politician would not have come from Ed.

He was good at it, though, very good. Being charming, talking to people as though he understood and shared their values, those were things that Ed had been doing for years.

But the plan, the original idea wasn't his. Ed McMather, successful politician, was someone else's creation. He was a tool, a pawn for more powerful interests."

"Who?" I asked.

She shrugged. "I was very careful never to know. But Ed was wary of them. And he wasn't a man who was afraid of much."

She sipped her coffee. "He must have found a way to take back control of his own life. Given the people he was dealing with, that probably meant information, something powerful enough to protect him, at least partially. And that information would be held in trust, to be used in the event of his sudden death."

"Why was he murdered, then?" I asked.

"Again, I don't know. My guess is he was set up by someone ruthless, patient and vengeful enough to have him shot down in his own home." She shuddered.

I was amazed that she could be relating such things so calmly. I now understood her move to Venice. If I had been in her shoes, I wouldn't have wanted to be on the same continent as the people Ed had gotten involved with either.

"What about Ted Hewitt?"

"Ted Hewitt?"

"He's been arrested for Ed's murder."

Vivianne frowned. "I knew a Ted Hewitt who worked for Ed for awhile, just out of law school. I only met him once. He seemed like a nice kid, shy. He had good manners."

"It's probably the same person," I said. "This Ted Hewitt was McMather's assistant."

"Then the police have made an error," Vivianne said. "The people responsible for Ed's murder would have hired someone unimportant to actually fire the gun. Never his assistant."

"Why not?"

"He'd be too visible, and it would be hard to make him 'disappear' if that became necessary."

Was it possible she was right? "Who would they have hired?"

"A hit man, a petty criminal. Someone none of us has ever heard of, with no connection to Ed."

That pretty much stopped that line of questioning.

Vivianne claimed not to know how her ex-husband's estate would be divided, or even how large that estate might be.

As far as she was concerned, they were divorced, Michael was dead and Ed's concerns were nothing to do with her. Except where they concerned Brian and Cassie. About Brian she was very worried.

"So you're afraid that whatever Ed knew, Brian now knows, or will soon?"

Vivianne nodded.

"And that will put him in danger?"

"I'm afraid so."

"Why?" This still wasn't making sense to me. "If the information was enough to protect Ed McMather all these years, surely it will protect Brian in the same way."

"Not if they can get to him before he realizes what he has. And once they learn he's the executor of Ed's will, they will get to him."

CHAPTER EIGHTEEN

I returned to my hotel after my encounter with the Delbert sisters feeling decidedly shell shocked. Between jet lag, the sense of urgency they'd expressed and all those cappuccinos, my nerves were jangling like a fire alarm, and I had an overwhelming urge to take immediate and decisive action. But in which direction?

Vivianne and her sister had given me a lot of information, but I wasn't sure how much of it to believe. Much as I'd appreciated the delightful duo, the notion of McMather's 'hostages to fortune' seemed a stretch.

Was Brian Stewart in danger?

I didn't quite believe it, despite Vivianne and Genevieve's persuasive story. I could have spent the morning being fed the mother of all lines, for reasons known only to those two tale-spinners.

And possibly to my client. I hadn't forgotten how quick Cassie had been to send me on this little adventure.

At least I had the answers I'd come to Venice for. Now the questions were pointing me back to Vancouver. Dammit.

I was only here to interview the sisters, but I'd hoped for an extra day or two to explore. Instead I was going to end up with a double case of jet lag. I knew a free trip to Venice was too good to be true.

I glanced at my watch. Maybe if I got an update from Jerry on the status of his investigation, it would buy me more time here. But nine hours difference made it the middle of the night in Vancouver. So much for that idea.

Instead I faced the inevitable. I was going home as soon as I could arrange a flight.

I tried the website first, and was drawn into menu hell. Then the connection timed out. With a sigh, I reached for the phone.

At least I had that option, and wasn't facing the interminable line-ups I remembered from my last visit. On reaching the front of the line, I'd invariably be told that the person I really needed to see was *al di la*, with a broad gesture—over there having another hour and a half line-up stretched before it. My jaw tightened at the memory.

I carried the phone out to the tiny balcony. Hot sunlight danced across the cobblestones as I waited to be transferred to someone who understood English, or even my high school French. It seemed to take hours, as I was transferred from person to person. *"Comé?"*

My eyes followed a lean black cat as it stalked leafy shadows in the small courtyard, while I was put on hold yet again. With all the caffeine buzzing through my system, it was hard to be patient.

When I finally got through, the good news was that the first available seat out was late the following morning, giving me the rest of the afternoon and the evening to enjoy Venice. Which I did. Thoroughly.

I strolled along the Canale di San Marco to the kaleidoscope of pigeons and tourists that is the Piazza San Marco. I was itching to sit in a nearby café and sketch some of the passing faces, but I didn't have time to do that and still see some of the Galleria dell'A-cademia. The Academia won, hands down.

I've always been a sucker for Venetian Renaissance art.

Six hours later, my feet gave out, my brain was overloading and

I was starving. I hadn't seen everything I wanted to see, but I was too hungry to care. I tore myself away and went in search of food.

I found it on a quiet canal just beyond the Academia, where I feasted on risotto terra mare paired with an amazing house white.

To celebrate having spent four hours without once thinking of my case, I ordered *tiramisu* for dessert, capping it off with more dark, fragrant coffee. Luckily coffee doesn't keep me awake, because I was exhausted. Content, but exhausted.

Dining alone, I got interested looks from more than one dark-eyed Italian male. But despite the little shiver I get when they address me as *Signorina* in that melting accent, I was too jet-lagged to do anything about it.

CHAPTER NINETEEN

At the airport the following morning, I joined the throng in the departure lounge, dug out the notes I'd taken the previous morning and re-read them, trying to ignore the babble of voices around me, all speaking different languages.

Then I read through my notes again, this time highlighting significant facts, especially names and dates.

It still wasn't making sense. Shaking my head, I started to go through my notes again, then caught the eye of a handsome dark haired gent seated across from me.

He smiled. I smiled back.

He smiled harder.

I winked.

At which point he giggled and hid his face in his mother's skirts.

You've got to love Italian men. Even the four year-olds are flirts.

Smiling to myself, I suddenly realized that this little by-play had caught the attention of several of my fellow passengers. Including another handsome dark haired gentleman who was matching my smile with one of his own. A smile that showed up the planes and angles of his chiseled face, that highlighted the tiny lines fanning out from his laughing dark eyes.

And this morning I wasn't feeling quite so jet-lagged. I smiled back and felt that little jolt of attraction.

It was all the encouragement Alessandro needed.

He moved to the seat beside mine, sat down and introduced himself. He was a businessman, importing goods from around the world, and traveling to Hong Kong via London and L.A. To say that the fact I was a P. I. amazed him would be to seriously understate it. It also appeared to intrigue him.

We talked non-stop until our flight was called.

As I settled back in my cramped seat and reached for my notes, a hand touched my shoulder. It was Alessandro. He'd arranged to trade his first class seat for one beside mine in economy. For a tall man, that was no small sacrifice—watching him trying to fit his long legs into the shoebox they call economy seating was almost amusing. I wasn't amused though.

It was my turn to be intrigued.

When we said goodbye in London, I had the feeling that he was about to offer to change his LA flight to a Vancouver one. He didn't, though, and part of me was relieved.

Relationships are complicated enough. Long distance ones are impossible.

He did leave with my phone numbers, though.

———

FINALLY THE LAST of the boarding passengers were herded aboard. I sat back in my narrow seat, trying to ignore my portly new neighbor's elbow, and began to review my neglected notes, fighting the tiredness and disorientation I'd been feeling since Alessandro left. I couldn't decide if he'd been a welcome distraction, or something more. And I really didn't want to think about it.

Closing my eyes for a moment, I opened them slowly and returned to the underlined items in my notes. Which suddenly looked blurry. I blinked, focused, then blinked again.

Tiredness, I decided.

I put my head back and closed my eyes, waiting until the seat belt sign finally blinked out.

Then I asked a passing flight attendant for coffee, lots of it. She smiled sympathetically—did I really look that bad?—and brought me my own carafe.

I guess I did look that bad. Oh well.

I poured a cup of dark brown liquid and took a fortifying gulp. Oops. This was definitely English coffee, not Italian. Maybe I should have ordered tea.

Still, it was coffee, I decided, taking another mouthful.

Putting the coffee aside, I was soon engrossed in my notes. Based on what the Delbert sisters had said, I had new questions about the Stewarts' car accident. I had even bigger questions about the nature of McMather's death.

Of course, if Ted Hewitt was the murderer, those questions were moot.

I began correlating the details Vivianne and Genevieve had told me with the facts I knew already.

According to them, McMather was Cassie's godfather. He'd also been Brian's mother's lover, and as a result was possibly Brian's father. And according to Viv, McMather had named Brian executor of his will.

Contemplating what I'd written, I remembered Brian's changed behavior, and wondered what McMather had told him any of this. If McMather had confessed to being his natural father, Brian Stewart would have been shocked. That was one possible explanation for his reaction to McMather's death.

It was time to have a chat with Brian.

Just as soon as I figured out a way to do so without triggering both his alarms and Cassie's.

I contemplated that thought off and on for the next several hours, debating my next move. That's one definite advantage of transatlantic flights—they give you the time to avoid making hasty decisions.

Should I tell Jerry about the possible threat to Brian Stewart's life, given that I mostly didn't believe it? If the danger Vivianne had talked about was real, though, I should to go straight to him with what I knew. Hell, I should probably be doing that anyway.

Still, Jerry likely already knew Brian was the executor of the will. And I'd feel like an idiot trying to explain the Delbert sisters to him.

Besides, I've always liked to figure things out for myself—Susanna has spent half her life calling me pig-headed. This problem was a little different than figuring out how to change the oil in my car or refinish a chair, though.

The wrong decision here could cost someone's life. It could even cost me mine. Did I have the right to see this one through?

Did I have the right not to?

Jerry is stubborn too, and sometimes he refuses to believe things that are clearly evident to me. Given my own doubts about what the sisters had told me, I suspected he'd just laugh me off. Making him less likely to listen later, if I discovered there really was a threat.

Just how much faith could I put in the sister's story?

Which parts were truth, and which parts were designed to serve some purpose of their own?

I worried about that one for awhile, wishing Alessandro were there to distract me. I'd seen the movie—it was too stupid to watch again and in-flight music channels give me a headache. I closed my eyes and tried to doze, but my mind wouldn't let go.

One moment I was replaying parts of Vivianne's story, the next I'd see Alessandro's laughing eyes, then my thoughts would shift a little guiltily to Susanna, wondering how she was coping with the absence of my so-wonderful brother-in-law. Then it was back to Cassie and Brian.

I had to trust my instincts. Which were telling me to answer a few more questions before I told Jerry anything.

That decision made, I must have dozed off, because the next thing I knew we were touching down in Toronto. After the hassle of customs and getting to the right gate, which, naturally, was halfway across the terminal, I was happy to settle into my new seat and close my eyes.

When the stewards came through offering the morning paper, though, I did open my eyes long enough to take a copy. And promptly wished I hadn't.

"McMather's Killer Still At Large" blared the headlines below the fold.

I scanned the text. Ted Hewitt had been released, his name cleared, and what the paper described as an all-out search was underway for the killer.

They'd let Hewitt go?

I wondered what had happened to Jerry's supposedly water-proof case? And what the implications were for my case.

If Brian Stewart had been named McMather's executor, then Jerry was likely to have a few questions for me, too. Questions I wasn't sure I knew how to answer.

CHAPTER TWENTY

Not surprisingly, I slept in the next morning. A hard run along the waterfront past Granville Island, followed by a steaming shower did a lot to reconnect mind and body. Considering my back-to-back transatlantic flights, I didn't feel too bad—nothing like the disorientation I usually suffer from.

Maybe my internal clock had never figured out I'd left town?

Whatever the reason, I was grateful for it. I couldn't afford to be slowed down by an uncooperative metabolism.

Over breakfast, somewhere between my first and second cup of coffee, I confirmed my decision to talk to Brian Stewart. It would make it almost impossible to follow him in future, but I doubted that would tell me much anyway. And I needed information that only he had.

I considered briefing Cassie first—for all of thirty seconds. Just long enough to realize she'd be likely to tell me not to talk to him. Why put her or myself in that position, when I was going to talk to him anyway?

Less than an hour later, I'd fast-talked my way past Brian Stewart's watchdog and sat in his spacious corner office, trying not to be distracted by the shadings of blue in his panoramic view of English Bay and the North Shore.

"So, Ms. O'Grady." He considered me over steepled fingers. "Is it Ms. O'Grady or Detective O'Grady?"

He didn't ask to see my ID, so I didn't correct his misconception. It was an odd thing for a lawyer to miss, though. Clearly my visit had caught him off-balance.

Good. "Ms. O'Grady is fine."

"You wanted to see me about something concerning my wife?" His expression wasn't friendly.

"Not quite. I'm sorry for the deception, Mr. Stewart, but your schedule is rather full, and I needed to speak with you. Actually, I'm looking into the murder of your wife's uncle. And godfather."

"McMather." His expression was hard to read, but I had the impression he was steeling himself for something.

"Yes. I've discovered that your father knew him quite well at one point."

"My father?" His shoulders relaxed just a hair. Whatever he'd been expecting, it wasn't that. "But he died nearly forty years ago."

"Yes, I know. But there seem to be some unanswered questions surrounding your parent's deaths. Are you aware of any of the circumstances?"

His look of shock told me he'd never questioned what had happened in his parent's tragic deaths. "Just what the police told me at the time. Their car went off the road on a particularly treacherous corner. It was an accident."

I leaned forward. "I'm going to be frank with you, Mr. Stewart. There may be a connection between Senator McMather's murder and your parent's untimely deaths. Is there anything you remember that might link them? Anything at all?"

Dead silence. I waited impatiently while Brian gathered his thoughts.

"I don't know what to say, Ms. O'Grady," he finally said. "I've never considered the possibility of foul play, but there are certain factors that I can't overlook."

Under stress, he talked more like a lawyer than ever. "Factors?"

"My parents' visit was a surprise to me. I hadn't been expecting them. I was studying hard, so it wasn't even a particularly welcome visit. I've felt guilty about that fact for years."

Another pause. His shoulders had tensed again, but his voice was firm and clear. A lawyer's trained voice.

I wondered what feelings hid behind that training.

"They were in town the whole weekend, but I didn't see much of them. I don't know what they did with the rest of their time. I think Dad may have had business interests down on the docks. He'd been a longshoreman for a time, and he kept up his contacts."

"Is that how he knew McMather?"

"Yes. They'd worked together, years before. They kept in touch."

Well, at least that checked out. "What about your mother? Did she know McMather?"

His shoulders tightened another notch, though his face didn't change. "I suppose she must have, through my father."

If he was lying, he was very good at it. "Nothing closer?"

"Not that I know of. They didn't exchange Christmas cards, if that's what you mean."

Not quite. "Would she have seen him, that last weekend?"

"I suppose it's possible, though I don't know why. And I fail to see the relevance of your questions."

Hmmm, he'd gone from shock to annoyance.

Could Vivianne have been right?

And if Brian was McMather's son, did he know it? "Sorry, just being thorough. Was McMather at the funeral?"

"I don't remember who was or wasn't there. Most of that day is a blank for me."

Remembering my own father's funeral, I could just imagine it had been. "I'm sorry. It must have been a traumatic time for you."

"Yes. It was."

"Did you see McMather after the funeral?"

"Only a few times, and only after I'd married Cassie. He didn't get on with her father."

From what Vivianne had said, that was an understatement. "Had you seen anything of him recently?"

Brian's expression closed immediately. The lawyer-mask was back in place. "I met with him several times in the last few weeks. It was a business matter, and strictly confidential."

"Even now the man is dead?"

"Yes. The matter in question has no bearing on his murder."

"I see. Well, thank you for your time and your patience, Mr. Stewart. I'll be in touch if I have further questions."

As I walked out of the familiar lobby, I put in a call to Jerry, got his voice mail.

Had Vivianne told me the truth about Brian being McMather's executor? I could have asked Brian directly, but it would have made him even more suspicious. And being a lawyer, he probably wouldn't have told me anyway.

Now, how about Ted Hewitt? I keyed in the number. More voice mail.

What about the loose ends I hadn't yet tied up?

I needed to know more about Brian's parents, but it was too late to head for Kamloops today—even driving the Coquihalla without stopping it takes more than four hours. And tomorrow was Sunday. Nothing would be open anyway.

I yawned hugely, wishing I'd stayed an extra day in Venice. The sense of urgency I'd felt there didn't seem quite so compelling now I was back. Cassie's mother and aunt were compelling storytellers.

I shook my head, yawned again. Delayed jet lag?

When I stopped and thought about it, I could feel in every cell exactly how exhausted I was. I wasn't going to get anything sorted out today. I was just too tired.

Plus I had a bad case of information overload, and my brain was refusing to function. I needed a break, and I needed a good night's sleep.

But first maybe I could solve the problem of Lisa Stern, the mysterious blonde who probably wasn't Brian's girlfriend, but had to fit in somehow.

As I walked the last half-block to my car, I keyed in the number Rob had given me. No answer. Where was everyone today?

I had a flash of that strange feeling you get when you've been away and on your return something seems to have changed, but no-one's told you yet. I always find it unsettling, but today I wondered if I'd missed something major.

———

LISA STERN LIVED in a restored Victorian a few blocks off Commercial Drive. Her street was leafy and quiet. I drove slowly by and parked several houses down, but still in view of the house. Twenty minutes of pretending to consult a map, then another twenty of faked phone conversation netted me exactly nothing.

Stowing my cellphone, I walked towards the house. Despite the darkly overcast day, I could see no lights on inside, nor was there any sound. I weighed the consequences for half a second, then strode up to the door and rang the vintage doorbell.

Nothing.

I rang once more, still with no response.

I checked my watch. Still early.

Another yawn decided me. I'd try again tomorrow. For now, nothing was going to keep me from a long soak in the tub and an early night.

But as I drove across the Granville Bridge, I found myself taking the cut off for Fourth Avenue instead of going straight.

Susanna's place wasn't far, I rationalized. Just off McDonald on Seventh. I could swing by, check whether she was home, then head back across Sixteenth and down to my place. Not even a detour, really. And I'd sleep better, just knowing.

Knowing what? I didn't ask the question. I might not have liked the answer.

As it turned out, I didn't sleep better. In fact, I didn't get much sleep at all.

———

AS I DROVE BY, I could see Susanna's lights were on. I was out of the car and up her front steps before I even thought about what I was going to say.

I rang the bell and listened impatiently for footsteps. I could hear her as she approached the door, then there was a pause. She had to be looking through the peephole.

Odd. That wasn't like Susanna.

When my sister swung open the door, I stared at her in shock. Her left eye was swollen shut and that side of her face was a rainbow of bruises. Against her pale skin the contrast was shocking. "Susanna, what happened?"

She shrugged, and gestured for me to come in.

I followed her down the narrow hallway, our heels clacking on the hardwood floor, loud in the silence. When we reached the living room, she collapsed into an overstuffed armchair and indicated that I should do the same. Her expression was resigned.

I couldn't stand it. "Susanna, are you okay?"

She nodded slowly, as if the movement hurt.

"Are the kids okay?"

"They're fine."

"Was it Godfrey? I'll deal with him."

"No, Barbara. You don't understand."

"Damn right I don't understand. Susanna, what's going on? What happened to you?"

She shrugged helplessly.

"Don't give me that." My sister is a survivor. We both are. There was no way she was going to give up over what some man had done to her. "Susanna, tell me what happened."

She knew that tone in my voice.

I hadn't let her hide from her pain when she was little, and I wasn't about to start now.

"It wasn't Godfrey," she said in a lifeless voice. "I was stupid, that's all."

"Susanna…"

"Barbara, I don't want to talk about it."

"I don't care," I told her. "I know how a woman's face looks when she's been hit, so don't pretend you haven't been hit. Whatever happened, you're not going to keep it bottled up inside. It'll tear you apart."

Susanna shrugged again, then her face seemed to melt.

"I wanted to get my own back," she said in a voice I had to strain to hear. "If Godfrey doesn't want me, I'll find someone who does."

I looked at her bruised, defiant face and my heart felt like it was cracking. We'd had this conversation before, in the days before Godfrey. "Oh, Susanna."

She met my eyes, then looked hastily away. "I know. I never did have great taste in men."

"Who was he?"

"Oh no, Barbara. Not this time. I don't need my big sister fighting my battles anymore." She swallowed, hard. "Besides, I don't even know his last name."

There was nothing I could say. "Where are the kids?"

"Grazielle and Mom took them to the cottage for a few days. To give us time, they said." Susanna made a harsh little sound that tried to be a laugh. "So far it's been a great help."

Grazielle was Godfrey's sister. If she'd taken the kids to her cabin on Salt Spring Island, she must see the problems between Susanna and Godfrey as pretty serious. "What can I do?"

Her voice sounded dead. "Nothing. There's nothing anyone can do."

"Have you talked to Godfrey?"

She shrugged. "Some. We're not getting anywhere, though. And I can't see him, not looking like this." Her voice had that hopeless sound in it again.

I stood up.

"Are you leaving?" Despite her determination that she didn't need help, Susanna sounded worried.

"Nope. Just thought this discussion would go better with some coffee. And maybe a little ice cream. You do have ice cream, don't you?"

"And chocolate fudge sauce."

For a moment I could see my daredevil baby sister peeking through the bruised version of the sophisticated mask Susanna had learned to wear.

"Perfect," I said, heading for the kitchen.

A pot of coffee and two large bowls of double chocolate ice cream with chocolate fudge sauce later, Susanna and I were sitting at the kitchen table bemoaning the end of the ice cream. We'd been chatting about nothing as we ate, but she did look better. Time for the next step.

"Susanna, have you talked to Godfrey since he left?"

That bruised face instantly set in defensive lines. "Why should I?"

My heart ached for her, but she couldn't keep hiding from it. "You said he felt stifled and he left. So what happens now? Is he coming back? Do you want him back?"

I found myself hoping she would. Much as I dislike my brother-in-law, I hadn't seen Susanna with bruises like this since she met him.

Susanna picked up her spoon, turning it over and over in her hand, as though it were the most fascinating thing she'd ever seen. "I do want him back," she said finally in a small voice.

"And what does he want?"

No answer, but she turned the spoon faster and faster.

"Susanna?"

My sister sighed deeply, put down the spoon and met my eyes. "I don't know what he wants. I've been refusing to talk to him."

My feelings must have shown on my face, because she suddenly grinned at me.

It must have hurt, though, because the grin vanished and she ran one long, polished nail gently down her bruised cheekbone. "I know, you don't even have to say it. I'm supposed to be a grown-up now. I'll call him. Tomorrow."

"You'll let me know how it goes?"

"Yes, I'll let you know. And thanks, Barbara. You've really helped."

I hoped so. "That's what sisters are for," I said as I shrugged into my coat. "I'll talk to you tomorrow. Are you going to be okay alone?"

She nodded, and I left.

As I drove home, I pondered patterns and relationships and how hard it is to leave some things behind. For all Jayson's emotionally destructive behavior, at least he'd never hit me.

And Andrea asks why I avoid relationships.

CHAPTER TWENTY-ONE

Sunday morning found me parked outside Lisa Stern's while the pale sunrise was still painting the horizon. My body clock was apparently still out of kilter after all that flying, and despite my late night I'd been wide awake at quarter to five.

My brain had immediately started churning over Susanne's situation, so no chance of getting back to sleep. I headed for the shower.

I left the house at five-thirty. There was no sign of Cat. Maybe he'd gotten tired of being thrown out. This was a good thing. Except that I missed his purring.

Of course, maybe Cat just didn't get up this early, which would be smart of him. Ridiculously early mornings had become and all too familiar pattern since I'd taken on this case.

A couple of hours later, I'd worked my way through an extra-large Americano and a not-even-remotely-healthy chocolate chunk muffin, a sure sign I was overtired. And the curtains had finally been drawn back in the Stern household.

When the front door opened, I was ready.

Or at least that's what I'd thought until I got a clear look at Lisa Stern.

She came down the walk towards me wearing yoga pants and a runner's singlet, and stopped for a moment to stretch out her quads. This time she wasn't wearing a hat, and I got a clear look at her face.

I knew her.

We'd met at the Private Investigators Association of BC conference a few months before, though I hadn't caught her last name.

Lisa Stern was a P. I.

———

CASSIE HADN'T EVEN ASKED why I needed to see her on a Sunday morning. She just appeared at my office door less than half an hour after I called her. She still looked pale, and there were shadows under her eyes that hadn't been there before. I showed her to a chair, got her a cup of coffee.

Apparently that exhausted her patience.

"Barbara, what is it? What have you found? Why am I here?"

It seemed easier to ask my own questions than to answer hers. I went for the kicker. "Why would your husband hire a private investigator?"

All color drained out of Cassie's face, and she grabbed onto the edge of my desk. "Brian hired a P. I.?"

"Yes. Lisa Stern, with Pritchard Investigations. She's the woman he met with last Saturday morning."

I watched her face closely. She hadn't known, and this was hitting her hard. I took a sip of my coffee and glanced out my office window at the rapidly building clouds, giving her a moment to recover.

Cassie's breathing was loud in the silence.

The constant construction noise of a rapidly changing downtown that plagues me during the week was absent on a Sunday. Even the swish and rumble of traffic was missing.

"I have no idea what is going on," Cassie said at last.

I considered her for a moment. Her face pale face, tightly clenched hands and the break in her voice gave lie to her words.

It was time to push her. "I think you do know."

I hadn't thought her face could get any paler. "I don't know what you mean."

"Why did you hire me?"

"I beg your pardon?"

"Why did you hire me?"

One beautifully manicured hand went to her throat, then fell back to her lap. "You know why. Brian had bought a DNA kit."

"That's only part of the truth, isn't it?" I said. "And we're at a decision point. Either you tell me what's really going on and allow me to do my job, or you fire me."

Her eyes hardened and she leaned forward. I held up a hand before she could speak.

"Before you fire me, though, you need to know two things. The first is that I think there's something wrong about the deaths of your husband's parents. The second is that your aunt told me Ed McMather was Brian's real father."

"What?" It was practically a screech. I hadn't thought she had such a sound in her. "Why did no-one ever tell me?"

I didn't say anything, just watched her face as she processed what I'd told her.

"So it may be his own paternity Brian is concerned about?" she said after a moment.

"At very least it's an interesting possibility."

Every muscle in her body seemed to relax and she leaned bonelessly against the chair-back. "So you've solved it."

"Maybe. I'm not sure I believe everything your aunt said. And Brian's conversation with McMather didn't seem to put his mind at rest. He's still not working, and he spent most of Saturday reading old newspapers."

"Maybe McMather denied it. Maybe he's trying to prove it."

"Then who told him about it in the first place? And who killed McMather?"

I waited to see if she'd mention Brian being McMather's executor. She didn't, so perhaps that wasn't true either.

As I spoke, the tension had crept back into Cassie's body. Her gaze fixed on the wall behind me, as though looking for answers in the cracks that ran near the ceiling.

"You need to tell me what you're worried about,"

Her eyes swung to meet mine. There was a long pause as she searched my eyes, then the words seemed to burst out of her. "Grant. Our son. He isn't—my husband's child. Brian doesn't know, but somehow McMather found out."

Even though the possibility had crossed my mind, it still came as a shock.

Grant was the middle child. I quickly calculated dates. When Grant had been conceived, Brian had been in the early stages of a very successful legal career and probably working eighty and ninety hours a week. Pretty tough on any marriage.

Obviously they'd weathered it, but with one—permanent—consequence. Which she'd never told him about, for whatever reason.

No wonder she was so tense. The strain of carrying that secret all these years must have nearly destroyed her.

Now that she'd told me, Cassie couldn't seem to stop. "He's so proud of him. Of Grant. Grantley Stewart."

She gave a fractured little half-laugh, half-sob. "Brian—he's so proud that Grant has become a lawyer, is carrying on both of the family names. At first I didn't know how to tell him, then I couldn't bear to. If Alicia hadn't been a girl... But Grant's our only son."

"You're afraid your husband suspects? And that it's Grant's paternity he's been testing?"

She nodded, and looked away. Her hand was pressed tight against her mouth, as if to hold back the tears I could see flooding her eyes. "I think he'll leave me if he finds out."

"You think that's why he hired a P. I."

"Yes." It was a bleak, choked sound.

"And when you talked to McMather? You said he knew?"

"I don't know how he found out. He didn't come right out and say that he knew Brian wasn't Grant's father, but it was clear that was what he meant. It was odd, he seemed almost—gentle. But he asked if Brian knew."

She couldn't meet my eyes. "I said he did, but that we'd agreed never to mention it, or discuss it with anyone. I hoped that might end it. But I was afraid it wouldn't."

No wonder she'd looked so strained on Saturday night. "You must have been relieved to hear of McMather's death."

At that she did break down. "Yes. God help me, yes."

My mind was busy arranging and re-arranging facts. "But if it were your son's paternity that Brian was having tested, he should have the results by now. A simple paternity test takes five days or less."

"Perhaps he knows and can't bring himself to confront me."

"With that on his mind, I can't see him spending time in the newspaper archives."

It took a moment to sink in, then she took a deep breath and drew herself upright. "So you think he might not be looking at Grant's parentage at all?"

"It's natural it would be the first thing you think of," I said as gently as I could. "It may not have even occurred to him."

A silence. Then she took a shaky breath and said, "Perhaps you're right. So what is he worried about? And what do you suggest I do now?"

"Can you just talk to him? Since it likely isn't Grant's paternity that he's worried about?" It wouldn't help my bank balance any, but it was the right thing to do.

She stared at me for a moment, then shook her head. "No. I just can't. Not without knowing for sure."

Shades of Susanna and Godfrey. "I'll leave for Kamloops tomorrow, then. I need to know more about your husband's parents, or at least his supposed parents, and their deaths."

She nodded, a jerky motion that looked almost painful. "I don't see how that relates to the DNA kit, but I'll trust your judgment."

Finally. "I'll be in touch."

After I saw Cassie to the door, I sat and stared out the window, seeing little of the parking garage next door that takes up most of my view.

That was some secret she'd been hiding. No wonder she hadn't wanted to tell me.

I wondered how it would affect our relationship, once she was no longer my client. It can be hard to be around someone who knows too many of your painful secrets.

And given her position in the art world, it was probably a good thing I wasn't painting anymore.

Not liking that thought much, I brought my focus firmly back to the case I'd been hired for. I didn't think Cassie's fears about Brian testing Grant's paternity were justified, but now more than ever I was determined to get to the bottom of Brian's behavior. My client couldn't continue much longer under the kind of strain she was feeling, and I suspected her husband wasn't much better off.

What I still didn't know was why.

CHAPTER TWENTY-TWO

Early the following morning I was on the road, headed for Kamloops. I had a long drive ahead of me, and planned to make this a one-day trip. Despite that, I'd be taking the old highway winding through the Fraser Canyon, rather than the newer, faster Coquihalla route.

The old route was where Joe and Maria Stewart had met their deaths.

I'd made careful note of the location, and I wanted a look at the spot where they'd gone over the edge so many years before.

The sky lightened and the clouds rolled away as I drove inland. It was going to be a gorgeous day. The radio was playing something with a Latin beat, which went well with the Costa Rican coffee I'd brewed while I had my shower. I yawned widely, and swallowed another mouthful of coffee.

From Vancouver to Hope, Highway 1 is a four-lane superhighway, carrying the normal burden of vehicles rushing to some unknown destination. From Hope north, Highway 1 becomes the mostly two-lane Canyon Highway, which widens to three and even four lanes in places before narrowing back to two as it twists through the mountains that rise steeply on either side of the Fraser River.

Spectacular as it is, narrow shoulders and steep drop-offs make it challenging for drivers.

In seven places along that route, the mountains rise so steeply that the road disappears into tunnels, laboriously blasted through sheer rock in the early years of the last century. As a kid I memorized the names carved above each of those tunnels, because they spoke to me of wilder days. Yale. Saddle Rock. Sailor Bar. Alexandra. Hell's Gate. Ferrabee. China Bar.

Those names still bring back the scary-magical feeling I'd felt as we drove into sudden darkness, dimly lit, or so it seemed to me then, by the lights on a roof of solid rock looming far above us.

The accident had occurred not far south of the now tiny town of Boston Bar and just past the Hell's Gate tunnel. I found a pullout and got out of the car, looking down hundreds of feet into Hell's Gate Canyon.

The river narrows here and the slow, muddy Fraser River becomes a roiling torrent, nothing but white water between narrow rock walls.

Now this is a favored spot for river rafting. Then it had been a fatal spot for Joe and Maria Stewart.

Whatever had happened, they'd had very little chance. Not here.

I stood looking down into the angry water for a long time.

Back on the road again, I kept picturing a car plunging off the road and down those steep cliffs.

I turned up the radio, but the signal faded in and out. When it vanished entirely, I put on 60's rock—good driving music. Mostly because it was so familiar I could ignore it.

I like to think while I drive.

On this particular drive, though, my thoughts were ping-ponging from that fatal plunge, to every nuance of the Stewart case, to Jayson's show the previous Saturday. And I was still worrying about Susanna.

I'd called her several times the previous day, and gotten no answer. I'd even called my mother, intending to ask her whether she knew if Susanna and Godfrey were talking. She wasn't home either.

And neither my mother nor Susanna had returned the messages I'd left.

Something was going on. But there was nothing I could do about it at that moment.

And then there was Jayson.

It had been deeply unsettling to see him again, in that room filled with his works and the people who'd come to admire them. I still didn't think the problem was Jayson himself. I've been over him for awhile, despite what Andrea thinks.

And my reaction to Alessandro is proof that I'm more than ready to move on, right?

Which meant my current angst was about Jayson the artist rather than Jayson the man. Could I be jealous of his ever-growing success as an artist? I chewed on that unnerving thought for about a hundred miles worth of dry hills and sagebrush.

It's pretty country, if you like a monochromatic vista of rolling hills baked by the sun. Which I do. Seeing it again always has me analyzing exactly which combination of shades I'd need to combine to paint the subtle gray-greens, browns and ochres.

I have a couple of tubes of paint I bought specifically for painting these seemingly desolate landscapes. This time of year, there's a blush of palest spring green overlying the dustier tones, creating a contrast that makes my fingers itch for a paintbrush.

It was well after ten when I passed the sign announcing I'd reached the outskirts of the city. Spotting an awning with the magic word "Café", I pulled in and parked. One cup of coffee, even good coffee, is no substitute for breakfast, and I was ravenous. Once I'd seen to the necessities and polished off a plate of eggs, sausage and home fries, I headed for the university.

Since the century-old *Kamloops Sentinel* hadn't survived a labor dispute in 1987, I'd be looking at microfilm. The archives wasn't open on a Monday, but the Thompson Rivers University Library, conveniently located uptown, was.

Fifteen minutes after finishing my breakfast I was busy scanning microfilms. Other than the account of the Stewart's "accident" I wasn't sure what, if anything, I was looking for.

The first few months turned up nothing of interest. Nothing of interest to the case, that is.

There's some quirky part of my personality that is fascinated by descriptions of weddings—elaborate ceremonies with white lace, flowing tulle and flower girls, or hippie ceremonies, all beads, long hair and incense. Which is odd because if I ever get married, I plan to elope—the idea of walking solemnly down the aisle gives me the heebie-jeebies.

When I read about someone else's wedding, though, I'm fascinated. I think it's the civilizing of pagan ritual, and how the trimmings change decade by decade that intrigues me. I heroically concentrated on my search for the Stewarts.

I found what I was looking for in the April fourteenth edition. A headline halfway down page three grabbed my attention.

"Rumors of Political Corruption" it screamed in large black type.

I scanned the text. Two candidates in the upcoming provincial election were accusing each other of vote-buying and character assassination, respectively. The supposed vote-buying candidate was none other than Joe Stewart.

There was an investigation into his behavior which turned up nothing, and the other candidate was forced to withdraw. I noted the pertinent details and scrolled forward.

Front-page news for May eleventh was the visit of the provincial Minister of Finance, Ed McMather. I grinned at the irony, given what I now knew of McMather's history.

McMather had presided over a ribbon cutting, a Lion's dinner and a ladies tea while making it clear he supported Joe's campaign. The article also noted that he was staying with Mr. and Mrs. Stewart.

Brian had told me Joe Stewart and Ed McMather kept in touch. But if Maria Stewart was an old flame of Ed McMather's, if Brian was their illegitimate son, what was Ed doing staying with Maria and her husband all those years later?

Did Joe not even suspect McMather was the father of his wife's child? Surely there must have been signs.

Perhaps Ed had bought them off, paid handsomely to have them raise Brian, and part of the deal was the political support? Otherwise, I'd be guessing Vivianne had lied, that Ed was not Brian's father.

Just how much of her story was true?

While my mind assessed and discarded possible scenarios, I kept scrolling forward until I reached the articles about the senior Stewart's deaths.

Here, that event was front page news. "Local Political Hopeful Dies in Fiery Canyon Crash," ran the headlines.

I focused on the facts.

The roads had been clear and dry, both weather and light were good. A small adjacent article detailed recent improvements to the highway itself, so it hadn't been due to the condition of the road itself.

The accident had happened early enough in the day that Joe Stewart, who was driving, was unlikely to be drinking. Or dozing at the wheel. No other cars were involved, and no-one had reported seeing anything.

Why, then, had the accident happened?

I scrolled on.

Joe and Maria Stewart had moved to Kamloops from the coast fourteen years before and become an integral part of the community. There were interviews with their neighbors, Joe's colleagues and supporters, Maria's gardening group. All expressed shock at the untimely deaths, and a sense of loss. I made note of the names.

Later articles gave more facts.

One article mentioned skid marks left across the road, and

stated that the RCMP were involved, but the case seemed to have been quickly closed.

The inquest was hurried and resulted in a verdict of accidental death.

Finishing the last article, I was left feeling unsatisfied, as if something hadn't been done, hadn't been covered. The author of the articles seemed to feel the same way.

I scrolled back through them, checking the names. All had been written by the same reporter, Doug Matthews. If he was still around, he might be worth talking to.

I scrolled forward to find the report of the funeral. The article was short, but comprehensive. It looked like half the town had been there.

Brian was present, of course, and so was Ed McMather. Robert Grantley was also present.

That last name stopped me short.

Brian and Cassie had barely started dating when Joe and Maria Stewart died. What was Cassie's father doing at that funeral?

And without his wife?

I'd been following a thread that linked Ed McMather to Cassie Stewart through Vivianne McMather on the one side, and to both Joe and Maria Stewart on the other. So where did Robert Grantley figure in?

I knew he didn't like Ed McMather—or at least that was what Vivianne and Genevieve had told me—but that was all I knew about him. I grimaced, made a note, and kept going.

Scanning through the rest of that year and the next one, I found nothing else of interest. On a hunch, I googled Doug Matthews. His by-line showed up in recent editions of the *Vancouver Sun*. Well, well.

Time to head home.

———

THE SKY gradually darkened as I neared Vancouver. For the route home, I'd taken the Coquihalla Highway—and while I missed the scenery of the old highway, I was very glad of the speed of the newer route.

Once I left the mountains behind me at Hope, though, it took forever to get through the farmlands and the suburban sprawl. Stuck behind a semi belching fumes, cursing the inevitable traffic tie-ups coming into the city, I called Susanna and got her answering machine.

Again.

Which started a whole other chorus of worries, and had me cursing the idiot driver in front of me with even greater fervor.

We crawled along Highway 1 until I turned off on East 1st, where I was actually going against rush hour traffic for a change. From there I made it to my office in forty minutes, including a stop at White Spot to pick up a Triple-O Burger and fries, which I called dinner.

Still no call from my sister, though. And no blinding insights into the Stewart case.

I sat cradling my mug of coffee while my eyes traced the long crack in the plaster on the wall opposite my desk. Despite an application of drywall filler and a coat of fresh paint, that particular crack keeps sneaking through. And whenever a case has stumped me, I tend to stare at that particular wall with grave attention.

I knew I was missing something, I just couldn't figure out what it was.

Was it something I'd heard, something I'd read, some fact that didn't fit?

Reaching for my notes from my conversation with Vivianne and Genevieve, I tried to stop a huge yawn as I began to check their story against what I'd learned from Brian and my trip to Kamloops. None of the facts disagreed.

Sometimes Vivianne had selectively left out the time frame, letting me assume things were happening at the same time when in fact there'd been months or even years between.

Several cups of coffee and numerous yawns and scrunched up sheets of paper later, I still didn't know what I was missing.

I suddenly wished that Sid Fluxgold hadn't unaccountably decided to go off on a cruise. Bouncing possibilities off him has often led me to the answers on some of my trickiest cases, and I could use his insight on this one.

My former mentor, with decades of P. I. experience behind him, is a shrewd, experienced judge of people. And he has an ability to ask the right questions, so that you find yourself telling him things you didn't realize you even knew.

It was how Sid trained all of us—kept asking questions until the answers were obvious, even to us. He gave his trainees confidence and at the same time honed our thinking processes.

I wished he was here, but I couldn't begrudge the fact he was finally taking the time to enjoy himself.

I couldn't picture him on a cruise, though. The idea of Sid and deck chairs is desperately incongruous. I know they have all kinds of entertainment on those things, but do they have smoky late-night poker games and strip bars?

If I couldn't talk to Sid, at least I could follow his precepts. What were the questions I needed to ask?

A few sprang immediately to mind. For starters, I'd left the whole question of Lisa Stern hanging. Why had Brian hired a P. I.?

And what was Robert Grantley doing at Joe and Maria Stewart's funeral?

I considered both questions for a moment, playing off one against the other, then picked up the phone and dialed Cassie's number.

"Hello?"

It took me a second to get my words in order. I hadn't expected her to answer. "Cassie, it's Barbara O'Grady. There are a few things I need to discuss with you. Can you talk now?"

"This is really not a good time," she said. I wondered who was listening. "I'll meet you tomorrow. Moka Café at one?"

It wasn't a question. "I'll see you then."

CHAPTER TWENTY-THREE

The following day was cloudy and threatened rain. Despite yesterday's exhaustion and my late night, I was up at six, waking before the alarm I'd set for eight.

This was getting to be a habit, and one I didn't want to encourage.

Still, I was wide-awake, so I got up and made coffee, taking it out on the deck. The cold, clear air was invigorating, and I had some thinking to do. Cupping my hands around the steaming mug for warmth, I stood and contemplated the gray, misty city spread before me.

What about Susanna, and the problems she was having with Godfrey? The problems she's always had with relationships.

I considered Cassie Stewart and the problems she was having with her husband.

I remembered Alessandro's smile, then Jayson's face drifted through my mind. Grimacing, I wrenched my mind to the notes I'd made the previous evening.

Despite my lack of sleep, I felt fresher this morning, and having some of my questions answered seemed sufficient reason to face Jerry's probing. I usually get at least as much information as I give.

By seven-thirty I was parked near the police station, waiting for Jerry to show. I'd ambush him on his way into the station.

With any luck at all, I'd get to him before he really woke up, and maybe get some straight answers.

Jerry's never been a morning person either.

It was nearly eight when I spotted his battered blue Chevy wagon. I was out of my car and across the street before he'd even parked. When he saw me, his expression wasn't exactly welcoming. I could tell this was going to be a difficult conversation.

"Morning, Jerry. Got time for a coffee?"

"We have to talk, O'Grady," he said, swinging away from me and striding towards the coffee shop around the corner.

Uh oh.

I hadn't seen Jerry this riled since the time in the seventh grade that I'd loosed his pet frog, Freddy. I'd decided that Freddy needed his freedom. Jerry hadn't agreed with me, and we'd almost come to blows. It had taken both his mother and mine to sort out that situation.

I didn't think that would be possible this time.

Although come to think of it, my mother had shared Jerry's outrage, while Jerry's mother had taken my side. Maybe she'd help me out again. It was a tempting thought and one that had me smiling as I followed Jerry's stiffly retreating back, ignoring the rush of traffic two feet away, heading for the Cambie Street on-ramp and downtown.

Jerry had already paid for two coffees and was headed for a table in the far corner. He didn't look happy. He watched as I pulled out the sleek black and chrome chair opposite him, then gritted out, "Just tell me, how do you do it?"

I drank a mouthful of coffee, which was awful. Jerry must be really annoyed with me—he'd ordered the weakest coffee going, and he knows I can't stand weak coffee. "Do what?"

A muscle in his jaw clenched and I could almost hear his teeth grinding. "The McMather murder. You told me you weren't involved. But Brian Stewart is the executor of McMather's will."

So Vivianne hadn't lied about that. "I just found out too."

"But you've removed yourself from whatever case you were working on, right?"

I shook my head, automatically taking another mouthful of coffee. Still terrible. I put the cup down.

"McMather was murdered. You're way out of your league."

"I'm just doing my job."

"Come on, O'Grady, you don't even carry a gun," he said. "You've got no business messing with killers."

"I'm not messing with killers, I'm simply looking for information. And you don't need to protect me."

"No, O'Grady?" he asked, drawling out the name just to irritate me.

He succeeded. I've often noticed to my chagrin that when Jerry and I argue, we both sound like we're twelve. No matter how determined I am to behave like a rational human being, when one of us is angry our conversations tend to degenerate into slanging matches.

I took a deep breath, and tried to get the conversation back on track.

"Look, I'm not in any danger here. And in any case, I can take care of myself."

"Ha," he said, folding his arms across his chest and sitting back.

Ignoring both the interruption and his body language, I continued, "I don't think my case is connected to the murder. But I think maybe Brian Stewart knows something."

Arms still folded, Jerry said, "Stewart says he doesn't know anything."

"You've talked to him?"

"Yeah, yesterday. Speaking of which, where've been, O'Grady? I've been trying to get hold of you for three days now."

"I went to Kamloops." I said. "And Venice. What exactly did Brian Stewart tell you? Did he mention why McMather named him executor?"

He ignored my question. "Venice? What were you doing in Venice?"

"That's where Brian Stewart's mother-in-law lives," I said matter-of-factly.

"So that's where Mrs. Grantley went. And I suppose you talked to Vivianne McMather as well?"

"They met with me together. But I suspect that most of what they told me was a tissue of lies they wove for some reason of their own." It was the conclusion I'd come to after yesterday's investigations. Dammit.

Jerry did not appear to find this information anymore helpful than I did. For a minute, I was afraid he was going to walk out.

He didn't. He took a deep breath and said very calmly, "Why were you waiting for me today?"

"Vivianne McMather told me Brian was McMather's executor. I wanted to confirm it with you."

He folded his arms and sat back. "So?"

"Since you've already talked to Brian, and concluded he isn't connected, I don't think there is anything else to say."

I watched him closely to see if my guess was right. His blank expression told me nothing. "But what happened with the Hewitt arrest?"

"We had to release him."

"Why?"

"DNA came back. It didn't match."

"Ouch. You must have some pretty strong circumstantial evidence, to have arrested him in the first place?"

He thawed a little. Or maybe it was habit. "Seems there was some tension between Hewitt and the Senator lately, and Hewitt wasn't shy about saying so all over town. He told four of his buddies, and half the bar they were in, that McMather had better keep his eyes on his ass or he was as good as dead. Hewitt had motive, means and opportunity. Only problem is he didn't do it,"

"Then who did?"

He ignored me, took a swig of his coffee. "So why did you talk to Mrs. McMather?"

I shrugged. "It seemed like a good idea at the time."

Jerry gave me that look.

"Okay, okay. I needed some answers on an unconnected case. I'm sure Brian Stewart isn't connected with the McMather murder, but the McMathers and the Grantleys are connected to my case. I thought the sisters might be able to give me some answers."

"And did they?"

"Nothing that checks out yet." Which I'd rather not dwell on. "Any idea why McMather would name Stewart as executor?"

"Not the foggiest. Stewart didn't seem to know, either. Or if he did, he's not talking."

"He didn't tell me anything, either," I said, still thinking about Vivianne and her story.

"You've talked to him?"

Oops. I hadn't meant to mention that. I nodded.

Jerry's face was not happy. "When? And what did he say?"

"Not much, actually. I asked him if his parents had known McMather." Which was true, as far it went.

"His parents? Why would you ask him that?"

"From something Vivianne McMather said," I replied, bending the truth slightly. "Apparently Ed McMather and Brian's father worked together, years ago."

"Seems a stretch."

I took another sip of that awful coffee. "Yeah, he thought so too. Either he doesn't know anything, or he doesn't want to talk about it."

"Good," Jerry said. He glanced at his watch, drained his mug. "Coffee's on me. Just stay out of my murder investigation, O'Grady."

He had the last word. I glared at his departing back, which was hardly satisfying. It had also started to rain.

How appropriate.

CHAPTER TWENTY-FOUR

Back in my office, I brewed a cup of real coffee, a nice dark Viennese roast. It was still pretty early, but I called Susanna anyway. And got her answering machine. Maybe she'd gone to breakfast with Godfrey.

Probably not. I'd try her again later.

Looking at my case notes, I wondered if I'd been an idiot to go to Venice in the first place, and once there, to return so quickly. Was I being manipulated by a trio of very clever women?

Cassie had hired me to follow her husband and find out what was wrong with him, and why he'd bought a DNA kit. I'd got so involved in looking for the link between Brian and McMather, I hadn't been focusing on the fact that Brian's behavior changed at least a month before McMather's murder.

There had to be a connection—it was too coincidental otherwise—but maybe I'd been too quick to focus on the obvious.

Something had caused a radical change in Brian's behavior, made him neglect a career that had been the most important thing in his life. It wasn't getting better, either, if my last meeting with him was anything to go by. What was significant enough to cause that kind of reaction?

I sat back and contemplated the crack in the wall, letting my mind drift.

Brian had gone to see Judge Rutledge as soon as he learned McMather had been murdered. Why?

He'd hired Lisa Stern. I had some work to do there.

Presumably the call to the library and the visit to the newspaper archives had the same purpose, to investigate some event in his past? Yet he'd seemed genuinely surprised to discover his parents might have been murdered.

So what event in his past was he suddenly so concerned with?

It didn't make sense.

And what about renewing his passport? Why would he have done that?

I kept running into mental dead ends. As I sipped my coffee, inspiration struck.

What if Brian had been planning a trip to Venice? It was after the meeting with McMather that he'd gone to the passport office, then done the research at the library.

What if he'd been planning to see Vivianne, then hadn't gone because McMather had been murdered first?

Trouble was, that got me no closer to knowing what he'd been looking into.

Could he have found out that McMather might have been his father? Surely that wouldn't have caused his behavior to change so drastically?

Unless there was some other factor involved, something I didn't yet know about.

And who had killed McMather?

I wondered how Brian had felt about Joe Stewart, about losing him so young. My father had been killed in the line of duty when I was only thirteen. Sometimes I think I'll never get over it.

I shook myself out of an uncharacteristic moment of melancholy, and back to the question of why Brian had hired Lisa Stern.

What was going on that both of the Stewarts felt the need to hire a private investigator? Each without telling the other?

That question stopped me short. Neither Brian nor Cassie had told the other what they were doing. Either the marriage was in more trouble than Cassie had told me, or both were trying to protect the other.

Which was it? And why?

I realized that I hadn't thought enough about how Cassie factored into this situation.

My interest had been in Brian's role. Natural enough, as he was the one I'd been hired to follow, yet all the connections I'd found led back to Cassie as much as they did to Brian.

And she'd been worried, maybe even frightened—enough to hire me under false pretenses, enough to send me to Venice to get Vivianne and Genevieve's story.

Or was that to get me out of the way following McMather's murder?

My head was starting to ache.

Time to stop thinking, Barbara, and take some action.

———

A QUICK PHONE call confirmed that Doug Matthews, the newspaper reporter from Kamloops, was still with the *Sun*. I drained my coffee, stuffed my notes into my purse and grabbed a jacket.

Presenting myself at the front desk, I was told that Doug wasn't in. When I pushed, the annoyed looking receptionist said I could probably find him at the Crown and Thorns pub. "It's just down the block."

Mentally shrugging my shoulders that anyone would be in a bar this early in the day, I sprinted across the street, head down against the steady drizzle.

Walking through the door into a dimly lit, dark-paneled gloom, it took a moment to orient myself. As I shook the rain from my hair, I took in a large room that looked like a bad cross between a faux British pub and a Munich beer-hall. At first glance, the place seemed deserted.

Then I spotted the man sitting slump-shouldered at a small table in the corner, with a pint of dark beer in front of him. If it weren't for Vancouver's strict non-smoking policy, I suspected there'd be a cigarette smoldering in an ashtray in front of him.

Even in the dim light I could see the deep lines carved in his face by years of smoking. What did surprise me was his age. Despite the lines and the gray hair, I'd guess he was barely sixty.

If this was the same Doug Matthews, he'd been pretty young when he covered the Stewart deaths.

I walked over to the table where he sat and stopped beside him. He didn't look up.

I couldn't tell if he was lost in thought and didn't know I was there, or if he was simply hoping I'd go away. "Doug Matthews?"

"Who wants to know?"

I slid into a chair opposite him, earning a silent stare in response. "I'm Barbara O'Grady, a private investigator here in town. I'm interested in the deaths of Joe and Maria Stewart, in a highway accident in the Canyon nearly forty years ago. I understand you covered the story."

Now I had his attention. "That was a very long time ago. Why do you care now?"

"Have you been following the McMather case?"

"It's a little hard to miss," he said. Then he looked at me sharply. "Are you implying there's a connection?"

"Let's just say I've found some unsettling links. I don't want to say too much until I know a bit more about what actually happened back then."

Shrewd gray eyes weighed me, judging my character and determination. Or at least that's how it felt. "Why should I talk to you?"

"Because if you wrote those stories, you have some unanswered questions, and I suspect you don't much like leaving questions unanswered. Between us we might just find some answers. Plus there might be a connection between that 'accident' and McMather's murder. And what a story that would make."

He nodded slowly. "You're right that I don't like unanswered questions. So what do you propose?"

"First, anything I tell you is off the record, for now at least."

"What makes you think you can trust me not to print everything you say, Ms. O'Grady?"

I grinned at him. I'm pretty good at assessing people, and everything I saw matched what I'd seen in his early work. "Call me Barbara. Right now there is no story, just a lot of unrelated facts. And I think you're too much of a newsman to ruin a good story by running it too soon."

And I didn't intend to tell him everything.

"Touché. Okay, you've got your pact of silence. For now. Just make sure I get the full story before any one else does."

"You have my word on it."

"Then I'm Doug." He raised his mug towards me, then drained half of it. "You mentioned connections between McMather's death and that of the Stewarts. What connections?"

"You may remember the Stewart's son Brian."

"The track star."

After all those years, he really did remember. I was impressed. "Brian became a lawyer. And he's just been named executor of McMather's will."

"So?"

"Brian is also married to McMather's goddaughter and niece by marriage, the former Cassie Grantley."

A frown creased Doug's forehead even further. "Both Robert Grantley and Ed McMather attended the Stewarts' funeral."

Now I was really impressed. "That's one of the things I've been wondering about."

"So when did Brian and his wife start dating?"

Doug Matthews was one sharp cookie. I wondered why I hadn't noticed his byline more often. "A few months before the accident."

"Did the families know each other beforehand?"

"Not as far as I can tell."

"So," he said thoughtfully.

"Exactly. I don't know what Grantley was doing at that funeral. But I'm beginning to suspect it ties into how the Stewarts died."

"Well, let's see what I can remember," he said, rubbing at his forehead as he spoke.

"Joe Stewart was beginning to make big noises in local politics. He'd been active municipally and he was close to getting the nomination to run for provincial office, get himself elected to a grander position. Joe was like that, had big ideas, never content with where he was. He was always looking for the connection, the next move, the right people. He wasn't above a little blackmail, either, if it got him what he wanted."

There was nothing wrong with Doug's memory. And he had a newsman's trick of telling a complex story clearly and concisely.

"Joe got into trouble with it," he continued. "That's when the corruption thing broke. He got accused of undue influence, basically bribing some of the local Social Credit party members to vote for him, rigging the nomination."

Doug took a swig of his beer. "It wouldn't have come out, except that his opposition, a loyal party member of long-standing, Grant, Graytham, something like that, got wind of it."

"Granger," I said.

"Yup. And from what I gathered, Granger was one of the few locals Stewart hadn't got any dirt on."

"What your stories didn't cover was exactly how the issue sorted out. Or how it related to Stewarts' death."

He snorted. "It was in the original story, the unedited version. At that point Stewart called in some muscle."

"McMather?"

"That's how I read it. McMather had too many connections, too much clout. I always wondered what Stewart had on him, to get him to come in like that. With McMather standing up for Stewart, the guys behind Granger backed off, and Granger had to as well. In fact, he withdrew from the race, ended up resigning from the party."

"I'm betting Granger didn't take his defeat well."

"Not well at all, especially when he'd lost so much face in front of all his buddies. And the worst of it was he must have known he was right. Eventually, he left town, just sold out, packed up his family and moved."

"Was that before or after the accident?"

"After. As you can imagine, rumors were flying. And Granger had been in Vancouver that weekend."

"So you think Granger was responsible for, or at least involved in the Stewart's death?"

"I did at first. The timing was just too coincidental. Then, as the reports came back, first the autopsy, then the investigation report, and nothing showed up, I began to wonder."

He tapped on the table with a thick, nicotine stained forefinger. "If it'd been me, I'd have been looking for tampering with the car, a hole in the brake line, something like that. With faulty brakes through Hell's Gate, a fatal accident was almost certain, especially if the brakes had been fixed so they went all at once when real pressure was applied."

"I thought the car caught fire," I said, recalling the garish headlines. "There wouldn't have been much in the way of evidence."

"Now that's an odd thing. The car caught fire, all right, or rather the engine did. They must have been running mighty low on gas though, or maybe there was a leak in the gas line too, because the fire didn't spread, and there was no explosion."

"The car didn't explode?"

"Nope."

I thought about that for a moment. "So what did the evidence show?"

"Aside from a few skid marks, the investigation turned up no evidence of any kind, and the autopsy was clean."

"And you began to believe it was an accidental death?" I prompted.

"No. But that level of tampering with evidence took a higher level of clout, either political or economic, than Granger had. Even back then."

"McMather again?"

"I've always thought so. It seemed to fit the facts. But there was no motive. Or at least not one that I could dig out."

"What about opportunity? Brian Stewart says he didn't spend a lot of time with his parents that weekend. Did you ever check where they went, who they saw?"

He shook his head. "Never got the chance. After I wrote that last article implying that something was being covered up, I got pulled from the story so fast it made my head spin. I spent the next six months covering weddings." He snorted. "Weddings."

He paused, looked around him for a waitress, and signaled for another beer.

I wondered if he always drank like that, or if it was the memory of covering all those weddings. Though he'd done some nice write-ups. I knew better than to mention it, though.

"Six months later," Doug said once the fresh mug was delivered and he'd taken a swig. "I got a job here and here I've been ever since. Once I was based in Vancouver, it would have been fairly easy to check up on that weekend, but it had begun to seem like a dangerous career move. And I hate covering weddings."

———

I SMILED at Doug's expression. He promptly buried it in his beer mug, as though desperate to get rid of a bad taste.

I took a drink of my own beer. Put it down in a hurry. It was still too early in the day for me.

Watching Doug drain his mug, I realized it was one of the things that'd been nagging at me on the drive home from Kamloops. After he'd covered the Stewart deaths, I'd only seen Doug's byline on various wedding stories for the rest of the year. I just hadn't consciously registered it until this moment.

"So whoever was involved in the Stewarts' deaths had enough clout to hush up the story completely," I said. "If it were McMather, what would his motive be?"

Dough put down the empty mug, glared at me. "Maybe Joe had something on McMather, something big enough to force McMather to help Joe clean up the nomination mess. Knowing Joe, that wouldn't surprise me. He could have known McMather before."

"He did," I told him. "Joe Stewart and McMather worked together as longshoremen in their early days."

"Wish you'd been working with me back then. Sounds like McMather had himself quite a number of reasons to kill Joe Stewart."

Somehow hearing the words spoken aloud made a difference. As my mind raced back over what I'd learned so far, I realized I'd been making some pretty broad assumptions. And missing a few things that should have been obvious.

"What if we're looking at this from the wrong angle? Both the Stewarts died in that car crash. Why are we automatically assuming that Joe was the murder target, and not Maria? I've heard rumors that Maria Stewart was once involved with McMather."

I considered mentioning the possibility Brian might be McMather's son, but I didn't yet know how far I could trust Doug's discretion.

Doug looked surprised. "McMather and Maria Stewart? Where'd you hear that?"

"I've got my sources."

"Reliable?"

"Maybe. Maybe not."

Doug looked thoughtful. "Still. A crime of passion, hmm? Never considered that."

"Not necessarily a crime of passion. Just a different motive for murder. What do you know about Maria Stewart?"

"Almost nothing. She didn't seem newsworthy at the time. I was more interested in Joe Stewart than Maria Stewart."

It was a typical reaction for that time. And I should have caught it earlier. Our culture still tends to assume that it's the male of the species that initiates action, and those thought patterns affect how we decipher situations and motivations.

"I thought any connection between McMather, Grantley and Stewart would be business-related," I said. "So McMather and Grantley being at the funeral without their wives made sense. But I didn't even consider that perhaps both of them came to Maria Stewart's funeral, rather than Joe's. Which has other implications."

"Still the world's strongest motivating factors. Sex and money. No, make that three—sex and money and power," Doug said. "That's what sells newspapers. Hell, that's what's in newspapers."

He frowned at me. "I thought back then that the death of the Stewarts was about power. But if Maria was the target, then maybe it's about sex. Interesting. Nice catch, Barbara."

He rotated his beer in the little circles of damp on the table, watching the patterns it made, seemingly lost in thought. After a moment he looked up. "So where does that leave us?"

"Still trying to follow a very stale trail. If you're with me on this?"

When he nodded emphatically, I continued, "We need to find out about the Stewart's last days. They were in Vancouver that weekend. Maybe if we knew why they came here, we'll know why they died. And I still think their deaths are the key to McMather's murder."

"Interesting."

"Since you did the investigation on the first half of the story, it seems fitting that you follow up on the second. Are you in?"

"I'm in. What'll you be doing?"

"I'll start with McMather's death. And his naming Brian as his executor."

"Fine." He drained his mug, set it down with a thump. "I'll need your numbers."

I gave him my card and took his, agreeing that we'd keep in touch.

As I left, Doug was texting something on his cell phone with one hand and signaling the waiter for another beer with the other.

This was no burnt out newsman, despite appearances. Feeling just a bit closer to solving this thing, I checked my watch. It was nearly time to meet with Cassie. Good.

I had some tough questions for her.

CHAPTER TWENTY-FIVE

Cassie had agreed to meet me at the Moka again, and she was right on time. I watched her walk in, shaking off a Burberry plaid umbrella, and noted the erect tilt of her head and the firm set of her lips. This was the public face she often wore as one of Vancouver's Beautiful People.

Now what? Was she going to pretend our last conversation hadn't happened—that she hadn't shared the truth about her son's parentage, which she'd been hiding all these years? Reaching the booth where I sat, she slid smoothly into the seat opposite mine.

Eyeing her closed expression, I decided to hit her with the hard questions before she had a chance to retreat any further behind those walls she'd erected.

"I've been looking into the deaths of Brian's parents," I said. "Did you know your father attended their funeral?"

The question caught her off guard, and the real Cassie I'd been coming to know peeked out. "What? My father? You're sure?"

"Yes. I confirmed it with the reporter who covered the story."

"He never mentioned it, even after Brian and I were engaged. Their accident was in the spring, I think?"

"Yes, that May."

"I don't remember him going." She glanced at the noisy booth full of teenagers one down from us and gave a little grimace.

I hid a smile. Their boisterous chatter was why I'd chosen this booth—it covered our conversation. I signaled to the waitress for coffee. It looked like Cassie could use a cup.

"Your uncle Ed was there too," I said once the waitress had left. "Any idea what either of them was doing there?"

"I think Mother might have mentioned something…"

Suddenly Cassie's eyes widened and all the color drained from her face. "They were both there? You're sure?"

"Yes. Why? What have you remembered?"

She shook her head wordlessly, all presence gone.

I watched her for a moment. "Your father must have known one or both of them."

"I suppose so." Her normally subtle application of blusher stood out oddly on her pale face.

"Would he have known Joe Stewart or Maria Stewart?"

She shrugged. It was a totally un-Cassie-like movement.

"Cassie?"

I could see her swallow hard. "Sorry, Barbara. It's something of a shock."

That harsh voice didn't sound much like my polished client, either.

What was going on? "What's a shock?"

"I had no idea my father had known either of my in-laws," Cassie said. "It's a little hard to take in."

The explanation didn't match her expression. "Why?"

"My father never mentioned knowing Brian's parents."

"And… ?"

She glanced at me. "And that wasn't like him. Why the silence?"

"Why do you think?"

She swallowed again. "I don't know."

"I thought you wanted to help your husband."

"I did. I do. Oh, God," she said, dropping her head into her hands.

This was so unlike her usual restrained behavior that I didn't know what to do for a moment. "Cassie?"

Nothing.

"Cassie, what is it? It'll be easier to talk about it than just fear the worst."

I wasn't sure I believed what I'd just said. I'm not much for talking about my own problems, but it seemed to have helped her to talk about her son last time. And I needed her to open up.

I had a feeling that Robert Grantley's presence at that funeral just might be the key this case had been missing.

"My father—he had an eye for the ladies, as my mother used to put it."

It sounded like neither of the Delorme sisters had chosen well when it came to their husbands. "Go on."

"She hid it well, but I think she was unhappy through a lot of her marriage. Looking back, I realize he must have had almost constant affairs. He wasn't home much," she added with a bitter little laugh.

Was she thinking about the similarity to herself and Brian? How could she not draw those parallels?

"And the funeral?" I prompted.

"Mother almost never said anything against Father, anything about his dalliances. That spring, I was just finishing third year, and Mother wanted the three of us to go to Seattle for a weekend. I remember now—Father couldn't go, he had to go to a funeral.

Mother was upset, and she made some remark about Father and Uncle Ed both still panting after the same woman. I remember it because the remark was so out of character for her, and because it was unheard of to hear Father and Uncle Ed mentioned in the same sentence."

"You think she was referring to Maria Stewart."

"Yes. Yes, I do."

"Why should that worry you? He could have met her at any time."

"Yes, but I remember Brian mentioning once that his mother

had been studying to be a lawyer, but left school when he was born. It was why he wanted to study law, I think. What if my father and his mother knew each other in law school?"

What if, indeed. "And your father never mentioned her when you began seeing Brian?"

"No, but how could he, if they had been intimate? My father wasn't one to talk about such things, and certainly not to me."

"They might simply have been friends."

"You didn't know my father," she said bluntly, a bitter tone in her voice. "He'd chase anything in skirts. If he knew Maria Stewart, you can bet they were lovers."

She barely seemed to be breathing and she was too pale. "What if… ?"

I waited.

"What if my father is also Brian's father? The dates are right." It came out in a rush, and she couldn't look at me.

"I think you're jumping to conclusions."

She gave a harsh little laugh. "Well, it would certainly explain Brian's changed behavior, wouldn't it? If he'd found out any part of this, I mean."

It could also explain why he'd hired Lisa Stern.

No point reminding Cassie of that little detail. She already looked like she might shatter at any moment.

Now seemed a good time to mention Vivianne's theories, though. "When I talked to your mother and aunt, they told me McMather had fathered Brian. They didn't say a word about your father."

"Knowing those two, they might be trying to cover it up. For my protection."

I could see that. "You're going to have to ask them."

Cassie was silent for a long moment, staring at the coffee that was growing cold in her cup.

"Would you rather I talked to your mother instead?"

Cassie sat in silence for a moment, then met my gaze. "No. I'll talk to her. It has to be me. I'll be in touch, Barbara."

She stood up as if afraid to say anymore. Grabbing her umbrella, she threw a ten on the table.

I sat watching her departing back, wondering how that conversation would go. I liked both Cassie and Genevieve, but it didn't surprise me that there was tension between them.

Funny how we never seem to outgrow our early dynamics with our mothers.

CHAPTER TWENTY-SIX

As I left the Moka, the darkening clouds told me we were probably in for a downpour. What I wanted to do was go home and curl up by the electric fireplace. What I needed to do was to have another chat with Judge Rutledge.

Maybe he knew something that would help sort this mess out.

A glance at my watch told me I'd make the next ferry to Bowen Island, if I rushed and the traffic cooperated. And if the weather didn't get too bad. It was just starting to rain again, so I made a dash for my car.

I was lucky. Several hours later, I was once again ensconced in Judge Rutledge's cozy front parlor on Bowen Island, having declined a glass of sherry. I'd explained I was running into some complications in researching the Stewart family tree.

Though a flash of irritation had crossed that lined face, he'd invited me in out of the rain, offered a towel, which I declined, made all the polite noises.

"Did you know Robert Grantley?" I asked when he'd seated himself on the brocade sofa opposite me.

"Certainly. He was one of my brighter students."

Cassie's fears danced in my mind. "And did Robert Grantley and Maria Delorme know each other?"

"They started law school in the same year," said the Judge.

He hadn't really answered the question. "And when was that?"

"More than fifty years ago."

Inside, I winced. The timing meant that chronologically, Robert Grantley could easily have been Brian Stewart's father. For Cassie's sake, I hoped it wasn't true.

I couldn't imagine how she would deal with it.

On the other hand, I couldn't imagine Robert Grantley allowing his only daughter to marry her half-brother, either. And it hadn't been a small wedding. He'd given his daughter away with all the trappings. I'd seen the pictures.

Still, a niggling little voice in my head was saying, Maria might not have told him. He was already married, after all.

Had Maria just married Joe Stewart and told no-one she was pregnant by someone other than her husband?

The Judge was nodding, unaware of my thoughts. "More than half a century," he said. "So many years. So many faces."

"Why did Maria drop out of law school?"

"It was the old story, at least for that time. She became pregnant, and had to get married." His tone was sad, but his eyes were shrewd.

I nearly missed it, distracted by relief that times had changed—and empathy for a bright, ambitious woman trapped in a world that didn't really want her to succeed.

But he was watching me too closely.

I re-ran his words in my head. What wasn't he saying?

"And she never completed law school?"

"No. There was no money. She was on a scholarship, one with a morals clause."

I winced. Just like that, all of her opportunities were gone. It was unimaginable now.

Wasn't it? "She was only in law school for one year?"

"Yes."

"Who was the father?"

"I always assumed it was Joe Stewart."

"How would she have met him?"

"I have no idea. As I've said, I didn't know her well."

So how had Rutledge's relationship with Brian come about?

"Cassie Stewart called you a 'family friend'. Did you keep in touch with Robert Grantley and Maria Delorme, and now their families, all these years?"

He smiled faintly. "No, no." Despite his years, his voice still had that note put there by decades of authority.

"I lost touch with both of them until Brian Stewart became my student," he explained. "Brian had all of his mother's brilliance and none of her weaknesses, and he was receptive to the few words of guidance I was able to offer him. I made a point of following his career. In fact, it flatters me to believe that to this day he considers me his mentor."

There was a softness in his voice that I found unexpectedly touching. At the same time, there was a false modesty in his words that I found annoying. But then I've never dealt well with those in authority, and despite being retired, the Judge exuded authority.

I still needed to know more about Maria Stewart and about Brian's birth, but he'd already closed that door.

And I couldn't afford to miss the last ferry. Spending an unplanned night on Bowen Island is not my idea of a good time.

I took my leave, thanking him politely for the sherry and the information. He was eighty-seven, after all. He graciously told me I was welcome anytime.

It was an invitation I wouldn't want to presume on, for any number of reasons.

On the ferry back to the city, I had some time to think, and no distractions. There wasn't much to see except fog and rain. I brushed absently at the dampness that clung to my cheeks as I considered what the relationship between Robert Grantley and Maria Stewart might have been.

Robert had likely attended the funeral for Maria's sake, after all. But how had he learned of the funeral? Had the respected lawyer and the beautiful law school dropout kept in touch all those years?

I hated that time and my incomplete information had turned them both into stereotypes.

Before the ferry was halfway across Georgia Straight, my thoughts were going around in circles, and I was giving myself a headache. Without new input, I wasn't getting anywhere.

I tried to shift my mind to something completely unrelated. Like painting and art openings, and why I'd stopped painting in the first place. That was headache territory too, so I pulled out my cell phone and called Susanna.

Getting her voice mail, I left another message telling her to call me as soon as she got in, then sat and stared at the seagulls dipping in the ferry's wake. What was I doing? Susanna and Godfrey's relationship problems weren't exactly a cheerful subject.

Not that I could talk. I hadn't managed a long term relationship since Jayson and I broke up. Now I was half-hoping Alessandro might call. And just how remote were the chances of that? Or that I could make a long distance relationship work.

I like being a P. I., and I'm good at it, but maybe Andrea's got a point. Maybe I do get too involved in my cases at the expense of the rest of my life.

I considered that thought for a while, idly watching two seagulls flapping and squawking over something floating in the water. On the other hand, the married couples I'd been spending time with lately seemed to be getting along about as well as those seagulls.

Maybe I'd think about making some changes in my life when this case was finished.

Or maybe not.

———

WHEN THE FERRY DOCKED, I followed an impulse and drove right through the rain-slicked city and out to UBC. I knew the annual student yearbooks were available on-line, but there's something about handling the actual pages created so long ago that gives me a different feel than staring at them on screen.

And scrolling through three hundred and some pages of digitized photos and text, when I don't know exactly what I'm looking for, is guaranteed to cement my almost-headache in place.

The University Archives is part of the old library complex, now expanded into the Barber Learning Centre. I find it an odd juxtaposition of very old and very modern, but I love the resources the new complex makes available.

Climbing those worn stone steps, I wondered if I was just giving in to a morbid fascination. I wanted to see what the young Maria Delorme and Robert Grantley had looked like.

Half an hour later, with *The Totem* year-books from nearly sixty years ago spread out in front of me, I realized I'd been following an instinct, not indulging in morbid curiosity. I'd found their pictures in the second book I'd opened.

Judge Rutledge had been right, Maria was beautiful, with curly dark hair and large soulful eyes. Robert was handsome too, with crisp brown hair and a big happy grin. Their Parliamentary Forum team won the national McGoun Cup for debating supremacy that year. They had obviously known each other very well indeed.

I stared at Maria's picture, wondering how a beautiful girl from Kamloops got all the way to law school in those days, when the usual occupation for a woman was wife and mother. She obviously had the brains and the ability to succeed. Yet having come so far, and worked so hard, she had to give up her dream.

I sat looking at the lovely face of the long-dead woman, wishing her picture could talk.

Again, I was struck by the conviction that Maria Delorme held the clue for which I was searching. The yearbook told me little more than her name and that she was twenty-one.

I flipped to Robert Grantley's picture. He'd been twenty-three in his first year of law school.

On an impulse I turned to the faculty section and found Gregory Rutledge's face. With thick dark hair and those piercing eyes, he'd been a striking man. Examining the pictured face, I wondered if his personal charisma had developed as his power and influence grew, or if he'd always had it. It was impossible to tell.

Then I flipped through the previous year's yearbooks.

No sign of Robert, but Maria was there. An Arts graduate, she'd been a volunteer on the student newspaper.

Shaking my head, I flipped through the previous year's students, and the year before that, and finally found Robert, graduating with a degree in Business. A business degree, followed by a law degree. No wonder he'd done so well.

I wondered where he'd been in the two years between his first degree and going to law school. I made a note to check on that.

Even more, I wondered what had really happened to Maria. If Brian was not Joe's son, was his father Ed McMather, as Vivianne had said? Or was he Robert Grantley, as Cassie feared?

Or had Maria met Joe, fallen in love and got married, giving up everything she'd fought for?

Judge Rutledge had implied Brian's birth was "premature." I made a note to check Brian's date of birth.

I looked at Maria's pictured face again.

She would have been a contemporary of Vivianne and Genevieve. I tried to imagine her sitting as a fourth at that cafe in Venice, and what the conversation would have been then.

Maria would have held her own, I had no doubt. I saw strength and a hint of passion in those pictured eyes, but who was she really?

Why had she made the decisions she had?

I returned the yearbooks to the friendly woman at the desk, and on another impulse asked for copies of the student newspaper from the same years. Paging through them, I reflected on how much life has changed in the last sixty-odd years. The pace of life was slower then, things we now take for granted were just ideas.

Yet the sense of intense possibility, of a whole new world opening before them, was almost tangible. There were the returned soldiers graduating, the army huts that had been pressed into service as temporary classrooms, the new buildings that were going up to house an expanding university.

In those days, university students were the cream of the crop, with their future stretching golden before them. For those graduates, finding a job was not a problem, only choosing from among the jobs available to them. A degree was a guarantee of a career, and a good one.

Unlike my degree. Which isn't worth the paper it's printed on as a ticket to a job. Times have indeed changed.

Several pages on, I found the article about the debating team's win. There was much "glory to our school" rhetoric, and interviews with both members of the team. Both Robert and Maria were articulate, both intelligent.

Robert had a sense of humor, and an intriguing turn of phrase. He came across as talented, enthusiastic, civilized.

It was Maria who surprised me. Even in an article written so long ago, her wit and charm sparkled off the page. Clearly the student interviewing her had been as impressed as I was. He kept giving her leading questions, allowing her to shine.

This was a woman I wished I had known.

More than ever, I wondered at the combination of circumstances that meant she had not gone on to finish her law degree, had never become the top lawyer the interview hinted she could have been.

If she had become a lawyer, would she have made a difference? Maria had only been forty-four when she died. What a waste.

Packing up the microfilms of the *Ubyssey*, I replaced them in their individual boxes before returning them to the desk, made a few last notes and decided to call it a day.

Now I had another goal in this case—I wanted to solve the mystery that was Maria Stewart.

Driving home along Twelfth Avenue through misting rain, I planned to order in pizza, open that bottle of Merlot Guido had recommended, and refuse to answer the phone for the rest of the evening. I figured I'd earned it.

Then I remembered Susanna.

CHAPTER TWENTY-SEVEN

Once I got home, I checked for messages. There were two. I hoped one of them was my sister.

No such luck.

The first voice I heard belonged to Jayson. I rolled my eyes as I heard that mellifluous voice inviting me to an opening on Thursday. Now what was he up to, I wondered, as I deleted him.

The next voice I heard had a beautiful Italian accent that made my knees go funny. Alessandro.

I hadn't thought he'd call. I wasn't even sure I'd wanted him to call. My knees were sure, though.

"Barbara. I had hoped you would be home. I did not think you would be, but I hoped. I am at the airport, here in Vancouver. We had a delay, and I am here for perhaps another hour or two. If you do not get this message in time, know that I am thinking of you. I will call you again. *Ciao, bella.*"

An hour or two. I live less than half an hour from the airport. But when had he called?

I frantically pressed keys, and that annoyingly perky recorded voice told me he'd called two hours ago.

I'd missed him.

But why hadn't he called my cell? Or had I given him the number? I pulled out my phone and checked. He'd texted me while I was reading yearbooks, and I'd obviously been too caught up in Maria's story to notice. Dammit all.

Picking up the phone, I ordered a pizza as a consolation prize and opened a bottle of Merlot to breathe. A small part of me was relieved that I'd missed seeing Alessandro, I had to admit it. He posed a complication I wasn't sure I had time for right now.

The other part of me, the weak-kneed part, just wanted to grab as much time as possible with him. Old-fashioned lust, that was. And probably long overdue.

I took a sip of wine, savoring both the taste of the wine and the thought of Alessandro's warm eyes and strong-looking hands.

The phone rang, and I jumped, then leapt to grab it. Alessandro had said he'd call me, but I hadn't realized he'd meant tonight.

"Hello?" I said, more breathlessly than I'd have liked.

"Barbara? Is that you?"

The shaky voice on the other end belonged to my sister and I promptly felt a wave of guilt. I'd been too busy thinking about Alessandro to remember to call her. "Susanna? What's wrong?"

There was a deep sigh. "Nothing is wrong," she said, her voice steadying and slowing. "I've just had a long day, and I'm tired."

"Did you see Godfrey?"

"Yes, I saw Godfrey."

"And?"

There was a small silence. She didn't want to tell me. I let the silence stretch.

"And we're talking," she finally said.

"Just talking? Is that good?"

"Oh, Barbara," she said on a sigh. "No wonder you're not married. Yes, talking is good. Not talking is when they walk out the door."

Hmm, hadn't been my experience. Of course, I was usually the one who walked out.

But Susanna didn't need to hear that. "And so?" I said as noncommittally as I could.

"And so we're talking," she snapped.

Then I could hear her taking a deep breath, and she said quietly, "Just let it rest, Barbara. I appreciate your help, your concern, but we'll have to work this one through in our own way."

Okay, I could accept that. "What did he say about your face?"

"It was carefully not mentioned."

And she called that talking?

Maybe it was a good thing she didn't want my advice. She wouldn't have liked it much. "Well, call me if you need me," I said carefully.

"Yes, I will. And Barbara? Thanks. I know you mean well."

I disconnected the phone and sighed. Damned with faint praise, again. Oh well, one day someone will appreciate all my sterling qualities enough to ignore those not-so-sterling ones. Like my tendency to interfere in other people's lives.

Luckily the pizza guy showed up with my dinner right about then, before I could get anymore introspective.

As I munched on a Manager's Special with the works, I focused on my case. It had got to the stage where it wouldn't leave me alone. I kept thinking about it, puzzling through the questions, trying to see the connections. It beat thinking about my life, which was my other option.

Pouring a second glass of wine, I went out on the deck and watched the rain and the headlights reflecting back from the wet pavement on Hemlock. I half hoped Cat would show up and distract me, but there was still no sign of him.

I stood breathing in the fresh, damp air and thinking. It didn't help much. There were too many loose ends, too many questions that I didn't have answers to.

The question I most wanted answered was the one Maria posed. What had happened to her?

If Vivianne were right in saying that Ed McMather was Brian's father, when had Maria and Ed met? And why had Maria married Joe rather than Ed, if Ed were the father of her child?

Unless Ed were already married? I did some quick sums and realized that no, Ed and Vivianne had married the following year.

So if Ed were Brian's father, why hadn't Maria married him?

And why was Robert Grantley at Maria's funeral, twenty-some years later? Granted, they'd been colleagues, maybe even friends, but twenty years is a long time.

I was going around in circles, and I knew it. I'd have given anything for a ten-minute conversation with Maria Stewart.

I hadn't even begun to answer the questions that I'd told Doug Matthews that I'd follow up. Why had Ed McMather named Brian as his executor?

If Brian were his son, it made some sense. And if Brian weren't his son? Nothing made sense. Perhaps Brian was Ed's lawyer.

But wouldn't Cassie have known that? Not necessarily, I realized. Another thread to follow up on.

When I started wondering how Jayson had managed to get a show at the Courtland Gallery and why he was now inviting me to another show, I finished my wine, turned on an old Katherine Hepburn movie that was playing on PBS and gave up thinking for the evening.

This case was going to drive me to drink. And I still had too many unanswered questions.

CHAPTER TWENTY-EIGHT

The next morning found me on the fifth floor of the library, looking at the microfilm records from sixty years ago, specifically at birth announcements. I was looking for anything I could find on Brian Stewart's birth.

I'd woken up thinking about Maria's life, realizing I needed to know more about the circumstances of her son's birth. I'd grabbed a coffee and a muffin, called them breakfast, and here I was.

It didn't take me long to find the record of his birth, though. He was a January baby, Brian James Stewart, been born to Maria and Joseph Stewart. He'd weighed nine pounds, two ounces.

I winced in sympathy.

Going backwards, I finally found the marriage record of Maria and Joe, in September 3 of the previous year. Four months before Brian was born, one day after Maria should have started back to law school.

Counting backwards on my fingers I worked out that Brian was probably conceived in early April.

Here was the reason that Maria had married Joe Stewart instead of becoming a lawyer. So where did Ed McMather fit in?

There was no article about the wedding, unfortunately, just the brief announcement. I would love to see a guest list. The bride and grooms' parents were listed and I made a note of both sets of names, then on an impulse started to scroll backward, looking for Robert Grantley's marriage to Genevieve.

I knew Cassie was a year younger than Brian. She was also two years older than her brother. I was assuming that Robert and Genevieve had been married in a year or so before Cassie's birth.

It was closer to three years. I found the write-up for their wedding in June, a society wedding with all the trimmings, given full coverage despite the various world crises that seemed to cover every front page. I scanned forward, looking for their son's birth.

What I found instead was a small article stating that Joe Stewart of Vancouver had been acquitted of stealing fish from his employer. No further details were given, but my interest was piqued to find him involved with the law just ten months before he married Maria.

Perhaps that explained how they met?

I finally found the birth announcement I'd been looking for. On March 14 a son named Gregory Robert had been born to Robert and Genevieve Grantley. At least they hadn't named him Robert Jr.

I found Cassie's birth notice for August 3, then packed up. Watching blurred newsprint race by was giving me a headache.

———

BACK IN MY OFFICE, I dialed Jerry's number. A phone call seemed safer than a personal visit, given our last conversation. Good thing, because Jerry's mood didn't seem to have improved any.

"Whaddaya want, O'Grady?" he growled.

"Nice talking to you, too, Jerry."

"This better not be about the McMather case."

"Not this time. I'm curious about a reference I came across to Brian Stewart's dad, Joe, having committed a minor felony."

"Recently?"

"No, sixty years ago. He was acquitted, and I'm curious about the details. Any chance you could get your hands on them?"

"With the chief looking over my shoulder on a major murder investigation, you think I've got time for this?"

"Please, Jerry?"

"Since it's such ancient history and you probably can't do any damage with the information, I'll see who I can dump it on."

I ignored the Barbara. "Thanks, I appreciate it."

"Just see that you don't get involved in my case."

Yeah, yeah. "You've got my cell number?"

"Of course," he said, and disconnected with a crash.

As I turned back to my computer, I was struck by a sudden thought. One of the first things Sid Fluxgold had taught me when I was training as an investigator was to always follow the money.

"No matter how people try to hide it, money always leaves a trail," he'd say. "And that trail can be followed."

The one question that I'd not thought to ask so far was possibly the most important question. Who inherited McMather's money? And how much money was it?

I knew Brian was the executor, but I didn't know who actually inherited.

I called Jerry back, and asked him. I could hear the hesitation on the other end of the line, as he debated whether or not to tell me.

Finally he sighed deeply, and said, "Okay, you'll find out any way. Cassie gets the lot, over ten million dollars."

"Cassie Stewart?" I said, so surprised that my voice rose to a squeak on the last word.

"Yeah. She was his niece, if only by marriage. Now, I've got work to do." And he disconnected on me again.

I sat and stared at the phone in my hand, while my mind raced, trying to connect this new information. Very gently I replaced the handset in the cradle.

"Brian is not McMather's son," I announced to the lines of sunlight on the wall.

A man like McMather would not will his money to someone other than his only living son. Not even to that son's wife.

So why would Vivianne McMather lie to me about Brian's parentage? Maybe she truly believed it?

Or maybe she was setting it as a red herring—to keep me from uncovering something else. Or to give me a plausible explanation for something I might otherwise question.

If I stumbled across the possibility that Joe Stewart wasn't Brian's father, then I was predisposed to believe that Ed McMather might be. When I find out that Cassie will inherit McMather's money, I am predisposed to believe it's because Brian is his son.

Except I didn't believe either of these things.

And I was left with two very interesting questions.

Who was Brian Stewart's father?

And why did McMather leave his money to Cassie?

I wrote these two questions down, then after some thought added the original two questions.

Who killed Ed McMather, and why?

Who killed the Stewarts, and why?

Staring at these four questions, I felt an excitement that usually means I'm close to solving a case. The elements of a solution were there, I could sense them.

Picking up the phone again, I put a call through to Doug Matthews. After a short wait, he came on the line, sounding annoyed.

I said I needed to talk to him in person.

He suggested his usual place.

With an inward sigh, I agreed. I could put up with the gloom if I got the information I was hoping for.

CHAPTER TWENTY-NINE

Doug shambled into the Crown and Thorns fifteen minutes late and predictably ordered a beer. I shook my head to his inquiring look. I was sticking with iced tea.

"So, what's up?"

"A couple of things. Maria Stewart was a law student, dropped out after first year. Looks like she got pregnant, and married Joe about five months before Brian was born."

I was watching his expression as I spoke. So far, he wasn't giving away a thing. "And Maria and Robert Grantley were in the same first year law class," I added.

Still no reaction. "And according to my sources, McMather's money goes to Cassie Stewart, Brian's wife. All ten million of it."

Now he looked interested, in a noncommittal kind of way. "Yeah, that kind of figures. She was his niece, wasn't she? And McMather was close to her mother."

"But I'd heard rumors Brian was his son," I began, then stopped. "Did you say McMather was close to Cassie's mother? To Genevieve Grantley?"

"Yeah. I did some checking around. It goes back years, but I talked to this retired guy I know, used to cover the society beat.

Genevieve Delbert and Robert Grantley were both well-connected —they were news from the day they married. He says he used to see Mrs. Grantley and McMather in little out of the way coffee shops, diners, places like that. Went on for about six months."

"When was this?" I asked, stunned.

"Sixty years ago, I guess. Something like that. Grantley himself was still in his last year of law school at the time, according to this guy."

" How reliable is this source?"

"I got the feeling the guy rather liked Genevieve Grantley, didn't want to rat on her. Didn't sound like he had anything concrete, he'd just seen them and drawn his own conclusions. Especially given that Robert Grantley had a reputation for playing around, despite being newly married. I'd say the information is sound."

I pieced it together. "And a couple of years later, Genevieve's young sister brings the same man home as her fiancé. Oh, poor Genevieve."

Then it hit me. "Wait a minute, Cassie was born the year her father graduated law school. In the summer. And McMather just left her millions. So whose daughter does that make her?"

Doug nodded. He'd already figured that one out.

"So. My source probably told me Brian was McMather's son in order to divert suspicion from Cassie's parentage," I mused, remembering in time that I hadn't told Doug that Genevieve and her sister were my source for this bit of information. "Did you get anywhere on what Joe and Maria Stewart did when they came to town that final weekend?"

"Joe Stewart paid a visit to the local party office and met with McMather, pretty much as we figured."

"And Maria?" I asked, not about to assume anything about her, not again.

"Had a long, private lunch with Robert Grantley."

"Robert Grantley?"

"Yup. And while she was still at lunch, it seems that Joe finished his meeting and went out to the University. Archive records show him checking out yearbooks from the year Maria had been in law school."

"However did you find all that out?"

Doug laughed. "Old newsman's trick. It isn't what you know, it's who you know. Plus, if there's a paper record of something, I'll find it."

I was impressed. And curious. One of these days, I'd get him to show me his bag of tricks. That kind of ability to gather information would come in handy.

"Anything else?"

"Joe met with Robert Grantley himself on the following day. And Brian and Cassie were already dating. Probably just coincidence Cassie didn't meet her future in-laws that weekend."

"Brian was in the middle of exams. He didn't have time," I answered absently.

Joe was meeting with Robert?

There was an idea nagging at the edge of my brain, brought on by the thought of those two meeting. Something I'd seen, or heard, something that wasn't quite right.

Doug studied my expression for a few moments. "Something on your mind, Barbara?"

"There's something I'm overlooking. I know it's important, but I just can't put a finger on it," I answered, unable to keep the exasperation I was feeling out of my voice.

"Yeah, I know the feeling. It'll come, though, it always does. Eventually. Sure you won't have a beer?"

By now, a drink sounded like a remarkably good idea, even at this hour. Regretfully, I declined.

I was going to need every brain cell I could muster.

———

HALF AN HOUR later I got back to my office, feeling clearer after the discussion with Doug. I still didn't have answers, but at least I was weeding out the lies. Though I had to shake my head in reluctant admiration at Genevieve and Vivianne's brazenness.

I was getting close, I could sense it.

I was also hungry. Checking my watch, I realized it was nearly one. I should have picked up some *pho* soup at that little Vietnamese place on Carroll on my way back here.

About to head out again, I noticed that the voice mail light was flickering. Impatiently, I picked up the handset and punched in the numbers.

"Barbara? It's Jerry. I looked into that arrest you asked me about, Joe Stewart. He was charged with and then acquitted of theft. He was defended by Gregory Rutledge through UBC's legal assistance program, assisted by a couple of law students. Robert Grantley and Maria Delorme."

Bingo. I promptly forgot all about lunch. Here was my explanation of how and when Maria and Joe had met.

Perhaps they'd begun an affair after the trial, then decided to marry when Brian was conceived.

So Joe Stewart was likely Brian's father, after all.

Except why had the marriage waited until she was five months pregnant? No way was Brian premature. Not weighing close to nine pounds.

And what about Robert Grantley?

I kept seeing his name and Maria's coupled.

First on the debating team, now providing legal assistance. And based on what Doug had just told me, at the same time Robert and Maria were working so closely together, Genevieve was meeting Ed at small, out of the way places.

And Robert had a reputation as a lady's man.

It was certainly possible that in the heady aftermath of their debating win Maria and Robert had begun an affair, and she'd gotten pregnant.

A new picture was gradually emerging, and I didn't like it very much. Unfortunately, it made a lot of sense.

It wasn't Maria Stewart with Ed McMather, as Vivianne had

suggested, but Maria Stewart with Robert Grantley, and maybe Genevieve Grantley with Ed McMather.

None of which got me closer to who had killed the Stewarts, but it did raise the strong possibility that Brian Stewart could be Robert Grantley's son.

And that Cassie Grantley Stewart could be Brian's half sister.

Or Cassie could be Ed McMather's daughter and not related to her husband by blood.

But it was just possible that Brian and Cassie were half-brother and sister.

What a mess.

———

I NEEDED A MENTAL BREAK. Stretching deeply, I got up and brewed a cup of rich Viennese roast. Leaning back in my chair, I sipped my coffee and let my eyes wander, enjoying the contrast between the sleekly efficient computer setup and the weathered oak desk and file cabinets on which they sat.

When it came to furnishing my office, I couldn't afford to pay retail, not if I wanted to eat. Which meant an auction.

I'd sauntered into Gray's Auction house on Broadway one hot sunny evening, prepared to stick it out. The secret to getting the real deals at an auction is timing—buying on those long hot days that turn auctions rooms into saunas send most people to the beach. The hardy few who do turn up seldom want to swelter for hours while the auctioneer drones on. And I do mean hours, because the best deals always come at the end of a four-hour auction, never at the beginning.

Every sweaty hour was worth it, though. The desk and filing cabinets were solid wood, probably dated from the forties. The real deal was a swivel desk chair and two guest chairs, all in a still-rich burgundy leather that looked straight out of a mid-century lawyer's office. As one of last lots of the night, they were ridiculously cheap—less than a hundred bucks.

Even at that price, I could barely afford them. I bought them anyway—they fit my vision of what a private investigator's office should look like. With a half grin at the artist in me that I can never deny for long, I finished the coffee, and turned back to see if I could find any sense in my case.

Slowly I laid out the connections between the three families, with all of the names and dates I'd gathered. Then I checked each against my notes, adjusting as needed, putting question marks for those things that I suspected were lies.

More than an hour later, my eyes were blurring and my hand cramping, but a picture was emerging. And all of the facts I'd been able to verify seemed to fit.

Perhaps it hadn't truly mattered who had fathered whom, until Cassie and Brian met and fell in love.

Doug had said that Cassie and Brian were dating before Maria and Joe made that last trip. If Brian were really Robert's son, Maria must have been frantic, thinking Brian was in love with his half sister.

And Robert? What would his reaction have been?

Had he known about Genevieve and Ed?

Had Genevieve known about Robert and Maria?

This was beginning to resemble a soap opera. Who knew, and when did they know it? And where did Brian Stewart and his DNA testing kit fit in?

There was no doubt in my mind that kit was connected—but if Brian was worried that he and Cassie were related by blood as well as marriage, what had raised that possibility for him?

And why had he been so upset with McMather?

If Brian had learned somehow that Robert Grantley was his father, he would have assumed that Cassie was his half-sister. Making his marriage both incestuous and illegal.

To say nothing of the potential genetic time-bombs that scenario could create for his kids.

Any of which would be enough to cause him to stop working and sit staring into space. It also explained the visit to the library.

But why the private investigator?

What would lead him to confide in a complete stranger, if he could search out the facts on his own?

Unless somehow time was a factor.

———

I TOOK a turn around the office, stared out the window at the thick clouds overhead. Maybe if I looked at the facts another way. Cassie and Brian had been married for nearly forty years. If they were indeed brother and sister, another few months wouldn't make any difference.

Except perhaps to Brian.

If he did think his marriage might be incestuous, his nerves must be shot, trying to preserve a normal front and keep Cassie from suspecting anything at the same time as he tried to verify his suspicions. That would certainly explain the air of desperation she'd mentioned.

But what had started Brian questioning who his father had been after all these years?

Could he have stumbled on something? Or had someone told him that Robert Grantley was his father?

I drew a question mark beside Robert Grantley's name, and a bigger one beside Maria Stewart's.

I'd suddenly seen another possibility.

What if Brian Stewart was being blackmailed, either by someone who believed he and Cassie were brother and half-sister, or by someone who wanted him to believe it? After all, his mother and the three men who might have fathered Brian were now dead.

Who was left to verify what was true and what wasn't?

Blackmail.

Now that was a factor I hadn't considered. It would explain why Brian's behavior had suddenly changed, and why he might have hired a P. I. And blackmail introduced the threat of exposure, even of violence.

I took all the names I had and drew a kind of chart, adding connecting lines where they seemed to fit. Then I sat looking at the result and thought some more.

If Robert Grantley was Brian's real father, did Joe Stewart, Brian's supposed father, know? What would have happened when he found out?

If Maria and Joe had met when she defended him, when and how might Joe have found out that Brian wasn't his son?

Could he have known all along and been willing to accept it in order to marry Maria?

Or maybe he didn't know until Brian was born.

Whenever Joe found out, and whether he initially knew who the real father was or not, I suspected he'd have resented the man who had fathered his wife's son, their only child. It was my guess he wouldn't have been above a bit of revenge, and he probably wouldn't have let Brian's real father off the hook easily.

Especially if Maria had tried to protect the man by keeping his name a secret.

It was a stretch, but it could explain both Maria's meeting with Robert that day, and Joe's meeting with him the following day.

Of course, that would mean that Robert was the logical suspect in the deaths of Joe and Maria.

Could Robert Grantley have murdered the Stewarts?

It fit all the facts as I knew them, except that I'd made a lot of suppositions and guesses. And, of course, it didn't explain Ed McMather's recent murder. Perhaps the DNA test the police had done was contaminated, and Ted Hewitt really had done it.

Or some as yet unknown assailant.

The other thing my Robert Grantley-as-the-killer theory didn't explain was who was blackmailing Brian Stewart. If my guess was correct, and he really was being blackmailed, that is.

I looked at my chart again, circling McMather's name this time. What if McMather had been the blackmailer?

Of course, that would make Brian Stewart his likely murderer.

But if I ignored that annoying detail, McMather as the blackmailer made sense.

If Joe Stewart had known who fathered Brian, it was possible he'd told McMather. But then why had McMather waited so many years after Joe's death before blackmailing Brian?

I got up and poured another cup of coffee. Took a deep breath, looked at my chart again.

Thought about Brian as McMather's killer.

No, that didn't make sense.

And nor was I making sense. McMather had been killed while I was still shadowing Brian at the play.

Looking at my watch I realized it was nearly five, and I hadn't had lunch. No wonder my thinking was getting fuzzy—I was fueling it on caffeine and not much else.

I had an early dinner at Guido's—he made me a dish of his special pasta, topped with a combination of tomatoes, roasted eggplant, olives, capers and garlic that is unbelievably good. The food, the atmosphere and several glasses of the hearty house red improved my mood considerably.

As long as I didn't think about who had really killed McMather.

CHAPTER THIRTY

I woke before the alarm the next morning, the chart I'd drawn the previous day fresh in my mind. Those disconnected facts had been jostling each other through my dreams all night.

I took a hasty shower, dressed and headed for the door. And nearly fell flat on my face.

"Oh, great going, Cat. You disappear for a couple of days, then reappear when I've no time for you."

He yowled.

"I didn't hurt you, did I?" I flipped on the hall light, crouched down.

Cat glared at me, wrapping his tail tightly around his front paws, as if afraid I'd step on it.

"Did I hurt you?" I reached out, ran a seeking hand down his back. Cat purred.

"Okay, I guess I just hurt your feelings. I'm sorry."

I ran my hand down his back again, then stood up, shaking my head. I was apologizing to a cat?

Cat yowled again.

"What is it?" I looked at him more closely.

Had he been hurt? I didn't see any sign of blood.

Cat gave me a disgusted look, then stalked towards the kitchen, stopping in front of the fridge. He looked at the fridge, looked at me and yowled again. Loudly.

"Oh. You want milk."

Cat purred.

"You're not supposed to understand English," I told him, getting out the milk.

His purr got louder.

"I don't even have time for my own breakfast. What makes you think I have time to feed you?"

Those amber eyes met mine. He waited.

"Stupid cat. You do know you're making me late, right?"

Cat ignored me. He was too busy lapping away at the saucer of milk I'd poured.

With a sigh, I grabbed my purse and headed for the office. I did pick up a *grande* Italian Roast coffee and a raspberry oatmeal muffin on the way, though. Watching Cat lap his milk had made me hungry.

Letting myself into the empty building, I sprinted up the echoey stairwell and down the dim hallway to my door. Switching on the light, I stared at the charts I'd left spread across my desk. Maybe it was because I'd taken a break from it, but what leapt out at me was the one piece I'd missed the day before.

There were the four couples, woven by chance and by marriage into a tight web—Robert and Genevieve Grantley, Ed and Vivianne McMather, Maria and Joe Stewart, Brian and Cassie Stewart.

And then there was Judge Rutledge.

He was not part of a couple, not related by blood or by marriage, yet he seemed to have been connected to most of them. Where did the Judge fit in?

He'd taught Robert Grantley, Maria Stewart and Brian Stewart.

He knew Joe Stewart through the legal aid program.

There was no indication he knew Ed and Vivianne McMather, but I'd bet money that he had, at least socially.

But what did it mean?

Gregory Rutledge was an old man now, long-retired and frail. In his day, he'd been a mover and a shaker, but even so, it was hard to see his impact on this case.

But everywhere I turned, there he was.

And he'd held positions of influence for a long time, probably still had connections to any number of the people who now held power in the legal and political spheres. It would be interesting to know whether he'd kept in contact with Robert and Maria after law school.

That thought led to another.

On impulse, I powered on my laptop and loaded a program that I'd never admit that I have, one that the phone company, not to mention Jerry and his colleagues, would have a real problem with. It was given to me several years ago by my friend Mark, a hacker with a penchant for information, and it gives me access to people's phone billings.

In essence, I type in a phone number, and I get a listing of all the long distance calls placed from that number. It comes in very handy.

Typing in Judge Rutledge's number, my screen was soon filled with dates, places called and phone numbers. I scrolled backwards, and found what I'd hadn't really expected to find.

Three, four, five calls to Venice in the last month. All to the same number, and all in the time period surrounding McMather's murder.

I picked up the phone, dialed the number and after a few moments listened with no surprise to a heavily accented voice saying, "*Casa* McMather".

I disconnected the phone, and redrew my diagram, with the Judge in the center.

He not only knew Genevieve and Vivianne, he was still in close contact with them. The *deus ex machina*?

After studying this new diagram for a few moments, I went back through my notes from my talk with Vivianne and Genevieve.

Their tale had been remarkably convincing. How much of that had been planted by someone else?

Someone who had convinced them that it was important that any questions be deflected?

My money was on the Judge for that one, though I'd bet they'd thrown in a few twists of their own.

Of course, I'm still prejudiced in favor of those two senior sirens, I admit it. And Judge Rutledge was too polished for words.

I couldn't see him as the villain of the piece, but he was the type who enjoyed manipulating and influencing others behind the scenes. I wouldn't be surprised if he knew the why on those murders, if not the who.

I looked at the screenful of information on his phone calls again. What if McMather's number were there? The Judge called McMather's ex-wife regularly. Did he also call the man himself?

I checked McMather's number then scrolled through the Judge's calls. No match.

So much for that idea. Unless—I referred to the online phone book again. From Bowen Island to Vancouver was a local call.

Unfortunately my very helpful program has a minor quirk. It'll give me long distance calls from any number, but it won't give me local calls. I made a note to have a chat with Mark about a possible update to the software.

I made a few more notes and wrote out some questions I needed answers for, then called Jerry. He wasn't in yet, so I left a message on his voice mail and called Doug. Who was also out. It was up to me.

––––––

LEAVING the downtown behind me I drove out to UBC, taking the scenic route along Cornwall and then down along Point Grey to Northwest Marine Drive and along Locarno Beach. I could probably have found most of the information I wanted at the *Sun* archives, but I needed some time to think, and that particular drive inspires me.

In my book, the panorama of downtown Vancouver framed by the North Shore Mountains and English Bay is unbeatable at any time of year and at any hour. It's as stunning at night when the lights of the city glitter against a surrounding dark blue as it is when the sun sparkles off the water and the sailboats are zipping between the freighters anchored in the bay.

Now the morning fog blanketed the mountains and the sea and sky were an understated symphony in silvers and grays. I had time to kill before the university library opened, so I drove slowly, savoring the view, and making mental notes about the color palette I'd need to paint this.

I wasn't fully caught up in the natural beauty around me, though. My mind and emotions were too focused solving an unnatural murder. The missing piece was knowing when the Judge and McMather might have met.

There was no question they would have met, professionally, socially or both. Both Gregory Rutledge and Edward McMather were prominent men in this province.

Had they met because of their respective positions? Or was there an earlier connection?

McMather and Grantley obviously knew each other by the time McMather married Vivianne. And I had two sources who confirmed that McMather and Joe Stewart had worked together before then.

Genevieve, on the other hand, must have met McMather several years before her younger sister's marriage. And presumably McMather had known Maria Delorme around the time he met Genevieve, or Vivianne's assertion that he had fathered Brian would not stand up to even the briefest of inquiries.

That left the Judge.

My hunch was that McMather had met Robert, Maria and the Judge while preparing for Joe Stewart's trial.

That had all kinds of implications about Judge Rutledge's role in this case, but I needed something more than just a hunch before I asked him anymore questions.

Which is what I was planning on doing, just as soon as I confirmed that he'd known, or at least met, McMather all those years ago.

But how deeply would I have to dig to get that confirmation?

The trial itself was a very minor event that had happened forty years before. Too bad it had been a trial rather than a wedding. At least at weddings back then, publishing the guest list was standard practice.

As it turned out, it was almost that easy.

I got to the university early, so I treated myself to another coffee and one of the justly famous UBC Cinnamon Buns, a huge, sticky indulgence that guaranteed I wouldn't be hungry again 'til dinner time. When the library opened, I headed straight for the serials collection and started going the microfilms of the *Province* news-paper from around the time of Joe Stewart's trial.

I found the write-up I needed fairly easily. The description of the trial was brief but complete, and included the mention of one Edward McMather, longshoreman, who'd been called on behalf of the defendant as a character witness. I found that fact truly ironic, given what I now knew of both men. But I had my confirmation.

Now I had a few questions for the Judge.

CHAPTER THIRTY-ONE

I made it onto the ten o'clock ferry, but only because it was running nearly fifteen minutes late. At least I wouldn't be arriving on Judge Rutledge's doorstep at noon. I'd hate to appear rude.

Pushy, maybe, but not rude.

I stayed in my car with the window partway open to catch the fresh, salty air and used most of the twenty-minute crossing to review my notes.

The Judge was no fool. I'd need my facts clear before I talked to him. I had a suspicion he wouldn't exactly be thrilled to see me again, even though he'd so graciously extended the invitation.

And I was right. He wasn't pleased to see me. His greeting was courteous enough, but without the warmth.

At least he didn't come right out and ask me to leave. Which was just as well, because I had no intention of leaving.

So there I was, seated in that cozy parlor for the second time in two days, but without the sherry this time. And the looks I was receiving made me feel very much like a criminal whose time has run out. I plunged in anyway.

"Judge Rutledge, as you know I've been working on the Stewart's family history. I've come up with some contradictory facts in researching Maria Stewart's life in the years just before her son's birth, and you're the only one I know who might be able to answer my questions."

I glanced over at my audience of one, but his face gave nothing away. "There seems to be some doubt about Brian Stewart's parentage, about whether or not Joe Stewart was his biological father. You knew both Robert Grantley and Maria Delorme personally. Did you have any reason to believe that Robert Grantley might have been Brian Stewart's natural father?"

He didn't even look surprised at the question. He gave me a slight smile, and in those soft tones replied, "I think you are getting rather carried away, Miss O'Grady. You'll end up doing more harm than you know. The only reason I am continuing this conversation is that you are here at Cassie Stewart's request. To answer your question, I know without a shadow of a doubt that Robert Grantley did not father Brian."

Well, that was certainly clear enough. If it weren't for the things I now suspected he knew, I would have been frozen by the contempt in his voice.

I hadn't expected him to be forthcoming, but I had hoped to shake him up a little. I should have remembered that in his day he'd dealt with far more accomplished manipulators than I'd ever be. Had probably been one himself.

"Then who did father Brian Stewart?" I asked.

"Joe Stewart was his father," came the calm reply. "I can't imagine why you would question it."

I chose not to answer that. "Did you also know Ed McMather?" I asked instead.

He made the smallest possible inclination of his head. "I knew him slightly."

Well, that was his version. It didn't matter, I just wanted him to know that I knew.

Now we were getting to the questions I really wanted to ask. "And the Delbert sisters? Genevieve and Vivianne?"

Again the slight inclination of the head, but he didn't bother to answer me this time. He eyes were steady, and focused on me.

"Why were you the first person Brian came to see when he found out McMather was murdered?"

He gave a small start of surprise, then raised one almost translucent hand to rub his right elbow, slowly, as if to say that the movement had been in response to a sudden twinge. It had been a twinge, all right.

He obviously hadn't considered that Brian might have been followed when he'd visited last Sunday. I wondered if he'd anticipated Brian's visit when he heard about McMather's death.

"It's very simple, Miss O'Grady. When Brian is in trouble, he turns to me. Over the years, he has confided in me on many occasions," the gentle voice explained.

"You speak of Ed McMather's death as if it caused trouble for Brian Stewart. How did it affect him?"

Judge Rutledge was silent. I watched his still face for a moment, and suddenly all of the pieces fell into a new and very unsettling pattern. One that was going to require a whole new line of questioning, one that in fact called for direct attack.

I followed my hunch, and was asking the next question before I'd even considered the wisdom of doing so.

"It wasn't the first time he'd been to see you about this particular problem, was it?" I said softly. "Someone had told Brian that Robert Grantley was his father. He jumped to the conclusion that Cassie was his half-sister. And in his panic he came to you, his mentor."

I let a silence fall between us. The Judge made no move to break it, just watched me, his face a calm mask.

"Why did you tell Brian that Ed McMather was his father?" I asked bluntly, watching for a reaction. Any reaction.

I still wasn't totally sure that he'd done so, but it made sense out of my jumble of facts.

He made no reply, and his expression of polite interest was firmly in place. Only the hands folded in his lap showed any sign of agitation. One of them shook slightly.

"Naming McMather as his father was quite a gamble," I said. "Thing is, it would only work if Brian didn't confront McMather. Unless you thought he wouldn't believe anything McMather said?"

I watched that impassive face—and the betraying hand—for a few seconds.

"But I'll bet you didn't expect McMather to claim paternity of Cassie," I said as I put it together. "Which, in case Brian didn't tell you that part, is exactly what he did."

I didn't know any of this for certain, but I was prepared to go with my intuition. I was still looking for the Judge's response.

I wanted to shake him enough to get at the truth.

It seems I had—I saw the shock register on his face before he recovered enough to cloak it. I guess Brian hadn't told him that part.

Still Judge Rutledge kept silent, but those cool silver eyes never left my face.

"Now Brian began to doubt you." I said, picking up momentum. "He hired a private investigator, started looking into exactly what had happened all those years ago. And he discovered exactly what I've just discovered."

I paused, then hit him with it. "Just how well did you know Maria Delorme?"

"As I have already told you, she was my student," was the smooth reply.

"And what else?"

His face gave nothing away, but again the slight quiver in his hands grew stronger, betraying the lie. The pieces were falling into place.

I dropped my bombshell.

"I don't think either Joe Stewart or Robert Grantley fathered Brian Stewart. Which leaves you."

"Nonsense." The Judge still had control of his expression but that hand was trembling badly now.

"Would you be willing to give me a DNA sample so we could verify that?" I asked, pulling out the one of the Gene-test vials and a plastic-encased cotton swab.

I'd known ordering that kit would pay off. Eventually.

He waved a dismissive hand. "As far as I can see, this is all ancient history. Whatever the truth might be, it is hardly relevant now."

I couldn't believe it. My long-shot hunch had been right. "It's relevant to Brian Stewart."

"Since he wasn't fathered by his wife's father, I hardly see why such an old story need concern him."

Was he really this immune to other people's feelings? "There's still the matter of three unsolved murders," I said, intent on shaking the truth out of him.

"Three?" he asked, with a slight frown. "I'm aware that they've temporarily had to release Ed McMather's murderer, of course."

"Three." I stated. "Ed McMather, Joe Stewart and Maria Stewart."

"My dear young lady, you have your facts confused, I'm afraid. The Stewart's death was a tragic accident. So young, so much potential wasted." He sighed.

"It was no accident," I said. And again my intuition got ahead of my common sense.

"Joe Stewart was blackmailing you, wasn't he?" I continued. "Even that many years later, you didn't want anyone to know about your affair with your student, the affair that resulted in an illegitimate child and the end of a very promising legal career."

I paused watching him. But thinking of Maria Stewart, all that promise gone, I couldn't resist it. "Her career, of course, not yours."

He made no response, but his eyes were tracking my every move.

It was a little creepy, but I ignored that too. I was too caught up in finally putting together the details of this awful case.

"I don't know how Joe found out," I said. "With fairly similar information, I leapt to the conclusion that Robert Grantley was Brian's father. Maybe it was fairly obvious in the early days that there was no sexual tension between Robert and Maria? But I'm curious why you didn't marry her? Maria, I mean."

The old man's face was all harsh lines, carved in stone. He made no answer.

I was on a roll. "Maria's feelings for you must have been very strong. Tell me, did she end up resenting the fact that you wouldn't marry her and she had to give up her career? In all their years together, Joe must have picked up something of how she felt about you, whether it was hate or love. After all, he'd have known from the start that Brian wasn't his child. Though I'm guessing he was willing to overlook anything to get Maria to marry him?"

Still no response.

I didn't let it stop me. "But I'll bet he resented the man who fathered Maria's son until the day he died."

Something in the Judge's expression told me that bit of deduction was accurate. "When Joe found out for sure it was you, did he decide to make you pay?"

"That's another interesting theory you have come up with, Miss O'Grady," he said. "I suppose you have overlooked the fact that I was appointed to the bench shortly after that, and that I have a spotless career record?"

"Not at all. In fact, that's the whole point. You weren't about to let anyone or anything interfere with the career that was just opening up in front of you."

"You have a bright mind, Miss O'Grady, and your theories all fit together so nicely. It's simply unfortunate you didn't spend more time studying logic," was his soft-voiced response.

"Oh, it's more than a theory. In fact, I managed to have a look at the initial report on the Stewart's car. Freedom of Information acts are wonderful things. Seems like the brake line was tampered with."

I was bluffing, but he couldn't know that. It was information I probably could have accessed, if I'd had a little more time.

"The final decision was that it was mechanical failure. Something was worn, and just snapped."

"Oh? I didn't think they released that information at the time."

As I watched the Judge's eyes grow flinty, I started to realize I might have gone too far, and that perhaps I should back off a bit.

It looked like some of my far-fetched theorizing may not have been so far-fetched after all—I'd just had the central character wrong. It wasn't Robert Grantley I should have suspected of murder, but Judge Rutledge.

An even more unlikely suspect, on the face of it.

It still didn't occur to me to leave.

Even if the Judge was a murderer, it had been a long time ago, and he was old and frail now. And even forty years ago, I couldn't picture this elegant man crawling under a car. Still, he might have paid someone else to do it.

Like McMather?

"In my position, or rather my former position," he was saying, "I have been privy to a great many things that were never released to the general public,"

"Really. Are you sure the murderer didn't just tell you?" As I heard myself ask the question, I finally recognized that if the Judge had hired someone to tamper with the senior Stewarts' brakes, then it was also possible that McMather with all his connections had found out and had been blackmailing him.

Which is a very valid reason for murder.

Especially if you've killed a blackmailer once before.

Unexpectedly nervous, I tried to read the Judge's face.

The changes in his expression were subtle, but I was suddenly certain this man was capable of murder and neither too old nor too frail to accomplish it if the need were great enough.

Too late, I realized the extent of my miscalculation.

"Look, this is all speculation, and I've no business accusing you in your own home. I'll just go."

"Oh, I think not, Miss O'Grady. I think you will be staying exactly where you are," he said.

He was right. And I was staring down the barrel of a small but efficient-looking gun.

CHAPTER THIRTY-TWO

My recollections of the next few moments have an eerie sharpness to them, as if I had the time to note every tiny detail. I remember the gleam of that deadly little weapon, held firmly in the Judge's frail, mottled hand. I remember looking into his eyes, now the cold color of some silvered metal, looking for some trace of mercy and finding none.

I remember thinking with some detached, ironic part of my mind that I should have settled for a boring office job. And being fiercely glad I hadn't.

If this was to be the end, at least I'd been living.

This man had killed before. McMather had been both larger and stronger than I, and it hadn't saved him. The only advantage I had was that I knew I was facing a killer.

McMather had died with a look of surprise on his face.

I was not going to die.

"You don't want to do anything sudden, Judge," I warned him.

"When you are as old as I am, Miss O'Grady, quick action becomes an asset."

"There is no need to kill me, you know."

"From what I've heard so far, there is every need."

Damn. What a time for my theories to prove right. "Killing me won't solve anything. I left word with the police."

"Of course you did. And you left a note, too. What woman wouldn't? Now, if you please..." and he waved me towards the kitchen with his gun.

What was it with this guy and kitchens, anyway? Maybe he just didn't like getting blood on the carpet. "You don't believe me?"

"It was a valiant effort, Miss O'Grady. But no, I do not believe you."

And he was right, dammit.

Maybe I could just keep him talking. I kept a wary eye on the gun, which had begun to shake slightly in his hand. Stall, until I could think of something.

"It's true, though," I said, fighting to keep my voice even. "See, Jerry Hawald and I are friends, we go way back..."

"Fascinating as I'm sure your life story is, my dear, it is another of those things I don't have time for. Now, move."

And suddenly the gun was pressed against my waist. I could feel a slight quivering, which started a much larger quiver deep inside me.

I moved ahead of him into the kitchen, my eyes darting from side to side, looking for something, anything, that might serve as a weapon or give me an advantage.

I had fifty-some years on this guy, after all.

The gun dug into my ribs again. "Don't even think about it," came that silky voice. "Out into the garden. And don't slow down."

Not the kitchen, then. Guess he didn't want blood in the house. Or was it that convenient drop at the bottom of the garden, the one that went off the rocks and into the ocean, he was headed for?

It would be a classy way to dispose of a body, always assuming the currents cooperated

I'd rather it weren't my body, though, thank you very much.

And I was running out of options.

"If you could move a little faster, Miss O'Grady," he was saying politely, digging the gun in again. "We really don't have time to dawdle, just in case you actually did call the police."

Dawdle. Now there's a word you don't hear much anymore.

I noted with alarm that my mind seemed to have numbed out on the struggle for survival, and kept wandering off on tangents.

NO! some part of me screamed.

I wasn't ready to die, to be dumped tidily off the nearest cliff. "It isn't so easy to just kill someone."

"No? It hasn't been a problem so far."

"Your odds are getting worse with every body. You must know that. And my body will be found in your own backyard. You'll have a hard time explaining that."

"In addition to genealogy, it might interest you to know that sport fishing is a hobby of mine. I'm very familiar with the tides, and this afternoon's tide will carry your body straight out to sea."

Oh, wonderful. Think, Barbara. There has to be something you can do. Say. Anything. "You won't get away with this."

As I mentally groaned at what my cartoon-soaked mind had come up with, I felt the gun nudging against my ribs again. "Just keep walking my dear, and let me do the worrying."

Fat chance. If he was that close behind me, I had to risk it.

Screaming as loud as I could, I stumbled. Falling back against him, I wrenched his gun hand away from me with my right arm.

"Damn you. Stay still," he yelled.

There was a loud bang. My left arm stung, then went numb.

I'd been shot? It was too much to process.

———

OUT OF NOWHERE THE hand holding the gun flashed towards my face. The blow clipped my cheekbone. Which nearly had me passing out from the pain.

A steely hand clamped itself on my left arm to steady me. "Don't do that again."

The gun dug into my ribs on the other side. "Now, just keep moving. I don't want blood on the path."

How could the old man be this strong?

I gasped in a breath. "The hell with your path. I'm the one doing the bleeding."

"Settle down. It'll be over soon."

If he didn't want to shoot me here, maybe I could use that.

But how? I could feel my legs starting to feel shaky under me. My face and my arm were throbbing in rhythm.

Which gave me an idea.

I let my feet falter, my body waver, until he was half holding me upright. I could feel the quivering in his hand increase as he fought to support my weight.

"Stop that. You're fine." He jabbed a little harder with the gun.

"I'm... I..." I let my voice trail off, sagged against him.

The second I felt his body shift to find balance, I turned into him hard, pushing his gun hand out away from us both.

I crumpled forward as I did so, ramming my head into his solar plexus.

I was nearly sick with pain, but I couldn't afford to stop.

As he gasped, I swung my right foot around behind him and swept his supporting foot out from under him.

We went down in a heap, me on top, and the gun went flying.

Fine with me.

Now all I had to do was restrain the Judge and stay conscious until help showed up.

A sharp stab of pain from my arm reminded me that I was probably losing blood. I still wasn't feeling it—too much adrenaline.

"You're not looking too good, Judge. Something to do with a head in the solar plexus?"

There was no reply.

That was okay, I wasn't waiting for one. Somehow I'd come out on top of this little episode, and I was busy trying to figure out how to stay that way.

There was no weapon in reach, not even a handy branch to hit him with. Not that I was sure I could hit him when he was just lying there looking old and injured.

Then those silver eyes opened and he gave me a look as cold as a January rain.

"Don't sound so sure of yourself, Miss O'Grady."

Okay, I needed to do something, and fast.

His expression told me threats would be a waste of time.

I rolled sideways, using the Judge's own weight to flip him, pinioning his arms behind him. I clipped him on the chin in the process, giving me a few minutes respite.

Now I needed something to tie him with. My arm was letting me know in no uncertain terms that I wouldn't be able to hold him for long.

The twine from a grape arbor proved to be my solution.

By the time the Judge opened his eyes, he was face down, trussed like the proverbial turkey.

"Enjoying the view?" I asked him.

He glared at me. "You're a very rude young woman. I shudder to think what your parents think of you."

"Hey, at least I don't go around killing people."

"What is it you do? You're certainly no historian."

"Private investigator."

He groaned. "Not a very good one, if your behavior to date is any indication."

"I found you, didn't I?"

"It certainly took you long enough. Not that it'll do any good. No judge would convict me. And may I point out, you're bleeding all over my lawn."

I looked. There was a small pool of blood at my side. I realized I didn't want to look at my arm. "I'll heal."

"At the rate you're going, you're more likely to expire right there."

"Then you would too—trussed up like that with no-one to help you."

"You aren't worried at the thought of bleeding to death?"

"I don't believe you. You just want me to go and find a phone so you can try and get free." Though now I came to think of it, I did feel a little dizzy.

How much blood had I lost?

"It's your life."

"Yeah, the one you were so busy trying to end a little while ago."

If I hadn't tied him so tight, he'd have given an elegant little shrug. As it was, he raised one thin eyebrow. "We all have our weaknesses. Mine is I'd like to preserve my spotless record."

"What record? You're a killer."

"Prove it."

"You shot me."

"Purely an accident. I was demonstrating my gun. My arm slipped."

"And McMather."

"No evidence."

"What about ballistics on the gun?"

"Surely you don't think I'm stupid enough to have kept the gun. Assuming I'd done anything at all, of course."

"I think maybe you're just that stupid. But surely you're not stupid enough to think you can talk me into letting you go."

"You're going to need some help for that arm."

"Oh, and you're going to provide it?"

"We're pretty isolated here. And you're bleeding badly."

I still didn't want to look.

But I probably did need to phone for help. I checked the knots. He wasn't going to get out of those in a hurry. "If it will make you happy, I'll go make that call."

"The phone is out," he said with a smirk.

"Maybe. But my cell phone isn't."

It shut him up, at least temporarily. I turned towards the house, had to put my hand on a nearby tree to steady myself.

Focus.

Just get to the phone.

Taking a deep breath, I walked steadily into the house.

———

I FOUND MY PURSE, and the cell phone. As I dialed 911, there was a loud pounding on the door. A voice that some part of my mind recognized as Jerry's shouted "Open up. This is the police. Open this door immediately."

I made my way to the door, leaning against the frame before flinging it wide.

"O'Grady. Are you all right?"

"Why wouldn't I be?"

"Your arm is covered in blood."

"Oh." I still wasn't going to look. "I'm sure I'll be fine."

Especially if I got to sit down really, really soon. "You might want to arrest the Judge. He tried to kill me. And he's the one who killed McMather, too."

"He what? Where is he?"

"Out back. Tied up." I sank into the nearest chair.

Jerry turned to the men who'd come with him. "Rob, call an ambulance. Mohammed, out back," he ordered, then crouched down in front of me.

"I told you to stay out of my case, O'Grady," he said as he reached for my arm. "Now look what you've done."

"I've solved it for you is what I've done. I'd expected a little thanks." Then I winced as he did something to my arm, and made the mistake of looking.

Things got a little fuzzy for a while.

I clearly remember Jerry reading Judge Rutledge his rights.

Jerry seemed to find informing the Judge that he was being arrested on suspicion of the murder of Ed McMather oddly satisfying. I guess for him it was the end of a case that had been far too high profile, with too few leads.

I was just happy I wasn't bleeding on the carpet anymore.

CHAPTER THIRTY-THREE

A long and rather blurred time later, I was back at the police station, against the hospital's wishes.

Against Jerry's wishes, too.

They'd put a cold pack on my cheek and stitched up the graze in my arm. The bullet had plowed a shallow channel through skin and muscle.

The good news was that nothing major had been affected and the bullet hadn't lodged. Nor was my cheekbone broken, though it felt like it.

The bad news was I'd lost a fair bit of blood and my arm hurt like nobody's mercy. And I was going to have a beauty of a shiner.

"Why are you here, O'Grady?" Jerry demanded, his worried tones cutting through the noise. "Why aren't you in hospital where you belong?"

"I hate hospitals. And they have sicker people to deal with than me. Besides, I want to make my statement, so I can put this behind me."

"It's not going to be that easy, O'Grady," Jerry muttered as he guided me down the hallway into his office. He pulled out a chair for me, and went to get his notepad.

I suspected he was right, but I'd deal with it in my own time and my own way. Just as soon as I was out of here.

"Okay, O'Grady," Jerry said, sitting down in front of me. "Why don't you tell me what you think you were doing."

"I was doing what I was hired to do," I said. Obviously the wrong thing to say.

Jerry lost it. "You're damn lucky to be alive. You had no right interfering in this case. What did you think you were doing, anyway, going to confront a murderer with nothing more than a smile to protect you?"

"Your murderer is nearly ninety."

"Who cares? Guns are effective no matter who's at the trigger end, as long as they still have their sight and enough strength to pull a trigger. As you found out."

"He barely winged me."

"Oh, and that's supposed to excuse what you did?"

"Okay, maybe I shouldn't have confronted him."

"Maybe you shouldn't have? Maybe?"

"But you have to admit I got the information I went for."

"I don't have to admit anything," he said. "What information?"

That's my Jerry. "When I left that message, all I knew was that the Judge was somehow connected to McMather's death."

"Yeah, I got that. Though I'm not sure how you knew to suggest I check his phone records," he said with a hard look. "But when I checked, I found Rutledge had placed a call to McMather the night McMather was killed. He called the number for the Bowen Island Ferries less than ten minutes later."

"And?"

"Rutledge reserved a space on the ferry leaving Bowen Island that evening, and a space on the last returning ferry. He was some-where in Vancouver at the time when McMather was murdered."

"Okay, that gives him opportunity. What about motive?"

"Motive I'm still working on. Means, however, is coming clearer. When I checked McMather's phone listings, I found out that McMather had placed several calls to the Judge earlier that same day. I also found out that Rutledge had a registered handgun, which was the same caliber as the slug they'd found in McMather."

"Was that the gun he used to shoot me?"

"Yeah."

So he had been that stupid. Or that arrogant. Somehow, the thought pleased me. "So then what?"

"It seemed worth talking to Rutledge. Especially as you'd said you were going to confront him."

"That's why you were there."

"Yup."

"And why you're so mad at me."

"Yup."

"Well, I didn't need bailing out. But thanks for the thought." Jerry looked ready to explode. I needed to distract him. "I might have some ideas about the Judge's motives."

"Give."

"I think McMather was blackmailing him. Remember I said I was looking into the crash that killed Brian Stewart's parents forty years ago?"

"I remember. But I thought it was an accident."

"Apparently not. Someone tampered with the brake lines. I think Judge Rutledge arranged it, and McMather knew about it."

"So you're saying Rutledge is responsible for three deaths."

"Yes. And he was about to go for a fourth. Thanks for talking me into that self-defense class, by the way."

"Barbara. You nearly died."

I was trying not to think about that.

CHAPTER THIRTY-FOUR

A week later, Doug Matthews walked up to the secluded table I'd chosen at the back of the Crown and Thorns. I was half-hidden behind a pillar, with my back to the wall and a good view of the door. No-one was going to be able to creep up behind me. Not ever again.

It seems getting shot does leave a lasting impact.

Doug's eyes moved from the glass of wine in front of me, to my bandaged arm, to my battered face.

"My God, Barbara, what happened to you?"

He should have seen it three days ago. "You'd better order a drink. It's a long story."

He signaled the waiter, then turned back to me. "Thanks for the tip on the Judge's arrest. If that's an example of the results you get, I'll be happy to work with you anytime."

"Just trying to keep my promises. And congratulations on the coverage."

"Yeah, I haven't had a front-page credit in a while. Plus the wire services picked it up, which was a bonus."

"You write a good story."

"Hey, I had some pretty good copy." He grinned. "Judge

Rutledge, old Hard Line himself, charged with murder. It doesn't get better than that."

"Has the Judge admitted guilt?"

"Of course not. He's still protesting his innocence, doing his best to look old and feeble, yet dignified and judicial. But they've got the murder weapon with his fingerprints all over it. Kinda hard to argue your way out of that one."

"Especially when he used the same weapon to shoot a nosy P. I. While trying to kill her."

Doug's eyes widened and dropped to my bandaged arm. "No kidding. That's what happened to your arm?"

"Yup."

"How'd you get out of it?"

"Basically I tripped him and sat on him. He is a half-century older than I am."

"Doesn't matter how old he is. He had a gun. And he'd killed before. Barbara, do you know how close you came to dying?"

I was still trying to come to terms with that fact. And failing. Time to change the subject.

"Are you interested in doing a follow-up story, tying in the deaths of Joe and Maria Stewart?"

"Are you kidding? Of course. What've you got?"

"A confession."

At his stunned look, I had to laugh.

"Oh, it's not good for much. He denies it now. But it's true all the same."

"Rutledge killed the Stewarts?"

"Had them killed. And the facts will bear it out. I know the police are working on it now. It should all come out at his trial."

"That wily old bastard. That'll be a spectacular trial. I just hope he lives that long."

I suspected Doug was alone in that wish. "Trying him could prove embarrassing. The man did hold a very high position in our legal system."

"You don't mean you think he'd get off?"

There was always the possibility a jury would acquit him. "Unless he has a lawyer who walks on water, I think the evidence will prove overwhelming. But I suspect the trial date may get bumped back a few times."

"Ah. I see. Much less embarrassing if he just dies in jail. Of old age."

"Exactly."

"Barbara, you are such a cynic. That's what I like about you."

"I prefer to think of it as being realistic."

"Yeah, whatever. So, what are these facts of yours?"

This would be tricky, because I didn't want to betray Brian and Cassie's secrets. There was no reason for Doug to know the details of their heritage.

"You were right all those years ago," I told him. "Someone tampered with the brake line on the Stewart's car. And the Judge paid them to do it, then put an abrupt end to the investigation into the deaths."

"No kidding?"

"The interesting piece is that somehow McMather found out. According to Ted Hewitt, McMather blackmailed the Judge for legal and political favors for years."

"McMather did? How did he find out?"

"Your guess is as good as mine. Maybe he knew the guy who sliced the brake line. Maybe one of McMather's many sources told him who had shut down the investigation and McMather put two and two together."

"So that's why the Judge killed McMather?" he said.

"Seems to be. The police found a lot of calls from McMather to Judge Rutledge in the week prior to McMather's death. Maybe the Judge finally had enough of McMather and his demands. Maybe the price McMather was asking was too high this time. Who knows?"

"So that old man just waltzed in and fired bullets into McMather until there was no way he could survive."

"Pretty much," I said. "It's no wonder McMather looked surprised."

"Yeah, most of us don't expect octogenarian killers. But why did Rutledge have the Stewarts killed?"

"Good question. Unfortunately, the only one left alive who knows for sure is the Judge, and he's not talking." Even if he had already confirmed my own suspicions.

"Hmmm. I wonder if I could get him talking."

I doubted it. But it might be fun to watch him try.

———

DOUG TOOK a swig of his beer, considered my bruised face for a moment. "It's been quite the case, hasn't it? Does Brian Stewart know his parents were murdered?"

"Yes."

"Must have been a real shock to hear something like that after all these years."

"Yes, I think it was."

I couldn't tell Doug, but that was the least of the shocks Brian Stewart had to bear.

When I told him that Judge Rutledge had been his natural father, Brian's expression had been one of overwhelming relief.

"Thank God." He'd turned to Cassie, who was sitting bolt upright on the sofa beside him in their ornate living room. "I was more than half convinced we were related by blood as well as marriage. It was becoming an obsession."

"Why didn't you tell me?"

"I couldn't bear to. Somehow telling you would have made it real. And I couldn't have borne that. If I didn't have you, I'd have nothing."

She put a hand on his arm, gripped. "Oh, Brian—you will always have me. Always. We would have gotten through it somehow."

He put his arms around her, held her in silence. I felt like I should be slipping quietly out, leaving them alone, but I hadn't told them everything yet. And I had a few questions I needed answers to.

Cassie leaned back in Brian's arms, looked up at him. "But what made you think…"

"That Robert Grantley was my father? I was told he was."

"By whom?"

It was what I wanted to know, too.

"By Ted Hewitt. Your uncle's assistant."

"Uncle Ed's assistant? But how would he know? He is much too young to have known your mother. And why would he care?"

"He was trying a small spot of blackmail. Apparently he thought I'd pay anything to protect my family, to protect you. He was right."

"Oh, Brian."

"Though I suspect not for the reasons he thought," Brian added.

"What did you do?" she asked.

"I gave him the ten thousand he'd asked for."

"But Brian, there's no end to blackmail," Cassie said. "Surely you didn't expect ten thousand to make him go away."

"Hardly. I knew Hewitt had been disbarred for some very questionable dealings a number of years ago. Why McMather hired him, I'll never know. I thought if I paid Hewitt the money, he'd go away long enough for me to figure out what to do. But no matter where I looked, I couldn't find anything to make me doubt the information he'd given me."

"But how would Ted Hewitt know who your parents were? And how did he convince you?"

"He didn't, not entirely. But he showed me proof that your father and my mother had gone to law school together, spent a lot of time together, visited for years afterwards. And that your father had attended my mother's funeral. Without your mother."

"Why would he my father do that?" Cassie said.

"I don't know. Perhaps they were just friends. Especially if you're sure Robert Grantley wasn't my father?" He looked at me.

"Yes, I'm very sure," I said. "You're Gregory Rutledge's son."

"But why didn't he just say so? Why the lie?"

Brian almost seemed to be talking to himself, but Cassie answered him. "Who lied to you? And about what?"

Brian gave her a crooked grin. "It seems as if everyone was lying to me."

Her face went white. "I didn't tell you I'd hired Barbara because…"

"I didn't mean you. I never meant you lied to me."

"But I did," she said.

"No more than I did to you, when I didn't tell you what was going on," he said. "If it was wrong, we were both wrong."

Her voice was definite. "It was wrong. We have to be able to talk to each other."

"Yes."

I couldn't stand the tension. I leaned forward in my chair. "So who did lie to you?"

Again the two of them looked at me blankly, as if they'd forgotten I was even in the room.

Brian was the first to recover. "Oh. Rutledge lied. My former mentor. My real father."

He gave a sharp snort of laughter. "He told me Cassie couldn't be my sister because Robert Grantley wasn't my father, Ed McMather was."

Cassie gasped and went pale. "He's wrong. He has to be wrong. Barbara, tell me he's wrong."

"Yes, he's wrong," I said firmly. "In fact, he was outright lying. Ed McMather definitely did not father your husband."

"I don't understand." Brian was looking back and forth between us. "Why should the possibility that McMather sired me upset you?"

Cassie sighed. "Because according to my mother, it was dear Uncle Ed who actually sired me, to use your phrase."

It was Brian's turn to look shocked. Then angry. "No wonder McMather denied paternity so vehemently when I confronted him."

Ah. That explained the body language at their lunch.

"You asked Uncle Ed if he was your father?" she said. "But you have never liked him."

"Yes, but I liked the idea of you being my half-sister even less. I had no choice but to confront him."

I had to know. "How did he react?"

"He was stunned, said he'd only met my mother twice, that she hadn't much liked him, either. He said it must be genetic. I couldn't believe he was making a joke of it. I nearly hit him."

I leaned forward to better read his face. "Did he ask who had told you he was your father?"

"He demanded to know," Brian said. "When I told him it was Rutledge, he got angry. He said the man would do anything to discredit him, no matter how underhanded. He said he, McMather was telling the truth, but I could believe what I chose."

"And what did you believe?" I asked.

"I didn't know what to believe," he said. "I didn't have any solid facts, but the fact that there were all these different stories meant there was something very wrong."

He frowned at the memory. "I didn't know which of the three had lied to me, nor to what extent they'd lied. On the face of it, Rutledge was the most credible of the three, and the one I'd trusted for years, but by that point I didn't even know if I could trust him."

"That's when you hired Lisa Stern," I said.

"How did you know about that?"

"She's good at what she does," Cassie said.

Brian gave me an assessing look, nodded. "Yes, that's when I hired Ms. Stern."

"What about DNA? Did McMather agree to a test?"

"How...?" He stopped, started again. "Yes, he did. Unfortunately we were to meet on Sunday and he was killed on Saturday."

He turned back to his wife. "Can you forgive me?"

"Of course. If you can forgive me."

"There's nothing to forgive," he said, taking her hand.

They needed to be alone. "Before I go..."

Cassie turned to me. "Thank you, Barbara. I mean that."

"Don't thank me yet. I still need to give you some tough news. Brian, it's been confirmed that your parent's death was not an accident."

Brian looked numb. "How...?"

"It looks like Rutledge paid someone to tamper with the brake-lines, so they failed in the Canyon. He also cut short the investigation. I'm fairly sure McMather found out about it, and blackmailed him for years."

"So when I told McMather that Rutledge was naming him as my father and he was so angry—Did McMather confront Rutledge? Is that why he died?" he asked.

There was no easy answer. "It looks like it."

Then the rest of it sunk in. "You're saying my father killed my mother. Why, in God's name?" he said.

"I don't know," I said. "Probably for the same reason he refused to acknowledge you. To protect himself and his career. Maybe someone found out, threatened to blackmail him. With both your parents gone, there'd be no proof."

I couldn't bring myself to tell him that Joe Stewart was the likely blackmailer, precipitating both his own death and Maria's.

"His career." Brian gave a bitter laugh.

"Your mother was his student when she got pregnant with you," I said. "Even back then, it would have reflected badly on him. He didn't want scandal touching him."

But I agreed with Brian. The man was and is a monster.

Once that combination of brains, beauty and forbidden sex that had drawn the Judge to Maria resulted in a child and a potential scandal, he saw her only as a threat to his own life and plans. Maybe in his twisted thinking, having both Joe and Marie killed was best way to ensure against any further blackmail attempts.

How ironic that Ed McMather then blackmailed him for more than twenty years. Served him right. I hoped McMather really made him suffer all that time.

"Nearly half a century later and he's still prepared to kill over it," Brian said, following his own train of thought. "You know, the worst thing isn't that I'm the bastard son of a murderer. It's that my real father is has absolutely no morals and fewer scruples. And I looked to him as a role model all those years."

He gave a bitter laugh, then turned to Cassie. "But I'd rather be the bastard son of a sociopath than your half-brother. It's worth anything to stay married to you."

She put up a hand to touch his face.

And I slipped out and left them together.

"So what are Brian and Cassie Stewart doing now, Barbara?" Doug was asking.

It took me a moment to come back to the present and understand his question. Then I grinned.

"They've gone on a second honeymoon," I said. "Using part of her inheritance from McMather, she's bought him a medium-sized yacht, complete with crew, and they've gone cruising."

What I couldn't tell him was the very private conversation I'd had with Cassie the day before they sailed. From somewhere she'd found the courage to tell Brian the truth about their son.

"The secrets in both our families have already done too much damage," she told me. "It can't continue into the next generation."

As it turned out, Brian already knew. He'd carried his own burden of guilt over his intense need to prove himself—and the resulting neglect of his wife—during those early years.

"Cassie inherited millions, didn't she?" Doug was saying. "Must be nice."

"Must be." If he only knew.

"What about you, Barbara? What's next for you?"

"We'll just have to see," I said.

———

A WEEK LATER, I was sitting in that same cafe in Venice, sipping a cappuccino, and contemplating a leisurely day of sightseeing. Savoring the smooth taste, I replayed the events of the previous month slowly in my head. Something I find myself doing quite frequently lately.

It's as though I need to fully understand what happened and my part in it before I can let it go. At least most of my questions are finally answered.

The trip was Cassie's way of thanking me—in addition to the very hefty sum now residing happily in my bank account. The very rich really are different. I'm not complaining, though.

I get to spend two leisurely weeks in Venice, just soaking in the city and all that magnificent art. And this time I've got Alessandro to show me around, the problems of long distance relationships be damned.

Another plus is Vivianne and Genevieve. Those two fascinate me.

I still haven't totally untangled their tale or the reasons for it. I gather the Judge had argued that Brian didn't need to know his true parentage, and convinced them to spin me their tale. Of course, they had their own reasons for spinning that particular tale, reasons of which he knew nothing.

He, of course, was the family lawyer they turned to when they were first investing their "household money". I wished I'd known that at the time, so I could've asked him what he thought of those two stock sharks. Though that might have ended up with me looking down the barrel of his gun even sooner.

No thanks.

If all my future cases had suspects pulling guns on me, I'd have to close my firm and go back to eating beans. Good thing being a private eye usually is usually pretty boring. I wasn't likely to be investigating another gun-waving murderer any time soon.

ACKNOWLEDGMENTS

Many thanks to my first readers Kelly Morisseau, Marie Connell, Graham Moore, Carla Lewis, Sandy Constable, Roberta Rich, Chris Petty, Bobbi Smith, Kayo Devcic, Brad Rowse and Travis Rowse for insightful comments on early drafts of the manuscript, and to my mother for her eagle eye for typos. Special thanks to Linda Roggeveen for copyediting and help with the legalese. All errors and omissions are, of course, mine.